THE MYSTICAL
ONES
RISE TO POWER

LAURA LYNN

Archway Publishing books may be ordered through booksellers or by contacting:

Archway Publishing
1663 Liberty Drive
Bloomington, IN 47403
www.archwaypublishing.com
1 (888) 242-5904

ISBN: 978-1-4808-6495-5 (sc)
ISBN: 978-1-4808-6494-8 (e)

Library of Congress Control Number: 2018907556

Print information available on the last page.

Archway Publishing rev. date: 06/26/2018

For my father who always
believed I could do great things.
I love and miss you every day!

PROLOGUE

There were nine dimensions, each one ruled by a different God. However, over a megaannum ago, they were all connected. Everyone could come and go as they pleased, except the mortals who did not have the knowledge or ability to travel beyond their own worlds.

Zeus had been the overlord of all the dimensions, since he, with the help of his brother, Hades, had overthrown his father and the other Titans. After trapping the Titans, Zeus turned on Hades, trapping him to spend an eternity on the Underworld.

Zeus thought himself to be a fair and just ruler. Most of the other gods disagreed, thinking he was arrogant and petty.

The gods gathered together and fought against Zeus to free their worlds from his grasp. The fight quickly turned into a war, one that the universe had never before seen and would not see for a very long time. Some of the dimensions were nearly destroyed because of the fighting.

Zeus grew tired of fighting, he split the dimensions, by putting borders up between each of them. He sealed all the portals connecting them all together. Zeus wanted to remain in control of them all, so he appointed his brothers and sisters to be the Travelers.

The Travelers were the only ones granted access to go between dimensions. They were to be the peacekeepers and report back to Zeus when things got out of their control.

There were ten Travelers in the beginning. At first everything was chaos but the Travelers restored order quickly. Ares had taken charge making sure that the Travelers did as they were told.

Ares had decided, the best way to keep the peace was to help the beings, they ruled over, as much as they could. Helping with crops and healing the sick, was easy enough for the gods.

After a few hundred years, some of the Travelers started to envy the beings they looked after. They saw how each creature fell in love and had children.

The Travelers wanted what the other creatures had and started having children with mortals and other beings from the different dimensions, these children came to be called the demigods.

Zeus became furious that the Travelers had been so careless. His anger diminished when he saw that the demigods were more obedient and naturally disciplined than the gods, so he decided that it was best to replace most of them with their children.

Zeus decided to take a mortal consort and he put his own half mortal son, Hercules, in charge of the new Travelers.

At one point there had been thousands of demigod Travelers. However, over the years Travelers had been mysteriously disappearing, leaving a mere twenty-five left.

Poseidon's daughter, Athena had been the last of the Gods and Goddess' to become a Traveler. Zeus hesitated in allowing her to go, afraid she would break her vow of celibacy. As Zeus had feared, Athena became pregnant shortly after she first left Mount Olympus.

When she had given birth to triplets, Zeus became so enraged that he forbid any of the Gods or Goddess' to ever travel again.

Zeus questioned Athena about how she came to be pregnant with such an atrocity as triplets. She had refused to speak a single word about the pregnancy or the baby's father.

Zeus then gave her a choice, kill her children or leave Mount Olympus forever.

Before the portals had closed the wolves had not feared the mortals. The wolves were more powerful than any mortal. Since the portals closed, the wolves' power weakened so they did their best to hide their true form from the mortals.

The wolves made homes among the mortals, in hope that being spread out they would remain hidden. That all changed, now the wolves lived in packs hidden away from every mortal.

When a mortal would happen to stumble upon a wolf pact, the wolves would allow the mortal to decide whether they wanted to join the pack or leave, depending on whatever they chose. The wolves did not harm mortals unless in self defense.

The wolf population had grown incredibly large on Alpha One in the past two hundred years, since most mortals were fascinated by the idea of being a werewolf, as they called it, almost every mortal that found the packs decided to become a wolf.

Once the war had started, every creature from all the dimensions either fought or hid like cowards. The wolves who chose to fight, left Mondo Del Lupo to stand alongside the gods, vampires, witches, and mortals that fought for their freedom from Zeus.

No one had foreseen that Zeus would seal all the portals to end the war. Every being that had left their homes to fight, was now trapped, unable to return home.

Wayne, the leader of the wolf army, did his best to gather all the wolves that had been fighting to protect Alpha One and the mortals living there. Once the wolves realized that the portals were closed, they started to try to find a way home.

Wayne had hoped that, his true love, Jade was still here, she had come here to help stop Zeus from destroying this world. Wayne searched for her for a long time. After the first hundred years, he had lost all hope in ever seeing her again and stopped looking. Instead, he focused on helping his wolves to survive in this world.

The mortals generally feared any and all beings that were different from themselves. Wayne decided it best not to allow the mortals to learn that the wolves were any different than any of them. However, there were a lot that were so fascinated by the idea of transforming into a wolf that they even had books about them.

Most of the books the mortals wrote about the wolves, were not even close to reality. First off, silver did not hurt the wolves and they did not change with the full moon. The mortals also believed that a wolf bite was all that was needed to turn people, but a bite from an average wolf, would only kill them.

If a mortal chose to become a wolf, they needed to drink Wayne's blood. For only the alpha's blood contained the toxins needed for a mortal to be changed.

However, a single bite, from any wolf, would kill a vampire in a matter of seconds. Which is the only real defense the wolves have against a vampire. The vampires have always been faster and stronger than the wolves.

The wolves and vampires had a peace treaty that lasted for thousands of years before the war. When Zeus closed the portals, ending the war, they had been trapped on the strange worlds they had been fighting on, it was every species for themselves.

Jade was the leader of the vampires, she was so beautiful that no man, mortal or otherwise, could resist her. Even if they could have, she could use her mind control on them, either way they had no control on what they were doing.

Her emerald green eyes were dazzling, like green diamonds in the sun. Jade always seemed full of life, even though her heart hadn't beat in over two thousand years.

She had only ever truly loved one man, Wayne. The union between vampire and wolf was strictly forbidden by Zeus. Zeus was concerned with what creation the two species could create.

Jade and Wayne both fought in the war to protect the love that they had. She feared that when the portals had closed, she would never see him again, yet she still hadn't given up hope that he was here, in this dimension.

After she had searched for Wayne for almost ninety years, she was ready to accept that he could not possible be on Alpha One.

Over time, the mortals had become aware of the vampires' presence in their world. Some of the vampires had separated from Jade and decided to create their own family of vampires.

The new vampires had no control over the hunger that now twisted their insides into knots. They killed without thought to what trouble they were causing. As the death toll rose, the mortals started to notice the vampires.

The fact that the vampires could not be in the sun without burning made it very easy for the mortals to identify each one of them.

Jade knew that the killing had to stop, the mortals had started fighting back and she did not want a war with them. Jade was afraid that if a war started between the vampires and the mortals, vampires would be the only creatures left on this planet.

She sent her strongest men to eliminate all vampires that were killing the mortals. As an extra measure she had the vampires who had created the new vampires killed as well. Jade knew that they would continue to create new vampires.

Jade decided that it was no longer safe for her kind to roam around freely. She found a beautiful island and moved all the vampires there. She decided to called it Bella Isola. She had made friends with a witch named Trisha.

Trisha spelled the island so that the vampires could walk in the sun without fear of burning in the daylight, they were also removed from any temptation to go against Jade's commands.

She built the island up as a vacation spot for mortals. There she could personally monitor all her vampires, making sure that no mortals were killed or turned.

Jade had sent her most trusted vampire, Vic, the leader of the Hunters, to find Wayne or any other wolves. She demanded that if any were found they be brought to her immediately. Once off the island, Vic ordered the Hunters to kill all wolves on sight.

Vic had ignored her orders. He knew that Jade was in love with Wayne and knew that if she ever found Wayne, she would leave him. Vic and Jade had been together for a hundred years now, ever since they came to the island to live.

Jade had tried over the years to convince Vic that she no longer loved Wayne. Vic knew she was deceiving him and even herself. After all these years she still searched for Wayne. Vic knew she would never stop loving Wayne.

Vic could feel that he was close to finding Wayne, and when he found him, he would revel in watching the life drain from Wayne's eyes. Then, he would end the wolves in this world once and for all.

Vic had always been a selfish soul. He could not stand by and allow a man that Jade loved to live. He would eliminate the, so called, love of her life, no matter the cost. He would have Jade to himself, without fear that someday Wayne would find her. He would not lose her, she was the love of his life. He refused to allow her to be with an idiotic animal.

After Zeus had given Athena the ultimatum, Athena had taken her three children away from Mount Olympus. She ended up on Alpha One, deciding that it would be the safest place for her daughters.

When Athena had left Mount Olympus, she had chosen a new home and with that her powers had left her. Athena had no other choice but to learn to live as a mortal. She met Wayne within the first few days of arriving in this world. The two of them became close friends.

Once Athena knew she could trust Wayne, she started telling him about her past and who she really was.

Athena told Wayne how she had met Bee, that she had fallen in love with him and had gotten pregnant.

Bee had told her that he was mortal, she later found out that he was much more than even she could have guessed. Bee had been banished from his home by his father and two brothers.

She had never learned the reason why he was banished, all she knew was that he could never return and he was very powerful. He had powers even a goddess like her had never seen.

She watched as he turned mortals into creatures that could not die, turn to smoke and could control other mortals. As they changed, their eyes turned black as coals with what looked like red, glowing diamonds for pupils. They had no remorse for the pain and torture they inflicted on others, attacking mortals and making chaos, seeming to enjoy wreaking havoc everywhere they went.

Bee seemed to enjoy watching the chaos but at the same time, Athena could see how empty he was inside. She could feel the pain he felt, losing his home and family.

He told her about his two brothers and how he had hoped they would stand with him. They, however, did not. They stood by their father's side and watched as their brother was thrown out.

When Athena had questioned Bee further about what had happened, he grew very angry. He used powers that Athena had never seen before. Then, everything began to shake, as if the ground would crumble apart and fall from under her feet. For the first time in her existence, she knew what real fear was.

She took a step back and immediately regretted it.

His eyes turned a burning red as he said, " You're scared of me? I will give you a reason to be scared."

He lunged toward her with his arms stretched out as if he wanted nothing more than to inflict pain.

Athena turned and ran from him as fast as she could. She could hear Bee call out behind her, vowing to find her, wherever she went. He had made a claim on her that she belonged to him.

Athena had returned to Mount Olympus to beg Zeus for forgiveness and help. Unfortunately, Zeus' personal seer, Beltra, had told him that there were three babes, born of Athena, that would cause his downfall. Beltra could only see them to the point of their birth, but she knew there was something different about the children.

PART 1

The Beginning

Chapter 1

Wayne had bought properties all over this world for his growing family. The wolves had to hide more than ever before. The mortals had wanted the wolves dead for a long time. Now, the vampires had started to hunt and kill the wolves as well.

They had lived peacefully alongside the vampires before being stranded on Alpha One. Now, the vampires would kill any and all wolves they could find.

Wayne had tried to find out what had caused things to changed. Wayne had talked to a lot of witches in hope that they could tell him why the vampires hated the wolves again. Not one seemed to know anything about it. He could ask one of the vampires, if only he could find one.

He knew that one or more groups of vampires wanted him dead. In the last year alone, the vampires had attempted to kill over a dozen of his kind, including his best friend James, to find Wayne.

James had told Wayne about how he had a run in with a vampire when he had been drinking at a local bar, as he walked out the door and turned down the alleyway, something swooshed past him. At first he thought it was his imagination from the large amount of alcohol he had drank that night.

James had decided he had imagined it and continued to walk but was quickly slammed to his back. Before he knew what was happening, someone had him by the throat, holding him to the ground.

He was shocked to see a beautiful woman hovering over him.

"Where is Wayne?" She asked in an even tone.

James shook his head, making it clear he would never tell her what she wanted to know.

He watched as her teeth slowly grew into sharp pointy fangs, dripping with venom. James tried, with all his might, to summon the wolf inside him but couldn't hold on to the rage while struggling to breath.

There was a loud growl and in a blur of color, the vampire was thrown backwards. James lifted his head and saw a huge brown wolf standing between the two of them.

James quickly caught his breath. In a blink of an eye, he had transformed into a massive black wolf, growling alongside his fellow wolf. Outnumbered, the vampire ran off knowing he was no match for two wolves.

Wayne shuttered as he thought about how James could have been killed. It was bad enough when the mortals had been hunting them. They had lost to many wolves to the mortals, when they had lived spread out among them.

Wayne knew that the wolves were no longer safe, when some of the mortals had discovered a small pack of wolves hunting one night. They had tracked the wolves back to their home.

When the mortals discovered that the wolves could take human form, they became afraid and started forming a plan to kill them. They watched the wolves every day for months until they were sure of the wolves' routine.

Then, late one night they made their move. They silently entered the home and decapitated everyone, even the children. Then they started searching for more wolves.

The mortals gathered in five groups of ten men, each with strong nets made of nylon and strands of metal, to capture any of the abominations. They each carried a gun on their side, to ensure their own safety.

After searching for a few weeks they came across two young wolves eating a small deer. The men took action, throwing nets over each of the wolves, capturing them.

The young wolves frantically started trying to free themselves. As their fear grew they started to change back into human form. The mortals drug them to an old barn, and using the same kind of rope, tied the now human looking wolves to chairs that were in the center of two small metal cages, they clearly had ready.

The mortals did not know anything about these creatures and were afraid that the wolves would attack humans.

After listening to the declarations from the creatures that they never attacked humans, they decided that they needed to know what the wolves could or would eat. They tested on the older one by connecting the food to a long stick, that could reach the now human looking boy. Meanwhile, letting the younger one grow weak and starve.

First, they fed him small pieces of cow and when nothing happened they tried to feed him chicken and turkey. The boy ate, thankful that he was being given food. When the wolf died they knew they realized that they had discovered a weakness.

The younger wolf had been forced to watch his brother wolf die, unable to help. He had sat there tied up starving for three weeks.

Every few hours a different mortal would come take over. Each one would sit in silence, watching over him and writing notes down in a small book.

News of the captured wolf spread through the small town quickly. The preacher gave a sermon on the beasts from hell. Some of the townsfolk were secretly fascinated by the wolves that could become human.

The most fascinated, by the transforming people, was a young girl, named Olivia. When she heard the preacher speak of the creatures, as if they were the devils creation, she knew that the men must have captured one.

She watched all the men in town over the next few days. She followed Zek, the most skilled fighter in town. She saw him enter the abandoned red barn that sat on the edge of town. Olivia knew then where they held the creature or creatures, if they had really captured any.

She decided to hide and watch what happened. Every few hours one would walk into the barn and moments later a different one would walk out. Every day she returned to watch the barn.

Then on the fourth day, she snuck into the barn and saw a young boy in a cage, he looked as if he had not eaten for a long time. She decided to gather some carrots for the boy and hid outside the barn, waiting for the sky to get dark.

She knew that the guard would need to relieve himself soon, since he had been in the barn for over two hours. Once he left, she grabbed the food and entered the barn. The boy looked up at her as she entered. Olivia tried to contain her surprise at the sight of him as he gave her a small, weak smile.

Olivia was shocked to see what the people of her town was capable of. The boy did not look much older than herself. She saw a stick propped against the wall. She picked it up and pushed a carrot on the end.

The boy did not look dangerous but she was not ready to bet her life on that. Olivia put the stick between the bars so the carrot was close enough for him to eat. He turned away. She knew he had not eaten in a long time, so she shoved the carrot at him.

He immediately started to growl. He broke free of the ropes and lunged at the young girl, slamming into the cage door with such force that it swung open as she fell backwards.

Olivia watched, in horror, as the boy turned into a black and grey wolf and before the she could react the wolf had sunk his teeth deep into her throat.

The man had returned and saw that the wolf-boy was gone. Then he saw the girl on the ground, dead, blood and carrots everywhere. He ran out of the barn to get help.

The men held a meeting and figured that the girl had been trying to feed the creature the carrots, they then concluded that the creatures could not eat vegetables. That would only leave red meat.

They took the dead wolf's body, tied a rope around his neck, and hung him off of the tower of the church as a warning to all other wolves that would dare enter their town again.

Wayne was roaming when Clara, a good friend, tracked him down and told him what had happened. She told him that the other wolves were seeking revenge.

Wayne then realized that he had to put a stop to this before they killed everyone in the town. They had to move some place away from the mortals. The wolves moved from place to place trying to stay away from any mortals.

Wayne hated that the wolves did not have a place to call home, he started searching for places they could all be safe and call home.

Wayne feared that the wolves would be hunted to extinction. Knowing that could happen, he had decided to buy land that had been abandoned for a long time so no one really knew about it. He then ordered all wolves to remain hidden from all mortals and vampires. The wolves were angry about only being able to hunt in groups and having to stay close to home, when before they could roam wherever they pleased.

More than fifty years after what happened with the mortals, he had bought multiple properties for his packs. Wayne made sure that the properties were spread out, that way there would always be somewhere for the wolves to run, if needed.

Wayne had moved to the three thousand-acre property, in a small town near Lancaster, Pennsylvania, that he had bought from a nice Amish family. There were ten farm houses scattered throughout the land, each with a family of wolves living in it.

Wayne had asked Athena to move onto the property with the wolves, but she refused. So, he had settled for getting her a house, somewhat, close by.

Athena had been living in Somerset, Pennsylvania, since Wayne had bought her the lovely, little two bedroom house. She was about an hour's drive away from Wayne's house in Lancaster. She knew that Wayne was not happy about her being a car ride away but she continued to reassure him that if she needed him, she would call.

Athena had gone to the farm, to visit a few times, always bringing her triplets with her. Wayne had been missing the girls so he asked Athena to have the girls' second birthday party at the farm house.

Athena agreed to have the party at Wayne's. The day of the party she gave the girls a bath and then dressed them. As she was putting the kids in the car she heard a voice say, "where are you off to?"

Athena turned around and saw Billy, a teenage boy that was always walking alone in the neighborhood. She assumed that he had no friends and not much of a family, even though he was a sweet kid. He had offered to mow her lawn on a number of occasions.

"We are going to see a friend of mine. He is having the girls' party at his house." She replied.

"Today is their birthday?"

She nodded.

Billy bent down and looked in the van window, "Happy birthday girls! Have a wonderful day." He looked back to Athena with a look of concern, "have fun and be careful."

He walked away before Athena could ask what he meant.

She shrugged her shoulders and got in the car. She looked down and saw that she needed gas so she turned down Kimberly street towards the gas station.

As she was filling up the tank she could hear the radio playing. The DJ started too announce the birthdays of the day.

"Happy twenty first birthday to Richard Anthony, from everyone at work. Happy fifth birthday to my sweet angel, Mary Beth. And A very special happy birthday Saina, Sandra and Samantha. Hoping to see you soon."

Athena gasped and looked at the radio. She put the nozzle back and got in her car. She was sure she heard the guy on the radio correctly. If she did that meant that Bee had found them or was close to it.

Wayne had all the wolves gathered together and working very hard to make it a happy birthday. The women made heart shaped decorations, covered in gold and silver glitter. Once that was finished they made three paper banners that said happy birthday, adding one girl's name to each.

The older kids used the helium tanks to blow up hundreds of pink and white balloons, tying long twisted strings to each one. The younger children would then take the stringed balloons to the men.

The men tied the balloons anywhere they could get the string tied to. They set up the swing set that Wayne had bought for the girls. There were streamers and twinkle lights hung in the trees that circled the yard. When everything was set up it looked like a fairy-tale scene.

Wayne had set up three long tables with white table-clothes draped over each for everyone to put the girls' presents on. He was grateful that it was not raining today, it had been raining for the last two weeks.

Athena pulled up the driveway in her silver minivan and saw how beautiful everything looked. She had been wanting to tell Wayne about what she heard on the radio but now decided to keep it to herself, not wanting to give him more reason to insist that she move here. She was touched that everyone had done so much to make a wonderful party for her girls.

Wayne saw the van pull in and walked across the yard to help Athena get the kids out of the car. Athena watched as he unbuckled each girl and gave them a kiss saying happy birthday. Each girl giggled as he put them down. They each wore identically styled dresses of different colors-Samantha in purple and green, Saina in blue and green, and Sandra in red and green.

It amazed Athena how the three girls were identical on the outside, but had totally different personalities.

Samantha was always smiling and never asked for help for anything. When Samantha wanted something she couldn't quite reach, she would pull a chair over. She was very independent for such a young child. Samantha never cried or threw tantrums when she didn't get her way.

Sandra was a very sensitive child, taking everything people said to heart. She would try to do things on her own, however, if she couldn't do it on the first try she would ask for help.

Saina seemed as if she was always unhappy. She wouldn't do anything for herself, she expected everyone to do it for her. Athena tried to teach her that she could not always get what she wanted. Yet, Saina would still throw herself, face first to the floor and scream as loud as she could until she got her way.

Wayne had called Athena, earlier that week, to find out what color dresses each of the girls would be wearing so the wolves could make the three cakes, decorated to match each dress, with small flowers and their names on them. Each of the three girls had her own stack of presents to open.

Wayne cooked hamburgers on the grill. After everyone ate, it was time for presents, the three girls each got their own tricycle. Samantha's was purple with pink stripes. Sandra's was red with white stripes, and Saina's was blue with grey stripes.

Each one had gotten a toddler bed, clothing, stuffed animals (mostly wolves) and a few baby dolls.

It took the girls over an hour to open all the gifts. Wayne and James went into the house and carried out the cakes. Once the cakes were eaten and the presents open, the girls ran off to play with the wolf kids on the swing set.

The whole day, everyone there tried to convince Athena to move, with the girls, to their community. Her response was the same every time. "It's too dangerous for us to be here."

She wouldn't answer why it would be dangerous but Wayne was sure that she was afraid that Bee would find her. The fact that she would protect him and the wolves proved that Athena was stubborn and brave.

Wayne had been trying to get her to stay close to him since he found out who she really was. He didn't like that she was alone with no powers to protect herself or the girls.

They had fought about it many times in the last two years, each time resulting in Athena getting mad and walking away. She would stop talking to him for a few weeks, but would always give in and call him, apologizing.

After the party was over, Athena had yelled at Wayne to stop nagging her about moving closer. She put the girls in the van and drove away.

On the drive home Saina and Sandra had cried that they did not want to leave the party. Athena knew that they loved being at the farm house surrounded by the pack. She herself felt safer there.

However, her fear that Bee would find her there and hurt or kill any of the wolves stopped her from accepting Wayne's offer. As she pulled in the driveway of her house, she saw Mr. Thompson watering his flowers that lined his walkway.

"Hello Athena." he called out politely, as he always did when he saw her.

Athena smiled, "Good afternoon. Your flowers are looking as lovely as ever."

"Thank you."

Athena unbuckled the girls and then helped each one out of the van. Saina and Sandra ran up the steps to the porch. Samantha looked up at Athena and pointed to the leftover food that Wayne had packed into the car.

"You want to give that to Mr. Thompson?" Athena asked her.

Samantha nodded her head. Athena handed a plate with a hamburger, potato chips and a piece of cake on it to Samantha.

The little girl walked around the flowers being careful not to step on any. She stopped in front of Mr. Thompson and handed him the plate.

He smiled at her, reached over the roses and picked a beautiful purple tulip. She smiled sweetly and ran back to her mother's side.

Athena always felt so proud when any of her girls showed such kindness to others.

Six months after the party, Athena was giving the girls a bath when she heard something crash and break downstairs. She quickly got the kids out of the tub and put them in their bedroom, pulling the door quietly shut.

She went to the top of the stairs and looked down, standing there in silence she listened for any movements.

After a few minutes she decided to go downstairs. She looked towards the front door and saw that it was open. Athena stood still and looked around, then she shut the door and checked each room to make sure no one was in her house.

Once she was sure no one was there she went back to the door and locked the handle and deadbolt. She started walking towards the stairs to go back up and finish bath time when she saw that the picture, she kept on the mantle of her and the girls, was lying broken on the floor.

Athena picked up the broken frame and was horrified to see the picture was missing. She ran up the steps and down the hall to the kids' room. She slowly opened the door and saw the girls were sitting on the round rug in the middle of the floor playing with toys.

She sighed with relief, she had been afraid that whoever had been downstairs had made their way to her girls.

Over the next six months she double checked that the doors and windows were secure every night before going to bed. Then in the morning she would check again.

She had put a small cot in the girls' room every night so that she could be close to them and make sure that nothing happened to them.

Athena had ignored all calls and checked the mail only to keep up with her bills, everything else she wrote, 'return to sender'.

He had not heard from Athena since the birthday party, a year ago. Wayne was concerned when three weeks had gone by and he had not heard from her. He tried calling her each day but she wouldn't answer his calls. After three months had gone by, he started writing her letters, all the letters he had sent were returned.

Wayne sat on the picnic table beside the swingset that he had hoped would show Athena that this could be a home for her children. He sat there wondering why she would be so mad that they all cared about her and the girls.

Wayne started to get a feeling that something was coming, something very bad. He held the black cordless phone in his hand, staring at it as if that would make her call.

As the sun started to go down, he tried one last time to call her. When there was no answer he pushed himself off the table and walked into the house.

Wayne walked into the kitchen and put ice cubes into a glass, filled it with water. Without realizing it, he had walked into the bedroom that he had set up for the girls. He had hoped after the party, Athena would see that she belonged here with the wolves.

He walked through the room touching the curtains and wishing for something to happen, anything that would bring Athena and the kids here.

Wayne looked out the window, there was no light left in the yard. He felt a cold chill run up his spine, ignoring it, he shut the light off and went to his own room.

He was sure sleep would come easily, however, the thought that something could be wrong had him tossing and turning. Wayne tried to ignore the urge that hit him, to get in his truck and drive to her house. After laying there for over two hours, he fell into a restless sleep.

Meanwhile, Athena was in a peaceful sleep. She had been so mad at Wayne and the wolves for using her daughters' birthday to ambush her. She knew she was being childish over this last year by ignoring Wayne's attempts to talk to her.

She had decided that Wayne was right, it would be better for her and her daughters to live with the wolves. The wolves could help protect the girls.

She would pack up what they needed and leave for Wayne's in the morning. The moment her head touched the pillow she fell fast asleep.

Down the hallway, all three girls started to scream. Athena jumped out of her bed and ran to their room. Before she could reach them, she was thrown against the wall by an invisible force. Still lying stunned on the floor, she heard a familiar voice that turned her blood to ice.

"You thought you could take my children from me?"

Then she saw him. Like her, he had not changed at all. His blond hair was still long, past his shoulders. His crystal-blue eyes looked at her as though he despised her. She knew he was searching for something inside her mind. She could feel him in her head.

She was mesmerized, lost at the sight of him. For just a moment, she forgot all the reasons she had run from him. She was so lost in his eyes that she had not seen the portal, in the wall just a few feet away, that he must have used to get there.

Then, in a flash, he grabbed Saina and Sandra. He disappeared through the portal with the girls.

Athena ran towards the portal as it closed, she slammed into the solid wall just as the last trace of the portal disappeared.

Trying to hold her anger and fear in, Athena picked up the crying Samantha. Doing her best to comfort the child, Athena knew she needed help. She thought about how Wayne had always wanted to help her so she went to the phone.

Athena had almost lost hope that Wayne would answer the phone when she heard him fumbling around, trying not to drop the receiver.

"Hello?" Wayne's voice said disoriented.

"Wayne, he took them. He took my girls. I know he will be back for

Samantha." She said with tears streaming down her face as she tried to remain calm.

"Athena?" he asked, rubbing his forehead.

"Yes, it's me. You need to help me."

"Who took..." The feeling that something bad was coming returned. "Take Samantha and hide. I'm on my way."

Before he hung up, he heard Athena scream. He heard a man's voice but couldn't understand what was said. He dropped the phone and ran to his truck. Wayne drove as fast as he could to get to her.

As he drove, he thought about everything Athena had told him and realized that the "he" she referred to had to be Bee. With that thought in his head, he pushed the pedal to the floor.

Less than an hour later he arrived at Athena's house. He could sense that something was very wrong. It was too quiet. The stench of death was in the air.

Wayne ran up the steps and slammed the door open. The smell was so strong inside that he took a step back. At times like this he wished he was a mortal. His heightened sense of smell could pick up odors days before mortals could.

"Athena," he called out. There was no answer. He walked toward the stairs, trying to convince himself that she was hiding as he told her to do, even though he already knew he was too late.

As he neared the top step, he heard something move. His brown eyes turned bright yellow. Wayne ignored the sharp pain as his teeth starting to grow into points and his ears growing bigger for him to hear better.

Transforming quick was always less painful, however, Wayne knew that sometimes you had to hold back. Right now he had to keep his anger in long enough to know what he was facing.

When he reached the top he looked down the hall in both directions. There was a light on in the room he helped Athena decorate for the girls.

Wayne walked slowly down the hall toward the half-opened door. Just as he reached out to push it open the rest of the way, he heard a man's voice. "I know you are there. Come on in, Wayne."

Wayne opened the door and saw a young man holding Samantha.

Athena lay in the corner, covered in blood. Wayne strained his ears, listening for a heartbeat in her chest, but there was none. Athena was dead. He fought the urge to run to her, but the child was more important.

With tears in his eyes, Wayne looked back at the man holding the little girl. There was something familiar about him. Wayne felt as if he had seen him before.

His hair was black as night. His eyes were as blue as the sea and reflected wisdom that didn't seem to suit such a young looking man.

"Who are you? And what happened here?" Wayne asked him as calmly as he could.

The boy nodded. "I am Hercules, son of Zeus. I was alerted to a distress call and arrived just before you. I do not know what happened."

"Why did you do this and where are the other children?" Wayne growled, still in shock, he did not believe a word the boy said.

Hercules looked as though Wayne had hit him. He had never been accused of murder. "I did not do this. As I said, I just arrived and found the girl crying by her mother's side. If there are other children, they were already gone when I got here. Whoever did this is a very powerful being, so powerful that not even I can track him."

Wayne's teeth and ears shrank to their normal size as he looked back to Athena's body. " Is there anything you can do? If you are who you say you are, you should be able to do something."

Hercules shook his head. "I did the only things I could. I stopped whoever it was from taking this child. I sent word to my father, and now I am waiting for Hestia to come retrieve the child. Zeus has welcomed her into his home."

"No," Wayne said. "I will take the child and raise her as her mother wanted."

Hercules shook his head. "You mean as a mortal?"

"Yes."

For a moment, Wayne thought Hercules would say no. Instead he said, "You have to take that up with my father."

"Zeus? How can I? I have no way to."

Wayne found himself standing with Hercules in what seemed to be a pure white space. There was nothing here, not even walls. The white went on for what looked like forever.

Wayne looked at Hercules. "Where are we?"

"We are in my father's meeting room. This is where you will make your case to keep the child."

In a blink of an eye, the room was filled with people. A few Wayne recognized from his home, Travelers and gods who came before the war. They were seated on benches made of white marble.

As Wayne slowly turned to look at all of them, he saw a man who was larger than any of the others. He had long white hair, a white beard, and eyes that matched Hercules'.

The man smiled, "Have a seat, Wayne."

Wayne turned to find that a chair had appeared in the middle of the room, just behind him. Wayne started to sit as the man sat down on a throne that had materialized behind him.

"How have things been on Alpha One?" The man asked Wayne, in a deep voice.

Wayne glanced around quickly at the others then answered, "Things are fine."

Zeus saw the questions in Wayne's mind, "I am sorry. Let me introduce myself. I am Zeus. No, I can not bring Athena back. Yes, I regret having banished her from Mount Olympus. However, I want her daughter to be raised here, among those like her."

Wayne was startled when he realized that Zeus had been reading his mind. "All due respect, Lord Zeus, she is not like those here. I feel it better if the child is raised on Alpha One, as her mother had wanted."

"What makes you think you could raise her? How will you control her powers?"

Wayne looked at the child that was clinging to Hercules. He saw Athena's eyes looking back. It was then that he felt the connection to her. A connection that would last until she was mature enough to look after herself.

He had never believed the other wolves when they said they had connected. They had described it as finding the one child they belonged to, the one person they were meant to protect. Even as an alpha, Wayne had never experienced the feeling before.

He wanted to protect her, he would do anything to make sure she was happy and safe, even if it meant giving his own life.

"Ah, I see." Zeus said, "you have connected. Most annoying thing about you wolves. I assume my choices now are to allow the child to return with you, allow you to remain here with her or kill you and keep the child?"

Wayne stood up, looked Zeus in the eyes without fear and replied, "Yes."

Zeus stood. "We shall deliberate now." He said looking around the room. All the others stood up at the same time, until that moment they had sat like frozen statues.

No one said a word for what seemed to be hours. Wayne stood quietly waiting for a decision.

Just when Wayne was about to speak, Zeus sat down.

"We have decided to allow the child to return with you. However, she will have more than you to watch over her. Someone who will be able to help guide her when she realizes who she truly is. She also needs a woman to raise her."

"That is hardly necessary, my Lord." Wayne replied.

"It is necessary. She is, after all a Demigod and a female. She needs a mother figure. Her fate is sealed. She will become a Traveler one day." Then, Zeus called out, "Summon the mortal, Kim McNeal."

Within a moment's time, a woman appeared beside Wayne. She was short, even for a woman, her long brown hair pulled to the back of her head. It took no time at all for her to recognize Zeus.

"My Lord." She said dropping to her knees.

"Kim McNeal, you are one of the few mortals from Alpha One that are still loyal to me. I have a job for you. Are you willing to help me?" Zeus asked.

"Of course, my Lord. Anything." She had tears of joy in her eyes. She was still on her knees, looking up at Zeus.

"Athena has been killed" he said casually, waving his hand. "This is her daughter, Samantha. I need you to take charge of her. She is a very special child. I will also be sending Tobinus along with you.

You will raise Samantha as your niece, Tobinus you will raise as your son. I believe you have longed for a child?" he continued before she answered. "I will teach him the ways of the gods, but hide it from the girl. She must not know anything, until I deem it necessary. Tobinus will be her shadow, her best friend. He will protect her. I will bring him here for training as I see fit. Are you willing and able to do as I ask?"

"Yes, thank you, My Lord" she replied.

Hercules had been standing quietly looking at Samantha. His mind seemed to float away from this place. He found himself lying on a bed holding Samantha, not Samantha now, but an older Samantha. He could feel the love between them. In that moment, he knew that he never wanted to part from her.

Everything changed and now he was standing at the altar with Samantha's hands in his own.

He blinked and he was standing back in front of Zeus holding her.

Hercules gently handed Samantha to Wayne. "Father, why send Tobinus? I could easily be her shadow, keep her safe."

Zeus laughed. "You are too valuable here. Also I see the hopeful future you see. If you are raised alongside her, you will have forgotten all that you know. The future that you just saw, among others, will not come true. You would have to give up all you have, I can not have that."

Hercules said no more, once his father had decided, there was no changing his mind.

Zeus looked back to Wayne, " You will be her protector, until Tobinus is ready. If anyone or anything should threaten her, it will be your responsibility to keep her safe." Wayne nodded. "Now, I would like to speak with Wayne alone."

Everyone disappeared instantly, including Hercules. Wayne was left holding Samantha, facing Zeus.

"You know of the other children?"

"Yes."

Zeus nodded. "I assume you know nothing about who has taken them?"

"No, my Lord."

"I will find them. When I do I will reunite them. I was wrong, when I forced Athena to choose between her children and Mount Olympus. I should have realized that the girls would be powerful, being three of them. There have never before been, as you call them, triplets born at one time on Mount Olympus."

"My Lord, may I ask, what do you know of the children's father?"

Zeus smiled, "Yes, you may. However, you will not receive any answer. That is my business to handle, your business is to protect the girl. Good bye, Wayne." He started to turn but stopped. "And by the way, Jade is on Alpha One."

Before Wayne could ask anything more, he was standing in a small living room that he didn't recognize. Miss McNeal was sitting on a tan couch waiting.

"So, now what do we do?" She asked him.

"Pack your things. You are moving in with the pack."

She nodded her head and went to pack some clothes. She didn't care that she was being uprooted or that she would lose most of everything that she owned. She didn't even care about the land and home that she had bought with her savings just last year. She had prayed, for years, for Zeus to grant her a child and her prayers had just been answered.

Wayne used the time to call a moving company to pick up the rest of Miss McNeal's belongings. He knew that she was giving up so much and wanted to be able to take as much as they could, she didn't have to lose everything.

Wayne looked out of the small living-room window and saw there was no car of any kind in the driveway, realizing that she must not own a vehicle. He went back to the phone to call James. The movers could take a few days to pack everything and deliver it.

As Kim was walking down the stairs, a man appeared, he was holding a small boy a little older than Samantha, with blonde hair.

The man looked at Kim, "you are Kim McNeal?"

She nodded.

"I am Hermes. I have brought your son."

Wayne couldn't help but notice the way Hermes voice cracked a little.

"Take good care of him." He said handing the boy to Kim.

"I swear, I will." She replied.

Wayne watched as Hermes hugged the child tightly, kissed his little cheek and whispered, "goodbye, my son."

Just as Hermes disappeared, Wayne saw the tears fall from his eyes. Wayne had seen the pain in Hermes' eyes, he wouldn't have given his child up freely. It had to be Zeus' doing, forcing Hermes to hand his child over so that Zeus could keep Hercules by his side.

CHAPTER 2

The next fifteen years, things were as normal as they could be for Samantha. She grew up with her cousin, Aunt Kim and Uncle Wayne. She always thought about what her mother may have been like. Her Aunt and Uncle had told her stories of her mother, she felt like she only got part of the truth.

She had one picture of her mother. The picture showed a beautiful woman smiling. Her long, brown hair billowing out behind her. The farmhouse, that Samantha had grown up in, stood in the background.

Her cousin, Toby was her best friend. He was more like an older brother. Samantha would sometimes joke about Toby being her bodyguard.

Toby always seemed to be close by if she needed him.

She remembered the time she had gone roller skating. She had been positive that Toby had stayed home. When a boy from school kept tripping her and laughing, Toby had appeared out of nowhere and hit the boy so hard that he flew over the divider wall.

No matter where she was, if needed, Toby would be there to protect her. Samantha called Toby a physic, always knowing when she needed him.

Everyone seemed to be over protective of Samantha. She wasn't allowed to go out in the yard alone until she was thirteen. Even then, Uncle Wayne or Aunt Kim would make up some reason that they needed to be outside too.

Samantha had gotten her driver's license two years ago, but Uncle Wayne was so protective that he had not let her take the truck out alone until last week.

"Uncle Wayne?" Samantha called down the basement steps. "Are you down there?"

"Yes, hun. I'm right here." He said poking his head out over the bottom of the steps, he had started spending more time in the basement than what he did in the main part of the house. "What's up?"

"Can I use the truck to go to town? I need to pick up a few things for the party."

"Sure, just come right back. I have a few things I need to talk to you about before everyone shows up." He replied.

"Okay, I won't be long. Thanks, Uncle Wayne."

She headed for the front door, grabbed the keys out of the bowl where Uncle Wayne insisted they be kept. She reached for the door but stopped when Toby called out from the next room.

"Sammy, where are you going?"

She smiled as he appeared in the doorway, "Just to town." The sad look he always got, when he was disappointed, appeared on his face. "Want to come with?"

From the basement, Wayne was listening to the two of them talking. He smiled to himself, he always did when Samantha and Toby spent any real time together.

Wayne had watched the two of them grow up, both of them without a care in the world. Until the day Zeus called for Toby, he was ready to start his training.

Soon after Toby started his training, Wayne noticed that Toby started to look at Samantha differently. Wayne knew that look, he just hoped that when Samantha learned the truth, she would see that Toby was in love with her.

Wayne hated that he had to lie to Samantha all these years, but he knew Zeus kept a watchful eye on them at all times. Zeus would stop, any attempt, Wayne made to tell her the truth.

Toby's frown turned into a huge grin. Toby was a year older, but he tagged along with her like a little brother normally does.

All her friends had crushes on him, they were all obsessed with his icy blue eyes. The only one of her friends that seem immune to Toby's charm was Gabby, Samantha's best friend.

Toby was six foot tall by the time he had turned sixteen. Outside of school, his sandy, blonde hair was always hidden under a black cowboy hat. Sometimes Samantha felt as though he was insecure and naive and other times, he seemed to be so confident that he came off as being cocky.

She didn't mind when Toby tagged along with her. She loved knowing that he was always there if she needed him.

Once Toby became a teenager, he started disappearing for days or weeks at a time, with no explanation where he went or why.

Once she had asked him about where he went when he left. He had told her that he was helping a family member. She knew he was lying because she had never heard of this person before.

Every time after that he would just say, "you already know where I was at."

Toby was unusually quiet on the trip to town. He played with the radio for a few minutes then just shut it off, content with the silence.

"What's wrong?" Samantha asked, glancing over at him.

"Not much." he said with a half smile.

"I can tell something is on your mind, Toby. You know you can tell me anything."

Toby looked out the window for a long while. When he looked back at her he said, "It's your eighteenth birthday, things are gonna change soon." Then he asked, "Did Uncle Wayne talk to you yet?"

"Yeah, I talked to him before we left." she replied confused. Her and her uncle had a fight the night before but they never stopped talking to each other for more than a few hours at a time.

"Oh, good. How do you feel about everything?" He asked relaxing a bit. "How much did he tell you? Did he tell you about your mother?"

Samantha looked at him in surprise. Toby never once spoke to her about her mother over the years. "What about my mother?"

Toby realized by the look on her face that Wayne must not have had 'the talk' with her yet. "Um, Nothing. Never mind."

She pulled the truck off the side of the road, shut the engine off and turned to look at him. "It's not nothing."

"You said you talked to him before we left and I thought you meant actual talk." He opened his door and put his feet out so his back was towards her. "If I would have known he didn't tell you yet…"

"Tell me what?" She interrupted. " Uncle Wayne said he wanted to talk to me about something. You already know what it's about though, don't you?"

"No, I.."

"Toby, don't lie to me." She said gently touching his shoulder.

He pulled away and got up. He walked to the front of the truck and sat on the bumper. Samantha got out and went to stand in front of him.

"Tell me what is going on, Toby." she demanded, crossing her arms over her chest.

"If I tell you, I could be in trouble. I don't know how much he wants you to know." he said pretending to fix his hat so he didn't have to look at her.

Samantha reached for his hand. She was happy to see he didn't pull away this time. "Please, if you know, I'd rather hear it from you anyway."

He squeezed her hand, "Let's take a walk."

"A walk?"

"Yeah, will you walk with me, Sammy?"

She nodded.

They walked far enough that they couldn't see the road. Then he stopped and looked at her.

"Okay. You want the truth?" he asked.

"Yes."

"Your mother wasn't, Athena Martin from Somerset, Pennsylvania." He started. "She wasn't from Earth at all."

Samantha started laughing, "So my mother was an alien?"

"No." He looked into her eyes and she saw that he was serious. Samantha stopped laughing. " Do you remember our Greek mythology class?"

"Yes."

"Do you remember learning about Athena?"

"The goddess of wisdom? Of course, she was my favorite. So what, my mother was named after the Goddess?"

"No, Sammy. Your mother was the Goddess. You are a Demigod."

"Tobinus, that is enough!" Toby heard Zeus' voice boom inside his head.

"No, she has the right to know." he answered out loud.

"Toby who are you talking to?"

He ignored her and continued talking to someone that wasn't there. "She should have been told the truth all her life as I was, not lied to by everyone who she loves."

Samantha took a few steps away from him. She thought that maybe he had went insane. There had been long periods where he would be gone. Maybe he had been in a hospital.

Now that she thought about it, that would make sense. He was always different when he came back home.

She was ready to go back to the truck when he reached out and grabbed her arm.

"I'm sorry" he said, realizing that he had hurt her arm. He let go of her, dropping his hand. "You have to listen to me Samantha. The truth is Wayne and Kim are not your aunt and uncle and I am not your cousin."

"What?"

"It's all a big lie. A lie that Zeus decided was necessary. I'm so sorry I never told you. I was following orders." He said looking to the ground with tears in his eyes.

Her head started to spin. She didn't know whether to believe in the craziness that now surrounded her or turn and run from it. She could tell that Toby believed in what he was saying by the pain in his eyes. Never before had she seen such pain coming from him.

"So, you are not my family?" She asked quietly.

Toby grabbed her hands gently. "Of course we are your family. Blood doesn't make you family. I love you Samantha, I always have." He released her hands. "Do you know how hard it is to live under the same roof as

you? Always knowing you're in the next room. So close yet so far away."
He turned away.

"Toby, I…" She realized that he was confessing his love for her. Not
the kind of love that a cousin feels, but real, true love. She saw pain in his
eyes and reached for his hand.

He knew that she was only trying to make him feel better. He turned
away and stood with his back to her.

"Where did you really go? When you left all those times?" she asked
trying to hide her concern.

"I didn't leave," he said looking to the sky. "I was summoned. I was
taken to Mount Olympus. Zeus has been training me to be your protector."
He turned back to face her. "I would never leave you by choice. Not for
anything."

"Is there anything else I don't know?" she asked.

"Um, yes but the rest really isn't my place to tell. I just want you to
know that I will always be here for you. No matter what happens, I'll be
by your side."

"We should get going." She said turning and walking away still not
sure if she believed all the ridiculous things Toby had said. She believed
that he would never leave her but the rest was to crazy.

He quietly followed her back to the truck and they continued their trip
to town in silence. As she drove down the road, she kept thinking about
what Toby told her and all the weird things that had happened in her past,
she decided that she did believe him. Too many things from her past didn't
make sense until now.

She thought about the time in school when she was sure she had left
her book bag at home but before first period she found it in her locker.

There was also other things that she needed and didn't have, but then
whatever it was would find its way to her.

They shopped in silence. Once Samantha had her dress and shoes for
the party, they got back in the truck and headed home.

She turned the radio on, unable to handle the silence. She had so many
questions she wanted to ask but didn't know how.

"Sammy, do you believe me?" Toby asked as he turned the radio down.

She thought for a moment, then realizing she truly did believe him she answered simply, " yes."

After a few minutes of complete silence between them, a question that she had asked her aunt and uncle repeatedly, popped up in her head.

She turned the radio off, "Toby, who is my father?"

Toby looked at her but turned away to look out the window. "I don't know." He said softly. "I don't think anyone does."

When they pulled up to the house, Wayne and Kim were on the porch waiting for them. Both of them with looks of fury on their faces. Samantha saw Cy standing by the swing in the yard.

As they got out of the truck Wayne said, "Toby, we need to talk."

Samantha glanced over at Toby and saw the worried look on his face. "No, we need to talk." She said to Wayne. "Why did everyone lie to me? Why didn't you tell me the truth about my mother?"

"Toby, you knew you were to remain silent. There are things we were never supposed to tell her. Things that 'HE' wanted to tell her." Wayne raised his voice.

In all the years, Samantha never heard her Uncle Wayne raise his voice like that. She could not recall a time that he was upset let alone him being mad as hell.

"We will have the party tonight and afterwards we will all sit down and discuss this. For now, let's get this party set up." Kim said calmly.

"How am I supposed to celebrate my birthday with all these questions in my head?" Samantha asked. "You lied to me. You all lied."

Wayne walked over and took Samantha's hand. " I promise after the party I will answer all your questions and more."

She pulled her hands away and went to the door, she looked back at the swing but Cy was gone. Shaking her head she opened the door and went inside.

People started showing up for the party at six. Samantha was glad that Gabby, her best friend, had come right after her and Toby had gotten back.

The two girls were in Samantha's room sitting on the bed. Samantha had decided to tell Gabby everything that she had learned about herself that day, but wasn't sure how to.

"What's on your mind today?" Gabby asked.

"Something Toby told me."

"Toby? What could he have said to make you so distracted?"

Samantha got up and walked over to the window. "I know who my mother was." She started.

"You always knew, Athena Martin." Gabby said with a puzzled look.

"No, you see, that's not right. Toby told me today that my mother was a Goddess."

"Well, she was very beautiful." Gabby absently started playing with the blanket.

Samantha shook her head, "not goddess like beautiful. A real goddess, as in Olympus and Zeus."

"That's awesome." Gabby said with a smile.

"You don't understand." Samantha said. "All my life they all lied to me. All of them."

"Maybe they were only trying to protect you."

Samantha turned to face her friend. "Protect me! By lying?" Gabby turned her head away. "Gabby? What do you know?" She asked, realizing that her friend wasn't being honest with her.

"What would I know?"

Samantha sat down on the bed facing Gabby. "You know something, so tell me."

"Oh, alright." Gabby said getting up letting the blanket fall to the floor. "I knew your mother. She was the most wonderful woman I ever knew."

"How could you have known my mother? We are practically the same age."

"Not exactly." Gabby said.

"Gabby?"

"Oh alright. I'll tell you everything. But don't be mad at me. I was just…"

"Following orders?" Samantha finished for her.

"Um, yeah. Okay, so here it goes. Your mother came to visit my mother when I lived on Mermaid Bay."

"What is Mermaid Bay?" Samantha questioned. She wanted all the details and the whole truth.

"It's where all the mermaids live. It's our home, our planet."

Samantha blinked in confusion, "So, you're not from Earth either?"

"No. I'm not from this dimension." Seeing the confusion in Samantha's face she added, "Guess I better start from the very beginning."

She told Samantha of Zeus, Athena, the dimensions and everything she could think of. She had wanted so badly to tell Samantha the truth for so long. But of course, Zeus had forbid it, so Gabby had remained silent until now that she knew. He had said that it was better that way.

Gabby finished by telling Samantha about the last time she had seen Athena.

"She came to Mermaid Bay, pregnant and alone. She wanted a way to get to Alpha One. Um, Earth. My mother gave her a spiral shrum, she couldn't travel any more because Zeus had stripped her powers. A few years later we were told that Athena was murdered. My mother found out where you were and sent me to help protect you."

"Wait, so you were never really my friend? And what do I need so much protection from?"

Gabby felt as though Samantha had slapped her, "Of course I am really your friend. Yes, I came here to protect you, but I am your friend. I don't know why you needed protection, but you just did."

Samantha could hear voices heading their way. "We will finish this conversation later."

Samantha's door swung open. Crystal, Jasmine and Sissy were standing in the doorway, Jasmine in front with the other two on either side of her.

Jasmine had always held herself with great poise. She was tall for a girl, with square shoulders and short black hair. Crystal and Sissy were twins, they were shorter with flaming red hair that touched the bottom of their backs. The three of them were always together.

"Happy birthday, Sammy." Jasmine said coming in to give Samantha a hug.

"Happy birthday." the other two chimed in.

"Thank you."

"Wayne said you were getting dressed for the party," Jasmine looked down at Samantha's clothes, a black tank top and a white pair of joggers. "Not again. Please tell me that's not what you are wearing tonight?"

Jasmine was referring to the last party when Samantha had shown up wearing torn up jeans and a tank top with flip flops.

Samantha looked down, "No. I bought a dress." She said laughing.

"Oh, thank God." Jasmine said.

All the girls started laughing.

Samantha went to the bathroom and put her dress on. When she was finished Crystal came in and did her hair in a swirling ponytail with curls falling along her face. Then Sissy started on her makeup. When Samantha looked in the mirror she hardly recognized herself.

They all headed down the hall to join the party. As Samantha got to the top of the stairs she saw that Toby was at the bottom of the steps waiting for them. When they reached the bottom he held out his hand to Samantha. She took his hand with a smile.

Together the two of them walked out to the back yard where it was lit up with bright lights hanging from all the trees. The music started to play as Toby pulled her onto the patio dance floor and twirled her around.

As she danced with Toby she felt like they were flying. They became the only two people in the world. Everyone else just faded away.

They danced to three songs then reality came back and Samantha said, "Toby, I need to socialize with everyone else too."

He smiled, "Do I have to let you go?"

"Only for now." She replied.

As she walked through the crowd, Samantha found herself wondering how many of the people here knew the truth about her. If Gabby had been hiding secrets then surely at least a few others were as well.

The party went on without any problems. Samantha was polite and did her best to include everyone into her night, even though Toby was the only one she wanted to be near.

She caught herself searching for Toby, every so often she would catch his eye. He would smile, wave, then wink at her. Now that she knew they were not related, she had started seeing him as other girls had always saw him.

"Samantha? Are you alright?"

Samantha turned her head and Sarah was beside her. Samantha had been standing there like a lost puppy, staring at Toby.

"Yes. I'm fine, Sarah. How are you?"

Sarah started rambling off a bunch of things about school. As her eye caught sight of Toby again, Samantha unintentionally tuned Sarah out. She had never noticed how he only half smiled when talking to someone that wasn't her.

He looked over at her and their eyes locked. She could see into his heart and soul. She could see how much he really cared for her and felt the love pouring out of him. It was as if the two of them were connected through time and space. As she stood there she realized he was totally in love with her. The feeling was so powerful she had tears in her eyes.

"Samantha, did you hear me?" Sarah asked.

"Um, No. I'm sorry. I'm a little preoccupied at the moment." she said forcing herself to break eye contact with Toby to look at the girl. "How are things with you and Ben?"

"That's what I was telling you, he broke up with me. He said he fell for someone else and that..."

"That's a shame. Can you excuse me?" Samantha interrupted before she walked off.

She looked at the place Toby was but he was now gone. She spent the rest of the evening looking for him but he was nowhere to be found.

When people started leaving, Samantha started looking for Wayne but couldn't find him either.

She saw her Aunt Kim and rushed towards her. "Aunt Kim, Have you seen Toby or Uncle Wayne?"

"I believe Zeus called them. I think they are both in trouble for letting you find out everything the way you did. Zeus wanted to tell you himself."

"Why would Zeus want to be the one to tell me? I don't even know him."

"No one knows why Zeus does the things he does. Who are we to question the king of gods?" Kim replied.

"Samantha."

Samantha turned at the sound of her uncle's voice.

"I'm so sorry. I'm sorry for everything. I should have told you this morning before you left. I should have known Toby would feel the need to tell you. I mean of course he would tell you. How could he not, being in love with you all these years." Wayne stopped abruptly.

"In love?" Samantha repeated.

"Where is Toby?" Interrupted Kim.

"Zeus, he's put Toby in prison. He said he had to make an example out of him. I tried to help him but wolves are no match for a God."

"Wolves? Wait what are you talking about?" Everything from the day started catching up to her, she started to feel dizzy. "Where is Toby?" She whispered before the blackness overtook her.

As she started coming to she realized she was lying on the couch. She could hear Wayne and Kim talking in the kitchen. Samantha laid there quietly listening to what they were saying.

"How are we going to help Toby?" Kim asked.

"There is no way we can. I have no way to Mount Olympus. Not without help."

"Have Samantha take you."

Wayne shook his head. "She's not ready. She is just finding out who and what she is. How could we expect her to use her powers?"

Samantha stood up and went to the doorway of the kitchen, "I will do anything to help Toby. He would do it for me."

Wayne looked up at her, "It's too dangerous. Zeus will not let Toby free." Then to Kim he said, "We will need help."

"I may have something that will help. I still have the spiral shrum that Gabby gave me. We can use it to go to Mount Olympus."

Kim hustled out of the room and up the stairs leaving Samantha alone with Wayne.

"Please tell me what is going on? And this time I want the whole truth."

Wayne sighed, looked around the room as if he expected someone else was there. He told her as much as he knew about what had happened to her mother.

He told her about his first meeting with Zeus and how Hercules had wanted to take Toby's place as her guard. He also told her all about himself and the wolves.

As he named some of the wolves he saw her eyes open, for the first time, in fear.

"Jasmine, Crystal and Sissy are werewolves?"

"Yes and no. Werewolves are cursed to turn with the moon, we have the power to transform when we have the need. We were blessed with the power to protect the mortals. Please don't be mad at them for not telling you, they were..."

"Just following orders. Yeah, I figured. Seems like everyone had orders to lie to me. What I don't understand is why? Why all the secrets? I already knew I was different, now I know why." She looked down at her hands.

"Samantha, you have to understand the situation. Zeus is afraid your father will come for you like he did....."

"WAYNE STOP!" Zeus yelled. Wayne and Samantha both jumped and turned, there was a large man standing by the doorway. "You go too far."

"All due respect, My Lord, I don't believe it enough. She deserves..."

"She knows what she needs to, for now. I know you are looking for a way to get Tobinus back. I have to inform you that it is not possible. I refuse to release him."

Samantha felt the rage grow inside her. She walked up to Zeus, looking up at him she said, "You will release him. You will tell me the truth about my mother."

Wayne took a step back, he knew he would fight for Samantha if it came to it but he knew he was no match for Zeus.

Zeus started laughing, "I will do neither. Your mother made her choice when she decided to have you. I owe you nothing."

You owe me everything, because you had everyone lie to me. You stole my life and who I am." She started to tremble with anger. She knew she should be afraid of Zeus. She didn't care who or what he was, he had Toby and that was all that mattered to her."

The walls started to shake, every light in the house shattered, the floorboards splintered apart.

Samantha took a small step back away from Zeus, "You will release him." she yelled.

Lightning shot through the window hitting the floor just inches from Zeus' feet. He jumped back, a look of horror on his face. "How did you do that?"

"Release Toby." She screamed louder, ignoring his question.

Zeus waved his hand and before her eyes Toby appeared. The house looked like new, as if nothing had happened.

Samantha grabbed Toby and hugged him as tight as she could. When she looked up she saw that Zeus was gone but was sure she had seen someone go around the corner to the kitchen.

"What happened?" Kim said as she walked into the room, unsteady on her feet.

"I don't know exactly. But I do know that Zeus was scared." Wayne said. Then he turned to Samantha, "You scared him."

"Zeus was here in this house?" Kim asked.

No one paid any attention to her.

"I don't know what happened. All I could think of was he had Toby and I was afraid I would never see him again and I, I felt …"

"Rage." Toby said lightly kissing her forehead.

Samantha looked up at him, "Yes." She was still holding both of his hands. "When he said he wouldn't let you go, I could feel the rage spill out and I couldn't stop it. I never felt anything like it before. I don't want to lose you, Toby. Not ever." she said as a single tear rolled down her face.

Toby raised his hand and gently wiped a tear away. "You will never lose me." He said pulling her back into his arms.

"Is anyone going to tell me exactly what happened here?" Kim said throwing her hand up in the air.

Wayne took her hand and led her to the kitchen, he was already explaining it as they disappeared around the corner.

Toby pulled back just enough to look at Samantha, "How did you get Zeus to let me go?"

"I'm not sure. I think when the lightning almost hit him…"

"Lightning? What lightning?" Toby said looking at her in confusion.

"The lightning I pulled down. I wasn't aiming for him, I just wanted…"

"You controlled lightning?" Toby asked.

"I think so. I could feel it and so I used it." she said.

Toby pulled away from her completely then. He walked over and sat on the couch.

"Toby," she said as she sat beside him. "What is it?"

Toby opened his mouth to speak then shut it again. He wasn't sure how to explain it.

"Toby?"

There was a knock at the door. They both jumped then Toby got up and without a word went to see who it was.

Samantha sat quietly, trying to figure out what had happened. Why would Zeus be afraid of her? Why was it such a big deal that she could control lightning?

She had read that many of the Gods could control different elements and had magic like powers.

Wayne and Kim came back into the room. "Where did Toby go?" Wayne asked her.

Samantha looked up at him, "He went to answer the door."

Wayne walked out of the room towards the door.

Kim sat down beside Samantha. "Are you alright, dear?"

"No, not really. I don't understand any of this."

Kim put her arm around Samantha, "I know. It's all confusing. Things will eventually make sense."

Wayne and Toby came back into the room, a man Samantha didn't know was right behind them.

He was short with dark brown hair and gray eyes that sparkled. He was wearing a tan trench coat that brushed along the floor as he walked.

He walked straight over to Samantha, "You look just like your mother."

Samantha stood up. "Thank you. Who are you?"

"Samantha, manners." Kim scalded.

The man gave a short laugh, "It's quite alright. She meant no disrespect." Then to Samantha he added, "I am a friend, my name is Kevin Killoran. I have been watching over you for your whole life."

"Why?"

"Because you're mother asked me to." He answered simply.

"I have never seen you before. So how could you have been watching me?" Samantha asked.

"I placed a charm on you, at your mother's request." He reached up and touched the charm on her necklace. "Your mother was afraid of something and wanted you to be safe. She wanted you safe so she recruited a few people to watch over you in case…" he trailed off then said, "When you are in danger, my charm burns red hot." He said as he pulled a matching necklace from under his shirt.

Samantha looked at both Wayne and Kim, "Did you know about this?"

They both shook their heads but neither said a word.

"If you're charm burns red hot when she is in danger, what took you so long to get here? She could have been killed waiting for you to turn up." Toby growled.

"I am embarrassed to admit that I stopped wearing it about a year ago. I knew to come because my desk, where I kept it, caught on fire. Everything was burnt to ashes. I found it when I was cleaning the mess."

"Yeah well, she didn't need you. She handled it herself." Toby said.

"So, you're like a warlock or something?" Samantha asked Kevin.

Kevin smiled, "No, there are no such things as warlocks. I'm a witch. I don't know where these mortals came up with the name warlock but all mortals that can wield magic are witches."

"So you can do magic?"

"Yes." he answered getting frustrated, "Now fill me in on what's been going on."

They filled him in on everything that had happened. After they finished talking, Kevin sat very quiet for a long time before asking, "Are you sure the lightning was your doing?"

"Yes, I felt it."

"Very interesting." Was all he said.

"What's so interesting?" Samantha asked.

"The fact that only Zeus himself has been the only one ever to wield lightning. But it sounds more like you created it. You say he looked scared?"

Yes, he was scared." Wayne answered.

"Well then. You have accomplished the one thing no one in the history of forever has ever dreamed possible. The questions that need answered are, Did you control or create the lightning and Why is Zeus, King of everything, afraid of you?." Kevin said.

Everyone exchanged looks but no one had any idea why Zeus would be afraid of a demigod. Samantha looked out the window and was sure she saw someone walk away.

"Did you see that?" she asked going to the window.

They all followed her to look out.

"There was someone standing there watching us."

Wayne looked at Samantha with concern, "Honey, there is no one out there. I would have heard them."

"Okay. Enough excitement for now. Who's hungry?" asked Kim.

They all went in the kitchen to eat sandwiches and chips. No one spoke but a lot of looks were exchanged.

Once they had finished eating, Kevin stood up and bid them a good night and left, promising to return when and if he was ever needed.

That night, Samantha lay awake, she was tired but couldn't stop her mind from working. She was well aware that in the next room Toby was still awake. She could hear him moving around.

She wanted to go to him but knew it would just cause trouble.

It was one in the morning when Samantha heard something hit her bedroom window. She really wasn't in the mood for Cy right now but she reluctantly got out of bed and opened the window.

Cy had a habit of waking her up all hours of the night to walk to the lake. He had become like a brother to her. Most nights that he showed up, she had needed someone to talk to, but tonight she just wanted to get some sleep.

As she put her head out of the window, a small rock hit her in the head.

"What the hell is wrong with you?" she yelled looking down to find that it wasn't Cy after all.

Wayne sat up in bed when he heard Samantha yell. He got up and and was turning the bedroom door handle when he heard a voice that sounded familiar, he turned and walked to the window to look out.

"I'm sorry. I didn't realize that you had opened the window." Said the boy.

She couldn't see him very well but she knew who he was just by his voice. Ben was Sarah's boyfriend, but before that he had a crush on Samantha. For years he would follow her around everywhere she went. Samantha was glad when he finally got together with Sarah.

"What are you doing here?" Samantha asked.

"Can you come out?"

She hesitated, she had not talked to Ben in almost a full year.

"Please, I need to talk to you. I know who you really are." He said.

Shocked at what he just said, she replied, "Oh, alright. I'll be out."

She got dressed and was headed to the steps when an uneasy feeling came over her. She turned around and went to Toby's door.

Knocking lightly she whispered, "Toby, are you awake?"

"Yeah. Come on in, Sammy."

Wayne was glad when he heard Samantha knock on Toby's bedroom door. He knew that Toby would protect her at all costs.

"Do you know why Ben would want to talk to me?" She asked.

Toby stood up faster than she had ever seen him move before. "Where is he?"

"Outside..."

Toby didn't let her finish what she was saying. Instead he walked past her and out his bedroom door, down the stairs with Samantha at her heels.

"Toby, What's wrong? What's going on?" She pleaded as she pulled on his arm trying to get him to stop.

"He has no business here" was all Toby said.

Toby pulled the front door open so hard that the handle stuck in the wall behind it. He stopped on the bottom step of the porch long enough to look around and spot Ben sitting on the swing under the big tree.

Ben saw Toby coming across the yard. He had been waiting for her, now he stood up. Samantha could tell if Toby wanted a fight he would not back down.

"What the hell are you doing here Ben?" Toby said pushing Ben back a few steps.

Ben regained his balance quickly and showed he would stand his ground. "I need to talk to Samantha. It has nothing to do with you. It's none of your business."

Toby took a step closer, the two guys were now face to face. "Anything to do with her is my business."

"I see, does she know yet?" Ben said sitting back down on the swing.

"Know what?" Toby asked innocently.

"That she is the daughter of Athena." Ben said with a smirk on his face.

"How do you…. Who are you? Really?" Toby questioned.

"Can't you tell who he is?" Toby spun around to find Hercules standing directly behind him.

"What are you doing here? I can handle this without your help." Toby snapped at him.

"Apparently not. Or this fiend would never have gotten close to her." Hercules turned to Ben, "What do you want with Samantha?"

"I just want to talk to her. I swear." Ben answered as he got up and slowly walked behind the swing trying to keep his distance from Hercules.

"Samantha, come over here." Hercules called over his shoulder without taking his eyes off Ben.

Samantha had been hiding on the porch watching Toby and Ben. She almost screamed when a third person appeared out of nowhere.

She slowly walked down the porch steps and in their direction.

Toby walked half way back to meet her in the middle. She took his hand as soon as he offered it. She clung to his arm like a small child.

She shyly looked up at Hercules.

Wayne saw the way Hercules was looking at Samantha. He had hoped that Samantha and Toby would find their way to each other but didn't know if it would happen with Hercules in the picture.

Hercules stood there mesmerized by her. He remembered the vision of him holding her but now facing the older version of the sweet baby took his breath away.

"Samantha." Ben said gathering his courage and walking towards her. . Toby grabbed Ben's shirt and pushed him backwards, once again.

"It's fine, Toby. He won't hurt me." Then to Ben she added, " Will you?"

"No, I would never hurt you." He replied.

Hercules still had not been able to take his eyes off Samantha but he tried to follow what they were saying. He knew at that moment, he would give his life for this girl. He had never believed in love at first sight until right now. Even his vision of her had never made him feel like this.

Samantha turned to face him saying something, Hercules shook his head, Toby and Ben were both starting to laugh.

"Shut up, both of you." Hercules scolded them. Then to Samantha he asked politely, "What did you say?"

"I asked you who you are and what you're doing here."

"Oh, yeah I guess you wouldn't remember me. I'm Hercules. And I am here to keep scum like him away from you." he said nodding towards Ben.

"Hercules." Samantha repeated looking at him. "They didn't do you justice in the movies." Then realizing she had said the last part out loud she turned away to hide the red in her face even though it was too dark for anyone to see.

Wayne shook his head and whispered to himself, "not him Sammy. Please not him."

Over the years, Hercules had approached Wayne asking about how Samantha was doing. Wayne grew very annoyed simply because he knew that Hercules still watched over her even though his father had refused permission, so he knew everything about her.

Each time Wayne saw him he had hoped that Hercules would give up and just stay away, but he always returned. Wayne had been thankful that Hercules never approached him when Samantha had been around, but now there he was, face to face with her.

Toby still stood between Ben and Samantha. Looking to Ben he said, "You have five minutes to talk to her, then you leave." Then looking at Hercules he added, "Both of you."

Hercules rolled his eyes but didn't say anything.

Samantha put her hand flat against Toby's chest, "I will be fine. We won't leave the swing. I can tell whatever he wants to tell me, he wants to say alone."

"Are you sure?" Hercules asked.

"Yes." Samantha answered with a smile.

"Alright, Sammy. We will be right over here." Toby said making sure Ben heard him.

Samantha and Ben sat down on the swing. She expected him to say what he had to say, but instead he said, "You really got them wrapped."

"I don't know what you mean."

"Of course you don't. You don't realize how to control it yet." Ben said with a heart throbbing smile.

"Tell me why you're here, Ben." Samantha said trying not to notice his beautiful gray eyes that didn't quite match his gorgeous brown hair.

Ben leaned back on the swing trying to relax a bit, "I am here to warn you. Word got to my father that Zeus backed down from you. Is that true?"

"Yes. Who is your father?"

Ben looked to the ground, "Hades." He expected her to get up and walk away but was surprised when she didn't.

"So, what does Hades want with me?"

"He don't want to remain trapped on the Underworld any more. He wants freed." Ben answered.

"And he wants me to... what, free him?" She asked.

"Yes."

Samantha didn't know why but she could physically feel sadness coming from Ben. She could tell that he cared for his father but at the same time he was terrified of him.

"Do you want him freed?" she touched his hand.

Ben looked at her his whole being felt the impact of her touch. He forced his eyes to the stars, "No." He answered in barely a whisper. Then looking back at her he said, "If he is freed, he will wreak havoc. He said as much. I don't want to see people hurt just because he has a score to settle."

"What do you mean? A score with who?"

"You're mother and all the other Gods that helped trap him."

"My mother? What does she have to do with anything?"

"Your mother was one of them that trapped my father. He thinks you owe him now." Ben said.

Hercules and Toby started talking as soon as Samantha had sat down with Ben. Neither of them taking their eyes off of the two sitting on the swing.

"Why are you really here, Herc?" Toby asked him.

"Same reason as you. I want her to be safe."

Toby glanced over at him, "I saw the way you were looking at her. Whatever you think she will never be with you. You don't deserve her and you are not entitled to her."

Hercules gave a small chuckle, "I don't think I am 'entitled' to her, but I will have her. She will see that we are meant to be together."

"See, the way you did when she was a baby?" Toby saw Hercules look at him for just a moment. "Yeah, Wayne told me about how you all but fought to be her protector. I'm the one that's been here for her, not you."

"That was not my choice."

"Your choice or not, she knows who has always been by her side. You can't muscle her into being with you." Toby said.

Hercules stood as still as a statue, "in the end she will choose me." Was all he said before he walked over to the swing, "Alright, times up. Get moving imp." He said to Ben.

Ben got up and started walking away. He turned and looked at Samantha, "Think about it, please?" Then he walked away.

Hercules offered his hand to Samantha. She reached up, as soon as their hands touched she felt her hand heat up. Within seconds his hand felt like part of her. She thought she should let go but couldn't. It was as if their hands had melted into one.

She looked into his eyes and tried to see into him the way she had with Toby, but couldn't. Something was there blocking her.

"May I walk you inside?" Hercules asked.

She nodded, not trusting herself to speak.

Wayne watched as Toby took her other hand and the three of them went inside the house. He was happy to see that Toby wasn't stepping back for Hercules to seduce Samantha.

Samantha went to the couch and sat down, the guys sat one on each side of her. As they sat down beside her, she burst out laughing.

Neither Toby nor Hercules knew why she was laughing. They looked at each other and both shrugged their shoulders.

Samantha couldn't stop herself, she laughed so hard she started crying, until Wayne came into the room and asked, "What's going on in here?"

She did her best to stop laughing, "It's just all so funny."

"What is?" Asked all three guys at once.

"Everything. Me, you, him, everyone." She said pointing to Wayne then Toby and then waving her arm around.

"Did I miss something?" Wayne asked Toby. "Other than the fact that Hercules is here in the middle of the night?"

"Ben was here. Said he wanted to talk to Sammy." Toby replied.

"I know that but why is she laughing?"

Hercules stood up and went over to Wayne, "I think her finding out everything all in one day was a little much. That's why my father wanted to be the one to tell her. She is having a mental breakdown so to speak."

"Why are you here?" Wayne asked him. "Did your father send you?"

"Not everything I do is for Zeus. I know what happened earlier and I know how my father can be. I am here now as I should have been the last fifteen years. No one, not even my father will ever hurt her while I'm alive."

"It was your father's choice to send Toby." Wayne reminded him.

Hercules looked at Samantha, "He doesn't always choose correctly."

Meanwhile, Samantha had stopped laughing and was wiping the tears off her face. She stood up, walked over to Wayne and slapped him across the face. Everyone was quiet waiting to see what would happen.

When Samantha swung the second time, Wayne grabbed her wrist.

"One was enough." he said.

Samantha yanked her hand out of his grasp, "It will never be enough. You lied to me. You both did. Everything I thought I knew about who I was, was nothing but a lie."

"Sammy, we couldn't tell you." Toby said.

"Bull shit, you chose to follow his rules, you chose to do his bidding. Now, here I am, with all this coming at me and I don't even know who I am or who my mother really was, or what she was like. That's on all of you."

Tears streamed down her face. She didn't care if they saw her cry. Maybe if they saw the pain that all their lies had caused they would feel some of the heartache they had caused her.

Hercules put his hand on her shoulder. When he spoke his voice was soft and sincere, "These people love you. They didn't mean to hurt you. If you are going to be mad at anyone, let it be me. I could have come for you at any time."

"Why didn't you then?" Samantha said as she pushed his hand away from her and walked away.

She walked out the door and out into the darkness. She could faintly hear them yelling to her to come back. She had no intention of going back, at least not yet.

CHAPTER 3

She needed time to clear her head and get a hold on everything that had happened.

Samantha walked for a short time before she reached the lake. This was where she came when she was sad or just needed time alone. Something about the water calmed her down inside.

She sat down under the willow tree by the water's edge and slipped her shoes off. She slid her feet in the cool water.

"Samantha."

She looked around but saw no one there.

"Samantha." Said the voice again.

She turned once more to find no one there. "If you're trying to scare me Ben, it won't work."

"I don't mean to scare you my child." A watery figure rose up from the lake.

"Who are you?" She said looking at him in disbelief.

"I am Poseidon." He replied.

"Poseidon? The sea god?"

"The very same." He said with a small laugh. "I have come to apologize for my brothers ignorance."

At that moment, everything hit her, " I don't know what to do or who to trust. How could they all lie to me like that?"

He glided across the water to the edge of the lake. The man that appeared before her wasn't as big as Zeus, but was bigger than an average man. He wore a bright blue chiton and his hair matched hers to perfection.

"Sweetheart, they did what they thought was best for you." When he saw the look on her face he added, " Wayne brought you back here to raise you as your mother wanted. She wouldn't have wanted you raised by Zeus on Mount Olympus. Not after everything that happened."

She wiped the tears away, "My mother wanted me to grow up here?"

Poseidon smiled, "Yes, after what happened. She lived here for a few years before," he hesitated, "Before she died." A single tear rolled down his cheek.

"You cared for my mother, didn't you?" Samantha asked.

"I would say so, she was my daughter."

It took Samantha a moment for that information to sink in, when it did she jumped to her feet, "You're my Grandfather?"

"I have never been called that before, but I guess I am."

"What really happened to her?"

Poseidon looked out across the lake. "I only know that who ever it was that killed her and took your sisters, is a very powerful being."

"My sisters? I have sisters?" Samantha said looking at him with disbelief.

"I never would have thought that my brother would hide that fact from you. I am very sorry you found out this way."

"Does Wayne know?" She asked.

"Yes, he knows." He said looking at her.

"The whole time, did he know the whole time?"

"Yes, Wayne knew your mother when you and your sisters were just babes. That was after Zeus had gave her that awful choice. Wayne was the one your mother called for help the night she died."

Samantha could see that no matter how horrible the truth may be, Poseidon would not lie to her. She was happy to see one person felt she deserved the truth and not just part of it.

Poseidon smiled when he heard the thoughts in her head. "You're very welcome." He said.

"For what?" She asked.

"For telling you the truth. That is what you were just thinking, was it not?"

She nodded.

They sat there, in silence, watching the sun slowly creep into the sky. "Who is my father?" Samantha asked breaking the silence.

"No one knows. Zeus believes it was your father that killed your mother and took your sisters. When the alarm sounded, Hercules was sent to your house. He was too late. You're mother was dead and your sisters gone.

He tried to track them but couldn't find a trace of them. They were gone. You were left behind, for an unknown reason. Maybe he meant to come back for you but saw we had beat him there. Zeus wanted to raise you on Mount Olympus but Wayne wanted to take you in and raise you here."

Samantha could hear the pain in his voice. "Why did my mother come here? Why didn't she stay on Mount Olympus?"

He lowered his head and replied, "That is the saddest part, none of it should have happened. When she became pregnant Zeus questioned her, you see, she was to remain pure. When she had three babes, he thought it a bad thing. He was wrong yet he gave her the choice. She chose to leave Mount Olympus."

"What were her choices?"

"Zeus made her decide between killing the three of you or leaving. She chose to protect her children." He touched her hand, "She loved you girls more then anything, including being a Goddess. Zeus had taken her powers and she left."

Samantha looked down as she processed the fact that her mother had given up everything for her and her sisters. But then a thought hit her, "You lost your daughter the day she left, didn't you?"

Poseidon did his best to smile, "I watched over her the best I could, but yes, I never got to speak to her again. Aphrodite and myself begged Zeus to allow Athena and her children back but he would not allow it.

Aphrodite was so distraught. When your mother died, She blamed Zeus for banishing her in the first place."

Samantha looked at him and saw the pain replaced by hope.

He continued, "When Zeus came to you and you used the lightning against him, he was scared. He is afraid of you, but no one knows why.

My guess is it has something to do with who your father is. Your mother refused to tell anyone who he was or even where he was from. I think she knew more than anyone of us ever imagined."

Samantha shivered. She had not felt the cold until now. She felt Poseidon's arm reach around her. She immediately felt warmth spread all through her body.

When she looked up at him he said, "I do more than rule the seas."

Samantha was glad that he had warmed her, she had so many more questions. "Thank you." She said.

Poseidon nodded. "I know you have many questions and in time I will answer every one of them that I am able to. For now I must go."

"What? Why?" She cried. She didn't want him to leave. Having him there made her feel closer to her mother and helped her accept that everything was now different.

He stood up to leave but stopped at the water's edge. "I want you to have this." He said holding out a photo.

Samantha reached up and took it. It was a picture of her beautiful mother and three small blonde girls.

"I returned to your mother's house and retrieved it. I needed something for you, when you were ready for the truth." He said.

Samantha tried and failed to hold the tears in. She hugged Poseidon and said, "Thank you, Grandfather."

"You are most welcome, my child." He turned and stepped out onto the water. The moment his foot touched the water's surface he turned to liquid once again.

"Wait." Samantha called to him. "Are my sisters alive?"

"No one knows, but I hope they are. Also, please let Wayne know that Jade is at Bella Isola." With that he disappeared with a splash in the water.

Samantha stood up knowing that it was time to go home.

On her way back to the house she thought about everything that had happened since she woke up on her birthday. Until now she didn't know how she felt about it all. Now she felt a sadness but also a contentment come over her.

She was sad because she knew the life she had was gone, nothing would be the same. When she thought about what her future could be she was amazed that something so extreme had been the truth about her life.

Samantha was excited about finding her sisters and her father. She didn't know how but she knew they were all alive somewhere out there and she vowed to herself that she would find them no matter what.

She looked at the picture again. Her mother was so beautiful. Samantha looked closer at the three little girls. They were so identical she couldn't tell which one was her.

As Samantha walked she got that familiar feeling that she was being watched. She turned and scanned the field for any sign of someone following her.

Like always no one was there. She was in the middle of an open field completely alone.

She walked past the swing and up the porch steps. The sun was completely up now and cast her shadow upon the door. She reached for the handle but before she touched it, the door swung open.

Hercules stood there looking at her and then grabbed her and hugged her tightly. He squeezed until she said, "ouch".

"I'm sorry. I didn't mean to hurt you." He said as he dropped his hands to his sides.

"It's fine. Where is Uncle Wayne?"

"I'm right here." Wayne said from the top of the steps. He walked down and stopped in front of Samantha. "Are you going to hit me again?"

She could feel her face turning red. "No, I'm sorry for doing it the first time."

Wayne hugged her then, "It was deserved. I should have told you the truth from the beginning."

Samantha looked around, "Where is Toby and Aunt Kim?" She asked.

"Toby is in his room and Kim is in the kitchen. Why?"

"I need to talk to all of you. Together." She answered.

Wayne went to get Toby and Hercules headed to the kitchen to get Kim. A few minutes later they were all gathered in the living room.

Once everyone, except Samantha, was seated she said, "I know why you all lied to me." She looked at Hercules, "I know why you didn't come for me. I understand it all so clearly now."

"Sammy, Where have you been?" Toby asked looking confused.

Samantha smiled. "I was with my Grandfather."

"Poseidon was here? On this planet?" Hercules asked.

"Yes. He told me enough of the truth for me to realize the situation all of you have been in. And he gave me this." She showed them the photo.

"That's your mother and …." Wayne started.

"Me and my sisters." Samantha finished. "I am going to find them all."

"There is no way to find them, Samantha. I have been searching for them for fifteen years. I have searched every place they could be." Hercules said.

Samantha shook her head, "They didn't just disappear. They had to have gone somewhere. I will find them."

No one said anything. They all sat quiet for a long moment. Then suddenly Samantha remembered the message Poseidon had asked her to give Wayne.

"Jade is on Bella Isola." She stated.

Wayne looked at her as if she had hit him again. "What? Where did you hear that name?"

"Poseidon told me to tell you."

"She's here! Zeus said she was but I didn't believe him. After all these years, there is hope."

Samantha knelt in front of him, " Help me find my sisters and I promise I will help you."

"You don't get it. Your sisters disappeared. We have no way to find them." Hercules told her then turned to Wayne, "But I know where that island is."

Samantha stood up, backed away from them and asked quietly, "So, that means I am on my own?"

"No. I am here for you Samantha. I will never leave your side again, unless you want me to. I will help you with whatever you want. I will support you till the end of time." Hercules declared.

"Same here." Toby said. "We are with you, Sammy. Till the end."

"Don't forget about me." Added Wayne. "I didn't take you in to raise you just to lose you now."

"Are you all sure? I don't even know where to begin."

"You go get some sleep. I will go check in with some people I know." Hercules said, "Maybe I missed something before. Toby, Do you want to come along? You may see something I missed."

Toby nodded in agreement, even though he knew Hercules just wanted to keep him away from her, but to Samantha he said. "He's right. You need to sleep. We will be back soon."

She nodded and the two of them walked out the door. She looked at Wayne, she could see something different in him. A new kind of light in his soul. She smiled at him.

Wayne looked up at Samantha, "Why are you smiling at me?"

"I see it."

"See what?"

"The love in your heart. Who is she, this Jade?" Samantha asked.

"She is the only woman I ever loved. Other than you." He answered. "Go to sleep, Sammy. I'll come get you when they get back."

Samantha went to her room and laid down but sleep wouldn't come. She laid there thinking about how much they were all doing for her and what they had already done for her.

Each one of them had given their lives up to protect her. They were always there when she needed them.

Samantha started feeling guilty for telling Wayne that she would help him if he helped her. He had already helped her in so many ways that she realized she owed him everything.

Wayne could easily have left to find Jade. In truth he probably should have. No one had seen her sisters in fifteen years, the odds of finding them now was very slim.

After lying there for over an hour, she got up and went to find Wayne.

Wayne was sitting in the dining room holding a piece of paper in his hand.

"Uncle Wayne."

He looked up and laid the paper face down on the table.

"I want to go find Jade. You deserve to be with her." She said.

"What about your sisters?"

She sat down beside him. "It could take years to find them. We know where Jade is."

"Are you sure?" He asked.

"Yes. You above all people deserve to be happy. I can feel the love you have for her. When Toby and Hercules returns we will go to find that island."

He hugged her tightly, "Thank you. We will find your sisters too. I promise."

Hercules and Toby went to Athena's old house. The house was still as it was the night Athena was killed.

Hercules showed Toby the room it happened in. The three small beds spaced evenly along one wall, each with a name engraved. The first bed read, Saina. The second, Sandra and the third had Samantha's name on it. There was a wooden toy box with a smiling clown painted on it and toys spread over the floor.

In the far corner, Hercules showed Toby where Athena had laid dead.

Toby pulled the purple curtains back to let the light in. Now that the room was lit up better he could see a grey circle that looked like someone smeared ashes over the wall.

"What's this?" He asked Hercules.

Hercules came over and slowly ran his hand over the mark. The wall, where the grey was, was warm on his hand.

"This part of the wall is warmer than the rest." He said.

Toby put his hand on the wall as well.

"This is the portal. I always wondered how he got here. How did I miss this?"

"Have you ever opened the curtains before?"

"No. There was no reason to." Hercules said.

"That's why you didn't see it. Look." Toby walked over and pulled the curtains shut. The grey circle disappeared and reappeared when he opened them back up.

"How did you know that would happen?"

"When we first came in, it wasn't there. When I pulled the curtains back, it was there. Common sense says it's not visible without sunlight." Toby explained.

Hercules stood a foot from the circle with his hands held up in front of him.

"What are you doing now?" Toby asked.

"Trying to reopen it."

The two of them tried for hours to open the portal with no luck. No matter what they tried, it remained sealed.

When Toby couldn't see anything else to do he sat down in the middle of the room.

Hercules turned and looked at him. "What are you doing?"

"Sitting."

"Why? We are not done here." Hercules said.

Toby stood back up. "Unless you know more to try, we are wasting time here. I wasn't raised as a Traveler like you. I don't know anything about portals or the other worlds. I was trained to protect Samantha. I can't do that from here."

"We promised to help her."

"Yes, but how is this helping? We can't get it opened." Toby said.

Hercules was ready to continue arguing then something occurred to him. Toby was in love with Samantha. Hercules had thought that Toby was just being influenced by Samantha's powers.

He had seen many boys at Samantha's school literally fall over themselves when she had walked past them. Now he saw that Toby, like himself, was not under her powers. Toby really loved her.

"Alright." Hercules said. "Let's go."

Hercules walked towards the door, Toby didn't move.

"Are you coming?"

"That was too easy." Toby said.

"What was?"

"You agreeing to leave. I could tell you wanted to stay but you changed your mind. Why?"

"It doesn't matter." Answered Hercules.

"Yes it does. Just tell me." Toby said grabbing Hercules by the arm.

"Let go." Toby dropped his hand. "You wanna know why?" Hercules asked.

Toby nodded.

"It's because I can see that being away from her is driving you crazy. I can see that you are in love with her. I don't know what will happen but I do know that me and you will eventually fight for her." Hercules said.

Toby stood there for a moment in silence then said. "You are right. I can't stand not being near her. But I don't think us fighting is needed. She will decide. And no matter her choice we will both have to accept it."

Hercules chuckled, "You really are the voice of reasoning."

They both laughed, then headed to the door.

Once they got outside they stopped on the porch. They stood there for a minute looking at the neighbor in his yard. There was an old man planting flowers along his walkway.

"Why hasn't this house been sold or rented out?" Toby asked, still looking at the old man.

"No one can see it. Zeus hid it from all mortals. Only we can see it."

Toby turned to Hercules and was about to say something, he turned back to look at the old man and saw that he was looking at them.

Before Toby could say anything to Hercules the man looked away.

"Did you see that?"

Hercules looked at Toby. " See what?"

"That old man, he was looking at us." Toby said.

"I just told you, no one can see us while we are here. " Hercules reminded him.

"Then he isn't mortal cause he looked right at us." Toby said walking down the steps.

"Toby? What are you doing?" Hercules asked as he followed him off the steps.

"If you are right then he can't see me and can't hear me." Toby walked over to the edge of the yard. "Hey. Hey you. Old man, I know you can hear me. Who are you?"

"Toby, knock it off. He can't hear you."

"Yes he can." Toby said over his shoulder. "He hears everything we are saying. Don't you, you old son of a bitch?"

The old man didn't look up but something in his demeanor changed. Instead of gently placing the last flower in the hole, he dropped it in and quickly covered the roots with soil. He dusted off his hands and stood up.

He started walking to his house when Toby said, "What are you?"

The old man turned and looked at Toby. His eyes were black and he smiled a sick smile.

Hercules had been watching, and now he jumped into action. He ran at the old man.

The man said something the other two couldn't hear and a swirling portal of purple and blue appeared on the door of the house. The old man disappeared into it.

Hercules reached the door just as the portal disappeared and left behind a big grey circle.

"It's the same as the one in the bedroom." Toby pointed out.

Hercules already had his hands up trying to follow the guy. After a few moments he dropped his hands and turned to Toby.

"I think that guy may have been the same one who took Samantha's sisters, I can't track him."

Toby shook his head, "he isn't the one who took them. Why would he be hanging around here?"

"I don't know, Toby. All I do know is, this is the same type of portal that is in the bedroom upstairs."

"But this is a new portal. It just closed. You should be able to reopen it or at least know where it leads to."

Hercules shook his head. "I can't!" he snapped. " I don't know what kind of beings they are. Have you ever heard of anything that has black eyes like that?"

"No. Never."

"Let's get back to Samantha. I have a feeling that we will see that guy again very soon."

CHAPTER 4

Back at the house, Samantha and Wayne sat waiting for the other two to return.

Kim was in the kitchen cooking as always when she was nervous. She didn't want no part of a war against Zeus, but she couldn't just turn her back on the only child she had ever raised.

On the other hand she would not have had the chance to raise Toby if it had not of been for Zeus choosing her. She owed Zeus but still couldn't turn her back on her boy or Samantha.

She had just put a batch of cookies in the oven when she heard someone at the back door. She set the timer for eleven minutes and went to answer the door.

Samantha had been listening to Wayne talk about how things were before Zeus closed all portals when she heard the timer go off. Kim was always quick to shut the timer off, but the timer kept on ringing.

Samantha got up and walked into the kitchen. She saw Kim lying on the floor in a pool of blood.

"NO!" She screamed running to Kim's side. "Uncle Wayne."

Wayne came through the door and saw Kim lying there. He pulled Samantha up and hugged her to him so she couldn't see Kim. He had been so involved talking to Samantha that he had not heard anything from the kitchen.

"Samantha?" Called Hercules. "Where are you?"

"In here." Wayne called to him as he tried to get Samantha to leave the kitchen.

Toby and Hercules both entered and saw Kim. They ushered

Samantha to the living-room. Wayne stayed in the kitchen to examine Kim's body.

After a few minutes Cy and James were coming in the back door.

"What happened?" Cy asked.

"I don't know. She don't have any trauma that I can see. But all this blood had to come from somewhere. I want you two to do a perimeter sweep and report back to me. Do not alert the others yet."

"Yes sir." They both said. As they went out the door they turned into two giant wolves and ran off.

Wayne got the table cloth and laid it over Kim's body. He shut the timer and the oven off. Then walked into the living-room where Samantha was still crying.

Samantha couldn't believe that Kim, the only mother she had ever known was dead. Toby had his arms around her. She knew he wouldn't let her go until he knew she wanted him to.

"Wayne, can I have a word with you, alone?" Hercules asked.

The two of them walked out to the porch.

"I think something big is going on." He started. Then he told Wayne about the old man and the portal.

"You think it's connected?" Wayne asked.

"It has to be. It can't be a coincidence that just when me and Toby discovered the portal in Athena's house, that man created one just like it and now this."

"You're right. There has to be a connection." Wayne admitted. " We need to get Samantha out of here."

Cy and James ran up to them. 'There is no sign that anyone or anything was here.' James said in his head.

"Let's get her out of here." Wayne said going back into the house.

"Samantha, go pack a small bag. We are leaving."

"Leaving? To where?" Toby asked.

"I have a house in Montana."

"No." Samantha said wiping the tears from her face. "We are going to find Jade. As I said."

"Samantha, that can wait. There is someone after you." Wayne said.

"More reason to find Vampires." Hercules said.

Samantha had got used to hearing crazy things, so finding out that Jade was a vampire didn't affect her that much. "They can help. And if I'm so strong that Zeus is afraid of me then why should I be afraid of who ever killed Kim?"

"And your mother." Hercules added.

Samantha turned and looked at him, "What?"

"I believe the man, or whatever, was the same as the one who killed your mother."

"How is that possible?" She asked.

"I think it's your father, or someone working for him. I think they are after you." Hercules said.

"We don't know that." Toby quickly added.

"Okay, so we find Jade and then figure it all out." Samantha said.

"Are you sure?" Wayne asked.

"Yes. Hercules, where is this island?"

"You are not leaving without the pack." Cy told Wayne.

"I will take you, James and Allen. The rest stay here." Wayne said. "Allen is on his way now. Terry will be in charge while we are gone."

It only took Allen a few minutes to get to the house. Followed by Jasmine, Sissy and Crystal.

Wayne told the girls to 'clean up' the kitchen. Then to Samantha he said, "Are you really sure about this?"

Ignoring him she repeated to Hercules, "Where is the island?"

"Off the coast of Australia. We can teleport to Australia but we'll have to take a boat to get to the island. There is a protection spell around it" He said.

"Alright. Let's go." Samantha said.

It took Wayne and Hercules only a few minutes to come up with a travel plan. Hercules, Toby and Samantha could just teleport the others to Australia, then they could take a ship out to the island.

They gathered in a circle around the map of Australia.

"Make sure you are thinking of Cairns. We will all meet up at the Coral Tree Inn." Hercules said pointing to a spot along the coast. Then he added, "Each of you will need to be holding on to either Toby, Samantha or myself. Samantha are you sure about this?"

"Yeah, how hard can it be?" She laughed.

"Alright. See you later." Toby said. He disappeared with Cy.

Samantha felt Wayne grab her hand. She closed her eyes and pictured the Coral Tree Inn. She had never felt anything like it before. It was like flying and falling at the same time.

She could still feel Wayne's hand in hers, but there was someone holding onto her right foot.

She looked down at her foot and saw Gabby.

Everything slowed down and she was now standing beside a beautiful swimming pool. She looked around, thankful that the pool area was empty.

Wayne stood by her side. Samantha turned to find Gabby lying on the ground behind her.

"Gabby, What are you doing here?" Samantha asked.

Gabby stood up and brushed the sand off her legs. "I came to check on you and I found Jasmine and Kelly cleaning blood off the floor. They told me that Kim was killed and you were leaving. When I went to the front door I saw Toby and Cy disappear. I ran and grabbed your foot as you were leaving."

Samantha went to hug her friend. "I'm so glad you are here."

"Well, you got us right where we need to be. This is the Coral Tree. Now we just need to find the others." Wayne stated.

Samantha looked around. There was a fountain with a statue of cupid in the center. Water was cascading down his shoulders making it look as though he was wearing diamond armor.

Jacaranda trees were off to each side, their branches making an arch of purple flowers around the statue.

"Come on Samantha. We have to find the others." Wayne said.

The three of them walked through the Inn and out the front door without seeing a single person.

Samantha saw Hercules walking towards them. She smiled at him. James and Allen followed behind.

Hercules went straight to Samantha, put his arms around her and hugged her tightly.

When he let go she asked, "What was that for?"

"Just happy to see you." He replied.

"Back off, Herc." Toby was walking towards them looking as mad as a bull. Once he was close enough he grabbed Samantha's arm and pulled her to his side.

"Really, Toby?" Samantha said.

"He has no right to touch you like that." He said to her.

"And you do?" She asked.

Toby removed his arm from around her shoulders. "No, guess not." then turning back to Hercules he added, "You were right."

"We need to have a serious talk, Toby." Hercules said as he started to walk away. When he saw that Toby wasn't following him he said, "Now boy."

Toby rolled his eyes but followed quietly.

Samantha couldn't hear what they were saying but could tell Hercules was getting madder by the second.

"Wayne?"

"Yeah."

"What is it with those two? Seems they are always at each other." Samantha said.

"Yes, well that's pretty obvious." He said smiling at her.

"Not to me. Tell me what I am missing here."

Wayne sighed. "Look closely at both of them. They are both in love with you, hun. They would do anything for you. Hell, they would die for you."

"Why?"

"Honestly, When I fell in love with Jade I was the same way as those two." He pointed to Hercules and Toby. "I never wanted to be away from her. Wanted her by my side no matter what."

Samantha smiled, "That's so sweet."

"Sweet or not, love is an obsession. It makes you do things you never thought you would do. Just be careful with those two. They may be tough but they can be broken."

Samantha was about to say, I don't want to break them, but didn't get the chance. Hercules and Toby were already by her side again.

Hercules looked at Wayne and nodded then said, "Let's get to the island."

Once they got on the boat, it didn't take long to reach Bella Isola. Samantha could see why people were drawn here to vacation.

The water was crystal clear, so clear you could see the seafloor and the fish swimming along it.

Gabby was standing beside Samantha looking down at the water. It was peaceful, until Gabby gave a startled scream.

"What is it?" Samantha asked her friend.

Gabby pointed to something out in the water, "There. Do you see it?"

Samantha's gaze followed where Gabby was pointing, there was a fish tail disappearing in the distance. "You mean the fish."

"That's not a fish. That's a merman." She said with terror in her voice.

"A merman?" Samantha was confused to why Gabby, the mermaid was afraid of a male version of herself.

"Yes. A merman. They are vicious." Gabby said.

"Isn't your dad a merman?" asked Toby.

"Yes, but I have never met him. Mermen do not come from Mermaid Bay."

"Where do they come from?" Samantha asked.

"No one knows. All I know is that when they came to the Bay they destroyed everything they came in contact with. They take what they want and burn the rest.

They come every few hundred years to mate with the mermaids. But the mermaids do not want to." Gabby started crying.

Samantha put her arm around Gabby. She hated to see her friend so upset. She looked at Hercules and with only her eyes, pleaded for him to help.

Hercules had been listening from behind them, now he saw the look

Samantha gave him, he stepped forward and reached out to Gabby. "That's what happened to your mother, isn't it?" he said gently.

"Yes. My father came to the bay looking to mate. He decided he wanted my mother so he forced her to…" She couldn't finish what she was saying. She was crying so hard that Samantha had to hold her on her feet.

"It's okay." Samantha said trying to comfort her best friend.

Hercules looked to Toby, "Help her." He whispered.

Toby nodded and placed his hand on Gabby's forehead. He looked through her memories for every bit that contained the mermen. Hercules handed him the small stone he had pulled from Gabby's pocket. Toby then put the stone against Gabby's forehead. The stone glowed bright pink and then dulled down to a light pink.

When Toby took the stone away, Gabby stood there silent.

"What did you do?" Samantha asked him.

"I took the bad memories and put them in here."

Gabby blinked as if she were just waking up.

"Here." He said handing her the stone. "You should hold on to this. Don't let anyone have it, ever. That stone holds all your fears, anyone can use them against you."

She nodded.

"You alright?" Samantha asked her.

"Yes. I am now. I feel so foolish. Crying like that for no reason."

"It's fine. Sometimes you have to cry to get the pain out." Samantha wasn't good at comforting people.

She looked back at the island. Now she could see some of the buildings. The ones closest looked newer than the ones farther in land. There was a huge castle in the middle of the island that looked hundreds of years old. Samantha couldn't tell if it sat on a hill or if it was just so big that it towered over the buildings around it.

She could see it had three tall towers and windows that had stained glass in them. There were trees of every color spread throughout the island. Samantha had never saw anything like this place. It seemed more like a fairy tale world than an island filled with vampires in the real world.

Toby came to stand beside her. He reached down and took her hand.

She looked up and smiled at him. She couldn't remember a time that he had not been there when she had needed him.

The thought of him not being there broke her heart. She never wanted to lose him. He was her best friend even more so than Gabby. She knew he belonged in her life no matter what.

"Why are you staring at me?" Toby asked looking out at the water.

"Am I not allowed to look at you?" She said looking away.

"Of course you are. But why are you looking at me like that?" He said turning her face back.

"I just realized how very important you are to me."

He turned away as he said, "And you didn't think so before?"

"You were always important to me. It's just now, well now things are different." She said.

He looked back at her. She had stopped smiling and now had a look of seriousness. "What's changed?"

She laughed. "Well for one you are not my cousin."

Toby laughed too. "That is true, but I have always known that." He looked down at his feet. "I wanted to tell you so many times. I thought if only you knew the truth you would see how much you mean to me."

"I do see it Toby. I know how you feel." She said. "I'm sorry I didn't see it before."

"Well before, you wouldn't have looked at me that way. You thought we were family. So I don't blame you for that."

"And now? Do you blame me now?" She asked.

Instead of answering he let go of her hand and walked away.

She thought about following him but Wayne shook his head as if to say, 'give him time'. It was then that Samantha realized Wayne could hear people and things from a distance. Then she felt like an idiot, he was a wolf, of course he had super hearing.

Samantha looked back out over the water. On the shore she could see people lining up to go water skiing and surfing. The beach was a perfect tan with people spread here and there sunbathing, a few were completely naked.

Samantha turned to look at Hercules, before she said a word he said, "You could use a tan." Then he smiled at her.

Samantha could feel her face turning red. "No. I think I'm good." She said with a forced laugh.

He saw the red in her face, and couldn't help himself. He pulled her to him to kiss her forehead and whispered in her ear. "One day you won't be so shy around me," before releasing her.

She looked into his eyes and was pulled into his thoughts and memories.

He was standing in a white room holding a baby, Wayne was in front of him. She looked up and saw that Zeus was there as well.

She looked back to Hercules and saw that he was looking at the little girl in his arms.

She could feel herself getting pulled in deeper.

They were lying on a bed, arms wrapped around each other. She could feel the happiness filling her heart. Hercules kissed her so deeply she could feel it in her soul. He pulled back from her and whispered, 'I love you'.

The scene changed again. Now they were standing beside each other holding hands. Poseidon stood in front of them speaking. She turned to see everyone she loved and a lot of people she didn't yet know sitting behind them.

There were beautiful purple and blue flowers everywhere. She looked through the people once more and realized Toby was not there.

It only took her a moment to realize that this was her wedding day. Now she knew why Toby wasn't there. He wouldn't want to watch her marry Hercules.

She closed her eyes and when she opened them she was in a room full of toys. Two small children sat playing both with curly blonde hair.

She was back on the ship looking at Hercules. "Was that real?" She asked.

"Not yet. But someday it will be." He answered.

Samantha turned back to look at the island. She did her best to hide what effect the vision had on her. She was more confused than she ever thought was possible.

Samantha knew Toby was in love with her and she thought she loved him too. But the vision felt so real and shook her so deep that she wasn't sure how she felt now.

That wasn't true, she knew exactly how she felt. It just didn't make sense. She was in love with them both.

Toby had seen Hercules pull Samantha close and whisper something to her. He watched as she blushed and then saw as the two stared into each other's eyes. He knew that Hercules was showing her his visions and worried that when it was over, he would have lost her forever.

As Toby was watching Samantha and Hercules, Wayne was watching Toby. He saw the jealousy in his eyes. Wayne felt bad for the boy. He had watched the two of them grow up together. He remembered the first time Toby came home with bloody knuckles.

Wayne had asked him what had happened, but Toby wouldn't answer. Later when Samantha had come home Wayne learned that Toby had got into a fight with some boy for taking a toy from Samantha.

It was then that he started suspecting Toby had more feelings for her then what he should have.

The ship was starting to dock. Samantha and the rest of the group walked through the crowd and waited for the ship to start letting the passengers off.

As they walked down the wooden plank that led to the docks, Samantha saw a man with almost pure white hair staring at them.

When they reached the docks, the man walked over to them.

"What is your business here?"

Samantha didn't let his rude demeanor bother her. "We are here to see Jade. I'm Samantha Martin." She said holding her hand out to shake his.

He hesitated for a moment then took her hand. His eyes met hers.

"You. I have seen you before." He said to her.

She smiled sweetly, "I don't see how that's possible."

"I don't remember when or where but," He shook his head. "Um, Jade don't usually meet with people. We have to be very careful who sees her. I will see if she will make an exception."

The man turned and was gone. Samantha looked at Wayne, "Where did he go?"

Wayne laughed, "He is a vampire. Very fast."

The other wolves had been silent the whole trip but now Allen stepped up to Wayne. "This may not be a good idea." It sounds like Jade is in charge around here. I don't think we should trust her."

"Cy, James, what do you think?" Wayne asked them.

They both shrugged their shoulders.

"What if she sees us and she was the one that put the order out for the vamps to kill you?" Allen asked.

"She would never have given an order like that." Wayne answered.

"You haven't seen her in a very long time, Wayne." Allen said.

Samantha couldn't help it, she couldn't remain silent, "I don't believe Jade would do anything to hurt Wayne. They are in love."

"Were in love." Allen corrected her. "They haven't seen each other in such a long time. How could you think that they still feel the same way?"

"I still love her. Same as I did all those years ago. Time does not change the heart my friend." Wayne said.

"Samantha Martin." Samantha turned and saw the man that had greeted them off the ship walking towards them. "Jade will see you and one of your companions. The rest of you are welcome to..." He stopped when he looked at Cy. He backed up a few steps and hissed. "You don't belong here." Then turned and ran back towards the castle.

"Great. See I told you." Allen started.

"At least he didn't attack Cy. Let's just go up to the castle." Wayne suggested.

With Allen's protests noted, they started walking towards the castle.

As they reached the steps of the castle, the doors swung open and four men stepped out blocking the entrance.

"We are here to see Jade." Samantha informed them.

"That one should not be here." Said the guard on the far left looking at Cy.

Toby turned to Hercules and spoke through thoughts. 'They don't realize Wayne, James and Allen are wolves too.'

'I wonder why tho.' Hercules thought.

'I don't know. Maybe the others don't smell as bad. Ha ha.'

Hercules looked at Toby, 'That's not nice. And makes no sense at all.'

"Who are your companions?" The same guard asked Samantha.

She stepped forward but Hercules grabbed her arm and pulled her back, "What are you doing?" He whispered.

"Showing them I am not afraid of them." She answered.

"You should be afraid, girl." Said the bigger of the four.

Hercules looked up at him. "Do you have any idea who we are?"

"I don't care who you are."

Samantha stepped in front of Hercules. "I am the daughter of Athena."

All four of the vampires looked at each other. The smaller one turned and disappeared through the door. The others turned back to look at Samantha and Hercules.

Within a few minutes the smaller one came back out. "Follow me, please." He said to Samantha.

"All of us?" She asked.

"Yes. Jade would like to speak to you."

They followed him through the door and down a long hallway.

Samantha, Hercules and Toby took the lead, Wayne, Gabby and Cy followed close behind them. James and Allen took the rear.

They stopped outside a big door that had flowers carved into it. The vampire knocked and the door swung open.

The room was immaculate. Samantha expected the room to be a library or study but instead it was a throne room. The woman sitting on the golden throne sat up straight. The guard beside her was the same one from the docks. He was standing with his arms crossed over his chest.

As she started to stand, her guard came to her side. Her bright red hair cascading down her back as she stood up gracefully.

She looked at Samantha, "Daughter of Athena?"

"Yes." Samantha replied.

Wayne saw Jade and his heart started to pound. After all these years, he had found her. His mind stopped thinking and his heart took over. "Jade."

Jade looked past Samantha and saw Wayne. Her eyes widened and her hands came to her mouth. "Wayne?"

The guard dropped his arms to his sides and looked from Jade to Wayne. "You." He said.

No one seemed to pay any attention to him as Jade slowly walked down the three steps. Wayne took a few steps and stopped not sure if Allen had been right.

Jade went to him and threw her arms around his neck. Wayne wrapped his arms around her.

"I have been looking for you, my love." She whispered.

The guard grabbed Jade's arm and she turned to look at him. "You can't.."

"Can't what? I can do as I please, Vic." She turned her back to him and was looking at Wayne now.

"How are you here?" Wayne asked her.

"I was here when Zeus sealed the portals. How did you find me after all these years?"

"Well truth is, I gave up a long time ago. Until Zeus told me fifteen years ago that you were here. I had the wolves out searching for any sign that you were really here. But everyone I sent out wound up dead, killed by vampires." he informed her.

Jade turned once more to Vic. "Is this true? You were killing the wolves?"

Vic stepped back. "Yes. I did not want you to find him. I did not want to kill them but they would not tell me where he was." He said looking at Wayne with pure hatred in his eyes.

"Kelly." Jade said in an even tone.

A young girl appeared beside Jade, "Yes ma'am?"

"Take Vic to the dungeons. I will be along shortly."

The girl nodded and followed Vic out of the room.

Samantha felt her heart go out to Vic. He had said he saw her before, now that she had taken closer look, he did seem familiar to her.

Wayne asked the others to leave him alone with Jade and so they walked out of the room and stood in the foyer.

There were leather covered benches on either side and a magnificent chandelier hung above them. Samantha had just sat down between Toby and Hercules when the girl, Kelly came out of a door that Samantha assumed went to the dungeons.

"Um, excuse me." Samantha said.

Kelly looked at her with a forced smile. "Yes."

"How long will he be down there?"

"As long as she wants him to be." Kelly answered walking away.

Hercules and Toby both looked at Samantha.

"What?"

Hercules looked as though someone had hit him. "What do you care how long he will be in there?"

Samantha shrugged her shoulders. Truth was, she really didn't know why. But there was something about Vic. Something about his eyes.

"There has to be a reason you asked." Toby chimed in.

"I don't know. Something about him." Samantha said looking straight in front of her, not wanting to look at either of them.

"What kind of something?" Toby asked.

"The way he looked at me and he said he saw me before. How could he have?" She said more to herself than to them.

"He couldn't have. I would have known if a vampire had been around." Toby answered.

"I don't know." Samantha couldn't explain it to herself let alone to the two guys who were in love with her. "All I do know is that I have to talk to him. Now."

Wayne and Jade came out of the room with big smiles just as Samantha stood up. Samantha had never seen Wayne so happy before. She was happy that they finally found each other.

Jade stopped in front of Samantha, "You may go see him. You have brought my one true love back to me, I owe you everything. All of you. I will be forever in your debt."

"Thank you." Samantha said. "How did you know..."

Jade pointed to her ear, telling Samantha that she had super hearing like Wayne.

She turned towards the door that Kelly had come from but Hercules stood in her way.

"I won't allow you to do this." He said.

"Herc, let her go." Wayne said.

Hercules stepped aside.

"The key hangs on the wall at the bottom of the steps." Jade called after her.

Samantha slowly made her way down the stone steps. She could feel it getting colder with every step she descended. There were torches to light the way.

She reached the bottom of the steps and found the key, just as Jade had said it hung on the wall. She decided to leave the key where it was, at least for now.

She walked along the cells until she saw him standing in the middle of one on the right. For a long moment she couldn't think of one thing to say.

"Why did you come here?" Vic asked her.

"To reunite my uncle with his true love. Why did you kill those wolves?"

He was hidden in the shadows, but she could tell by the way he shifted his body, he wasn't very happy with her answer.

"I…" He started but then paused. He stepped out of the shadows and Samantha looked into his eyes.

She did know him. He had come to see her before, in her dreams.

"I, I know you. I remember you." She said.

"As you said, there is no way for us to know each other. If I would have known you, I would have found him and he would be dead." He said, not taking his eyes away from hers.

"No, we didn't meet. You were in my dreams. I dreamed of you every night."

"You? You were the one that pulled me." Vic said stepping closer.

"Pulled you? What do you mean?"

"Vampires don't sleep but when someone, other than another vampire wishes to see us, we get pulled from our bodies and can be in someone's dream or nightmare. I remember you pulled me almost every night for almost two years. It stopped just a few days ago."

"I found out I'm a demigod a few days ago." Samantha said. "Is that why I haven't seen you in my dreams?"

"I don't know but could be." Vic stepped closer, he was at the bars now. He reached his hand through the bars and touched her cheek with the back of his hand. "I didn't think I would ever really see you."

His hand was cold as ice but she didn't even flinch. She put her hand over his. "I didn't think you were real. How did I pull you?"

"I don't know. Usually the person pulling had to have seen the vampire. For example, anyone that had visited the island would still hold memories in their subconscious. So they would be able to pull one of the vampires they had met."

"But I have never met you." Samantha said.

"No. I have never heard of a Demigod dreaming of a vampire. We can't feed on you. We can only feed on mortals." Vic said.

Samantha took a step back.

"Don't leave." Vic pleaded thinking that he shouldn't have said anything about feeding.

She reached through the bars and touched his face. "I'm going to get the key."

She went back to the bottom of the steps and grabbed the key off the wall. She walked back to the cell, held the key to the hole then pulled it back away.

"Why did you want Wayne dead?" She asked.

"Because I love Jade." He said.

Samantha looked in his eyes again and this time she was searching for the truth. She found what she was looking for and then said, "No, you don't love her. You have convinced yourself that you love her." Samantha reached for his hand. "You don't belong with her."

Vic shook his head. "I do love her."

"Vic you will need to let her go. She belongs with Wayne. You see that." She said.

Vic looked in her eyes and saw the truth staring at him. This girl was the one he was suppose to be with. He saw it so clearly now. He should have known the first time she pulled him into her dreams.

He had been lying in bed with Jade when all of a sudden he was in a strange room with a beautiful girl. There was music playing. The girl walked over to him and they had danced. He had held her tightly in his arms until the music ended.

The girl had looked up at him and smiled so sweetly. He lowered his head and kissed her lips. Her kiss tasted so good, a sweet but sour taste lingered on his tongue even once he was back in his body.

"It's always been you. Hasn't it?" Vic asked mesmerized.

She put the key in the hole and turned. The cell door opened and they instantly fell into each other's arms. He kissed her lips but this time it was different, real.

Vic pulled back to look at her. "You are so beautiful."

"Samantha? Where are you?"

Samantha pulled away from Vic just as Hercules approached them.

"What are you doing?" He asked her.

"Talking to Vic." She answered.

"Well, put him back in his cage and let's go. We found a lead on one of your sisters." Hercules said.

Samantha looked at Vic. Then said, "No, he is coming with us."

"The hell he is."

"The hell he ain't." She said back to him.

The two of them stared at each other for a long time.

"Fine, I guess we could use the help since Jade has asked Wayne to stay here." Hercules said.

"He isn't coming with us?" She asked.

"Take it up with him." He turned and started to walk away. "But, Toby won't like him coming with us."

The three of them walked up the steps and back into the foyer. Wayne was standing with Jade. Gabby, James, Allen and Cy were standing on the opposite side of the room. Toby stood alone in the middle waiting for Samantha.

Samantha looked at Wayne. "What's going on?"

"Jade has asked me to stay here but I told her I made a promise to you. I am going with you." Wayne said.

"Are you sure?" She asked.

"Yes. But I am sending James, Allen and Cy back home. Toby has agreed to take them."

Jade touched Samantha's hand, "I've had Trisha take down the barrier temporarily. That way he can get back."

"Thank you." Samantha replied with a smile.

"Toby, we will be waiting for your return, but hurry back." Hercules said.

Toby walked over to Samantha and pulled her to him. He kissed her cheek, " I won't be long. I love you."

Toby released her and took a step back the three wolves each laid a hand on Toby and they were gone.

Samantha looked at Gabby, "You should have gone with them."

"Are you kidding me? Like I would leave you now." Gabby said giving Samantha a quick hug.

"So what's this new lead?" Samantha asked Hercules.

It was Wayne that answered. "There is a vampire here who says he's seen a black eyed man before. He says the man makes visits to the mainland every few years to make deals. They have a meeting today at 5:30. So we are going to try to talk to him and see what we can find out."

"Okay. When do we leave?"

"As soon as Toby gets back." Wayne said. " Are we good?" He asked Vic.

Vic looked at Samantha and smiled, "Yeah, we're good."

Wayne was concerned with the way the vampire was looking at Samantha. Then he remembered Athena telling him that her mother was Aphrodite, that thought made it all clear to him. Samantha was unknowingly putting these guys under her spell.

However, it was impossible to tell if they were all being persuaded by her powers or if they truly cared for her. He hoped that Toby's feeling were real, they had always been so close and he would hate to see them lose the relationship they had.

They waited for a long time for Toby to return, When the clock chimed at five o'clock Hercules said, "Something is wrong. I am going to find out what happened."

He disappeared before anyone could say a word.

Hercules appeared in front of Wayne's house. There were a dozen people standing around. He stopped a young girl, "What's going on here?"

She had tears running down her face. "We were attacked."

"By who?"

"No one knows. All I know is the men who attacked us had black eyes and were stronger than anything I ever heard of. They killed all but the few of us here." She ran off crying.

Hercules saw Cy standing by the corner of the house covered in blood. Hercules ran over to him. "What happened here? Where is Toby?"

"They were here when we got here. They were slaughtering people. We didn't stand a chance. Toby fought as hard as the rest of us but…" Cy pointed to a sheet lying over a body. Hercules went over and pulled the sheet back.

Toby laid there staring up at the sky. Toby was dead. Hercules stared at him. He dropped to his knees at Toby's side.

He was sad for the loss of his friend, before Toby had come to protect Samantha, Hercules and Toby had been close. Toby was always willing to go with Hercules when he had wanted a companion on a mission.

He thought about the pain of losing Toby would cause Samantha but also for Hermes who had given his only son to help protect Samantha.

Samantha looked at her watch for the hundredth time. "How long should we wait? We are going to miss the guy."

"You're right. Let's go. We'll fill Toby and Hercules in later." Wayne said.

"Gabby, stay here with Jade please?" Samantha said.

Gabby nodded.

Jade looked to Vic, "You will go along with them. Make sure everything goes well. The sun is going down so make sure you stay on the west side of the hotel to avoid the sun."

Vic smiled, "Yes ma'am."

The three of them left the island and went back to the Coral tree to meet with the Black eyed man. Teleporting was easier the second time for Samantha.

Once again Samantha was standing by the pool. Most of the pool area was now in the shade. She glanced over at the fountain but something was different. The water flowing down Cupid was now a light pink.

Samantha looked at Wayne, "Do you see that?"

"Yeah, Something happened here."

Vic took a few steps towards the fountain and held his hand up, "Stay there. You don't want to see this."

"What is it?" Samantha asked.

"I don't know yet. Stay here." He said lying to her. He could smell the blood in the air.

Vic walked around the back of the fountain. There was a woman lying in the water behind Cupid. Her blood was mixing with the water.

He peered out from behind the fountain and said, "Wayne, come help me."

Wayne walked around and saw the woman's body. The two of them pulled her body out of the water and Wayne checked for wounds but couldn't find any.

"Samantha, We have to get out of here." Wayne called out.

Samantha didn't answer. Wayne and Vic both looked at where she had been standing but she was gone. They both yelled her name and started looking for her.

Samantha had been waiting while the guys were behind the fountain until someone grabbed her from behind. A cold hand went over her mouth and she was dragged backwards.

She was blindfolded and put into a vehicle. Who ever her captor was he or she wasn't very smart, her hands were still free. She waited until the vehicle started moving then took the blindfold off.

She was inside a van. There were papers and candy wrappers all over the floor. She looked to the front seat. A man was driving. She had never saw him before.

"What do you want from me?" She asked.

He glanced back at her. She saw his eyes were black as coal. He turned back to the road without answering her.

She decided to remain silent until they got where they were going. She thought that this man, or whatever he was could lead her to her father.

Half an hour later the van stopped. The man got out and went around the van to open the door.

"Get out."

"Not until you tell me why you kidnapped me." Samantha wasn't too worried since she could just teleport back to Wayne, which he must not know.

"I needed to get you away from the wolf and vampire." He answered.

Samantha noticed that he had what looked like a tattoo on the left side of his neck. She couldn't see it well enough to know what it was.

"Okay. Here we are. Now tell me what you want."

He motioned for her to get out of the van. She sighed and got out.

She looked around and saw that they were at an old farm. There was a house that looked as though no one had lived in it for a very long time. The paint had started to peel off and some of the windows were broken. Vines had overrun most of the front porch.

As she looked at the house she saw a curtain move in an upstairs window. She stared waiting for anything else to move, when nothing did she continued to look around the property.

The barn looked a lot newer. The paint looked fresh and there was a clear path from a car or truck coming and going.

"Who are you?" She asked looking back at him.

"My name is Kappas." He closed his eyes and when he opened them, they were black. He blinked and they were back to blue.

Samantha backed away, pretending to be afraid. "You know they will find me. You can't run from a wolf or vampire."

"How long do you think it will take them to follow our trail? The vampire could have kept up if the sun wasn't out." He said laughing. "By the time the wolf finds this place we will be gone. We just have to wait a few more minutes."

Samantha looked around again. The only road was the dirt path they came in. There was a field and beyond that woods. Samantha thought she saw something moving at the edge of the woods. She stared at the spot where she thought she had seen it.

Just as she decided that she was seeing things again, she saw it, a huge grey wolf was slowly creeping its way across the field.

Samantha looked back at Kappas to make sure he didn't see the wolf, hoping the wolf was Wayne. He was busy fiddling with a small blue box that had a white double cross on the top of the lid.

When the wolf reached the edge of the field it started running towards Kappas. There was no sound from the wolf's feet as it ran.

Kappas turned just in time to see the wolf leap at him. It tore into his throat. Black goo oozed out from the wolf's mouth. Samantha turned away but only for a moment.

When she looked back, Kappas was lying on the ground and the wolf was slowly walking towards her. As it got closer, it began to change. By the time it reached her, it was a man.

"Uncle Wayne." Samantha said as she threw her arms around him.

"It's alright. I'm here now." Wayne said.

"Where is Vic?"

"He is stuck at the hotel. He can only be in the sun on the island." Wayne explained. "What happened? Who is that?" He pointed to where Kappas had been lying.

His body was gone.

"He said we were waiting for something or some one. I don't think we should be here when whatever it is arrives." Samantha said still looking at the place Kappas had been.

Samantha and Wayne teleported back to the Inn. Vic was waiting for them by the pool. He was being very careful to stay in the shade. When Samantha and Wayne appeared Vic almost forgot the sun. He took a step and the sunlight touched his hand. He pulled back quickly.

Samantha ran to him and he hugged her tightly. "Don't ever disappear again." He said.

She pulled back and looked at him. "Not like I had a choice."

Wayne walked over to them. "What did you find while I was gone?"

Vic dropped his hands and walked back around the fountain. This time Samantha followed as Wayne walked around the fountain too. She saw the woman lying on the floor.

"Well the body is drained of blood but there is no punctures in her skin. It almost seems like someone is trying to make it look as though a vampire did this." Vic said.

Wayne looked at the woman's neck, there were no bite marks but there was a black ring just above her left collarbone. "What is this?" He asked showing the mark to Vic.

"No idea."

Samantha heard someone walking towards them, "I think we better leave now."

They both grabbed a hand and they teleported back to the castle.

When they got there Jade and Gabby were still in the foyer. They had waited there for them to return.

"Did Hercules or Toby come back yet?" Wayne asked Jade.

She shook her head. "No. What took you so long?"

Wayne told Jade and Gabby about the guy who kidnapped Samantha and finished with what they had seen on the dead woman.

"A black ring?" Jade asked.

"Yes. Have you ever heard of something like that?"

Jade nodded, "It can't be possible though. They were eliminated by the Titans."

"Who was?" Samantha asked.

"The Forbidden. They were the cruelest of all creatures. They went from world to world draining all the life and killing the planets. Kronos created them so he had the strongest army. But he couldn't control them so he had them all destroyed." Jade answered.

Wayne rubbed his forehead. "Well he missed one. How do we kill it?"

"We can't." she said. "Only the Titans have the power to stop them, but they are still in Tartarus on the Underworld. They have been locked up there since Zeus overthrew his father. We have to free them to stop the Forbidden."

Samantha had read the stories of the Titans. She always thought they sounded scary and mean. After all Kronos was said to have eaten his children. She couldn't imagine what they would do if ever released.

Gabby stood up and said, "There is no way we can release them. We would need to go through the Underworld. Which means…."

"Hades." Samantha finished.

"What about Hades?" Everyone turned to see Hercules standing by the door. He was covered in blood and dirt.

Samantha ran to him. "What happened? Are you alright?"

"I will be fine. There is so much I need to tell you but I don't know how to." He said sitting down on the closest bench.

Samantha sat beside him and put her hand in his. She looked at him and saw a tear roll down his cheek.

"Tell me what happened." She said gently.

Wayne had come over and knelt down in front of Hercules. He opened his mind, took Hercules hand and thought, 'Can you think it and I will tell her? I can tell it's something bad.'

Hercules started thinking of everything he had seen in the last few hours. Toby lying dead along with more than thirty of the wolves. He thought of the conversation he had with Cy.

Wayne saw everything as if he was there himself. As he watched all the bodies being buried he started to cry. He let go of Hercules hand and the room came back into focus.

He looked at Samantha but couldn't get the words out. He didn't want to tell her that Toby was dead.

Wayne took Samantha's hand, "Sweetie, I am so sorry." He swallowed and wiped the tears from his face. "Toby, Toby is dead."

Samantha pulled her hand away and stood up. "NO!" She screamed.

Wayne tried to pull her in to hug her but she pushed him away.

"This is my fault. It's all my fault and now he is gone." She cried as she slid down the wall. "Toby, I am so sorry." She put her head on her knees and wrapped her arms up around her head.

Gabby slowly sat down beside Samantha and put her arms around her. She didn't say a word. She understood what real loss like this felt like and there were no words that would comfort her.

"Hercules." A loud voice echoed through the castle.

Hercules looked up. "Poseidon!"

Samantha raised her head. She saw her grandfather standing in front of her. She got up and he embraced her. As soon as his arms closed around her she felt better.

"What has been going on here?" Poseidon asked.

Between Wayne and Hercules they told him everything. Hercules told him what had happened to Toby and the wolves. Wayne told him how Samantha had been kidnapped by a black eyed man and also about the dead woman.

When they both had finished, Poseidon looked to the ceiling as if he were talking to someone they couldn't see and said, "The Forbidden have returned." Then to Samantha he added, "Are you alright, my child?"

"Yes Grandfather, but Toby.." she cried.

"Toby is gone and as sad as that is we can not change it. It's time for you to come home. This is not your fight. Any of you." He said looking at each one in turn. "The planets will all be destroyed. I will transport all the Behemoth and Vampires home to get loved ones."

"The what?" Samantha asked.

"The wolves." Jade answered. Then to Poseidon she added, "What home would you send us to? Our home was destroyed by Zeus during the war."

"That is irrelevant. We will stay and we will fight. This is our home now." Wayne said.

Poseidon shook his head. He knew that Non Morti was still as alive as a planet full of vampires could be, but decided to remain silent about that fact. "The only way to stop the Forbidden is to release the Titans. After being imprisoned for so long, how happy do you think they will be to help us? They would rather kill us than stop the Forbidden."

Samantha said. "We don't know that. If we free them, they should help us. We have to at least try." Then to Hercules she asked, "Is that what killed Toby, the Forbidden?"

"No, The black eyed people killed Toby. How many Forbidden are there?" Hercules asked.

"Kronos had created six." Poseidon answered. "I, myself saw three of them killed. As for the rest I do not know for sure, but was told they had all been destroyed."

"Well, it seems at least one got away." Hercules said.

Wayne and Jade had backed into the far corner secretly whispering. Wayne stepped forward and said, "We need to release the Titans. This is a fight that we can not go into alone."

Poseidon shook his head. "I will have nothing to do with this. I must now tell Hermes his only child is dead." He disappeared.

"It seems as though your grandfather is a bit of a coward." Vic said to Samantha.

The doors swung open and they all turned to see Ben walking towards them. He walked up to Samantha. "I can help. My father holds the key which opens the cage door. I will help you free the Titans."

Samantha looked at Ben with disbelief. "How did you know we were here? How did you get here?"

"I have been following you. I was on the ship that brought you to this island. I have to admit, I am impressed. I thought all the vampires would have been long dead by now." Ben said looking at Jade.

"How can you help us?" Samantha asked.

"I can take you to my father. He will help you, if you help him."

"No way." Wayne said. "Samantha will not be dealing with Hades for any reason."

Samantha looked at Wayne. "I don't have much of a choice. We need the Titans to stop the Forbidden."

"Yeah but who will stop Hades then?" Hercules butted in.

"We will." Once again they all turned towards the door. Kevin stood in the doorway. "Once the Titans destroy the Forbidden we will deal with Hades. And don't forget, it was Zeus and Hades that imprisoned the Titans. They will not allow Hades to destroy this world like he did the last one."

Hercules didn't say a word, but Samantha thought she saw anger flash across his face. She started to doubt the reason he was there. After all he was Zeus' son. Would he really help them against Zeus, or would he turn against them when the time came?

"So, are we going then?" Ben asked.

Samantha looked back at Hercules, "Yes. Let's do this. But I don't think everyone should go. Just me and Vic."

"Are you crazy? I'm not going to sit here while you go poking around the Underworld." Wayne said in protest.

Gabby was too worried to be angry. "Samantha, How do you know you can trust Ben or his father?"

"I don't. But I don't have a choice."

"Yes you do." Hercules said. "I am going with you."

Samantha didn't say anything, she just nodded her head.

"Well if he is going, then so am I" Gabby said.

"Fine." Samantha said. "We will all go."

"That won't work." Ben said. "Only Travelers can Travel to the Underworld and back. Anyone else would be trapped there forever."

Hercules smiled. "Well that settles that then."

Samantha looked to Wayne. "I will be alright."

"I don't like it but I guess I don't have a say in it." Wayne said.

"I will keep her safe." Hercules told him.

Vic pulled Hercules aside. "If anything happens to her, I will be the last thing you ever see."

Hercules laughed, "Like I'm afraid of you. She is safer with me than you." He turned and walked away. "Samantha are you ready?"

Samantha nodded.

Ben reached for Samantha's hand. She pulled away quickly.

"It's better if we are connected so we don't get separated. The Underworld is tricky." Ben said.

"Oh, alright." Samantha said grabbing each of them by a hand.

"Don't try to take control." Ben said and they disappeared.

PART 2

The Underworld

CHAPTER 5

Samantha looked around in the darkness, she saw there was no sign of life on this planet. The ground was dead and black to the point that nothing could grow, there were no trees, hills or valleys. It was so cold that Samantha started shivering, she was sure the sun had never touched the planet.

She turned to Ben, "Are you sure this is the right place?"

Ben nodded, "Now you see why my father wants freed, because nothing grows here, nothing can live at all."

Hercules turned his head so Samantha wouldn't see him rolling his eyes. He hated seeing Samantha show any compassion for Hades or Ben. He could feel Samantha softening up to Ben and he didn't like it one bit.

"Yes, I can imagine he would after being trapped here for so long." Samantha said as she started to feel sorry for Hades.

"This way." Ben said with a soft smile as he started walking.

As Samantha followed Ben she felt as though she was walking in place. Everywhere she looked was dark. She started thinking what it must be like for Hades, being trapped here.

When she had learned about Hades in school, she thought that he had deserved what he got from Zeus. Now looking around at this empty world she decided that no one should be so isolated with so much death surrounding them.

Samantha wished Toby was here right now. She had always felt safe when he was around. She looked ahead, past Ben and saw someone standing up ahead.

She turned to Hercules, "do you see that?"

"See what?"

"The person…" She started as she pointed and looked back to where she had seen the figure. There was nothing there.

"There isn't anyone here but us." Hercules said with concern.

Samantha started walking again. She was sure she had seen someone ahead of them.

Hercules and Samantha continued to follow Ben in silence, for what seemed to be a long time until he stopped.

Ben pulled a dagger out, Hercules quickly got in front of Samantha. Hercules thought that Ben had tricked them into coming here to possibly kill him and keep Samantha prisoner here like his father had done to many others.

He wouldn't allow that to happen. He was willing and ready to fight Ben if he made one move towards Samantha.

Ben laughed as he put the blade to his hand and with one smooth pull he sliced his palm, blood started to drip on the ground. He turned to Hercules, "you are not worth it, but I am surprised that you would ever think I could ever hurt her?"

Hercules knew he had not spoke his thoughts out loud but somehow Ben knew what he had been thinking. The realization that Ben was reading his mind was very unsettling to Hercules. He didn't like anyone getting inside his head.

The ground started to shake and crack.

Samantha grabbed onto Hercules to keep herself steady. Hercules had been here before and knew the shaking would only last a moment. He decided to take advantage of the situation. With a smile on his face, he put his arms around her and held her tight.

Hercules watched as Ben's smile faded into a look of pure hatred. Hercules almost laughed and would have if it wouldn't have made Samantha mad. Which he knew she would be mad since Ben was doing his best to help her.

Samantha watched the ground as it opened up. When the shaking had stopped the faint stench of death made her stomach turn. She had never smelled anything so repulsive. She did her best to ignore the feeling that she was going to be sick.

A staircase now descended down into the depths of the planet.

She tried to catch Ben's eye but he turned his back to her as if the sight of her now made him sick.

Samantha had no idea why Ben was upset with her but decided that now was not the time to ask. She decided that she would ask him once they got back to the castle. For now she would have to just let it go and do what she needed to do.

Ben started to go down into the darkness. Samantha hesitantly followed with Hercules close behind her.

Samantha was about to ask Ben if he had any type of light, when torches suddenly lit themselves along the walls.

Everything was damp and Samantha could now smell the repugnant odor of rotting flesh. Trying to keep her stomach under control she asked Ben, "what is that horrible smell?"

Ben stopped to turn so he was facing her, "that is the smell of all the dead being tortured and rotting away." He regretted answering in such a way the second he saw the look on her face.

"Oh," she said as he turned around and continued to descend the steps.

She thought she heard something breathing heavily. She wanted to ask Ben about it but was afraid to hear the answer.

Once they reached the bottom it opened up into a large cavern. There were different tunnels leading in all directions. In the center was a big black creature, clearly asleep.

As they got closer three gigantic dog heads lifted up and started to growl. As the creature came at them, Samantha was startled and stumbled back into Hercules and would of fell if he wouldn't have steadied her.

"You alright?"

"Yeah, I'm good." she replied, feeling embarrassed.

Ben shook his head. He couldn't believe that Samantha was falling for the act Hercules was putting on.

He reached into his jacket and pulled out three bones and tossed one to each head. "Good boy!" He said patting the head that was closest to him. "Come on. Let's keep moving."

They followed Ben as he started down a tunnel.

"What was that thing?" Samantha asked.

"That 'thing' is Cerberus. He's my dog." Ben told her. "You remember him, don't you Hercules?"

"Yeah, I remember."

"Do you have any scars?" Ben laughed. He remembered when Zeus had sent Hercules to kill Cerberus.

The moment Hercules had shown up on the Underworld, Ben wanted to go stop him from entering.

He knew that Hercules wasn't there to just visit. Hercules had his sword drawn ready for a fight. It wasn't until later that Ben found out that Zeus had ordered Hercules to kill Cerberus.

Hades had refused to allow him to seal the door or interfere in the fight, so he had sat by his father's side and watched as Hercules tried his best to annihilate Cerberus.

The battle took only a matter of minutes and ended when Cerberus had grabbed ahold of Hercules' side and tossed him back up the stairs. For the first time ever, Hercules had gone home without a victory.

"No, Ben. He didn't get ahold of anything but my shirt." Hercules answered obviously annoyed with the fact that he had lost.

Ben knew that Hercules was lying, he remembered the blood on Cerberus' face and on the ground by the steps. He thought about calling Hercules out on his lie then decided that the truth would eventually come out.

Samantha wanted to hear more about what had happened, but figured asking would just make things worse. It was clear to her that her two companions despised each other.

She could tell that there was a lot of history that neither of them was ready to let go of. Her being here with just the two of them was obviously making things worse between them.

She decided to remain quiet and try to stay neutral between them.

The tunnel started to get more narrow as they walked. It wasn't long before they were single file. With Ben in front of her and Hercules behind her she started to feel trapped.

"This better not be a dead end." Hercules growled.

"We are almost there." Ben snapped back.

Samantha looked over Ben's shoulder and saw a red light glowing ahead of them.

The tunnel finally started to widen and she could now see what looked like a river of fire. They had entered another cavern, this one was a lot bigger than the one Cerberus had been sleeping in.

Once they were fully out of the tunnel, Samantha could see that it wasn't a river of fire but a river of lava that ran along the edge of the cave to light the space.

There were stone statues of gargoyles, each with a fierce twisted look on their faces, spaced evenly in front of the lava. Directly in the center was a black throne.

"Father?" Ben called out.

At first nothing happened. Then with a whoosh, a blue and black swirl of dust appeared in front of them. As the dust began to settle, a man appeared.

He stood towering over the three of them like a skyscraper. His long black hair hung down just above his knees. His piercing gray eyes seemed to see through them as he looked down.

Ben bowed on one knee. "Father, I have delivered Samantha to you."

Without acknowledging that Ben had spoken or that he was even there, Hades addressed Samantha, "You, are the daughter of Athena?"

Samantha nodded her head.

"Ignorant child! Speak when spoken to." Hades scolded.

Samantha could swear that she saw his eyes flash bright red. "I apologize. Yes sir, I am Athena's daughter."

"Why have you come?" He asked.

Ben looked confused, "Father, you told me…"

Hades silenced Ben with a single look of fury. Then turned back to Samantha waiting for her to reply.

"I am here for two reasons. The first being that I need your help." Samantha answered.

"And the second?"

"Because you need my help." Samantha replied as she took a step forward to not only show her seriousness but also to prove that no matter how big and intimidating he seemed, she was not afraid of him.

Hades took a step back and sat down on the throne. "And you are willing to help me?"

"Yes, but only if you help me." Samantha said. She wasn't sure if he knew that she had noticed the way he backed up when she had stepped towards him.

"And what is it that you need from me?"

"I need the key to release Kronos."

"You moronic child, do you know what you ask of me?" As Hades spoke, gold and blue flames burst from his head, his eyes now a flaming red.

"Father, please just listen." Ben pleaded standing to face Hades.

"I will not hear of it. Kronos will have all our heads if he were to be released. Ben, you know the role I played in trapping them. Have you forgotten all that you have learned?"

"If you help us free them, they may show you mercy." Ben continued to beg. "Please father, a Forbidden has returned. If you do not help now, it will eventually reach you."

Hades remembered what happened when Kronos had first created the Forbidden. Whole worlds were devoured. Endless life forms wiped from existence, including the one being that he truly loved.

He still blamed Kronos for her death. Kronos had swore that he did not know the Forbidden would be so destructive. Hades had still helped Zeus trap all the Titans in the darkest part of Tartarus.

After the door had been shut and sealed, Hades was imprisoned within the planet by Zeus to guard the door.

Over the thousands of years trapped on the Underworld, Hades had thought about how his own father had apologized. A few times he had almost had himself believing that Kronos had been telling him the truth.

Then he would remember, the summer breeze making Mileena's

(mee-leh-nah) golden hair fan out behind her. Her beautiful blue eyes dancing with love as she looked at him.

Just the thought of her was enough to fuel his rage. When she was killed he had turned every ounce of love he had into pure hatred of everyone and everything.

He also knew that if Zeus had not had declared war on the Titans, Mileena would still be alive. The only way he could get to Zeus was to be freed of this place.

"I will help you. However, you must complete three tasks for me."

"What tasks?" Hercules asked.

"You will need to collect the shell of judgement, a vial of blood from the undead and a tear from a ghost." Hades said with a grin.

"How are we supposed to get all those things?" Samantha asked.

"That is for you to figure out. Gather the items and return them to me, I will allow you to free Kronos. Now go." Hades disappeared in a puff of smoke.

Hercules, Samantha and Ben started to make their way back through the tunnel. When they reached the outer cavern Cerberus was gone. As they ascended the stairs the torches extinguished themselves behind them.

"He knew we were coming didn't he?" Samantha asked Ben.

"Of course he did." Ben smiled. "He knows everything that happens here."

After they resurfaced, the opening vanished as if it was never there.

They returned to Bella Isola to start figuring out how to collect the items that Hades had requested.

Samantha told Wayne about the deal they had made with Hades. She didn't realize he would be so mad at her.

"Why would you make a deal like that? Do you realize that Hades will betray you? He will do and say anything to escape the Underworld." Wayne yelled at her.

Hercules stepped in front of Samantha, "She did what she had to do, so back off."

"Uncle Wayne." Samantha said stepping around Hercules to stand between them. "I didn't have much of a choice. A deal with Hades is the only way to stop the Forbidden. I can't release the Titans without his help."

"Maybe you won't need the Titans. There are other powerful beings that might be able to…"

"Where? Where are these powerful beings that are as strong as the Titans?" Samantha retorted.

"Alright, Sammy. You do what you need to." He said as he turned and walked away from her. "But, good luck convincing Jade to allow any vampire to give you blood."

As Wayne disappeared around the corner to find Jade, Samantha turned and went up the wide staircase.

"Where are you going?" Hercules called after her.

Samantha turned around and replied, "I need some time alone."

Jade had given each of them their own suite to stay in. Samantha walked down the hall and entered the sixth door on the left side. Jade had called it the Lilly suite.

Most of the castle had stone walls and floors but all the private suites were modern and up to date.

The Lilly suite was a bright white with painted lilies scattered here and there on the walls. The canopy bed had purple lace that draped down touching the floor.

Windows that opened wide allowed sunlight to flood into the room. A warm breeze swept the room making it seem more like a dream than reality.

A sitting area with a fireplace included a matching set of furniture, a black leather loveseat and a recliner. A light brown coffee table sat in the middle of the light purple area rug. The rest of the floor was a white shag carpet.

Samantha couldn't have decorated the space any better. She felt relaxed in this room. Right now that's what she needed, so she went into the bathroom and ran a hot bath. She was glad that it was an old claw foot tub that was deep enough to submerge her whole body in the steaming hot water.

As she laid in the hot water, she thought about everything that had happened since her birthday. She thought of Toby and how he had said he would never leave her and she started to cry.

He had left many times before to train with Zeus but he had always returned. This time it was her fault and he would never return. She should have never let him take the wolves home. If only she would have went with him or went in his place he would still be here with her.

She could still feel his arms around her and wished that the feeling was real, that he was here right now with her. Holding her close.

She laid there crying until she started to fall asleep.

She heard someone whisper, "I love you."

"Toby?" She said sitting up in the tub.

She looked around hoping against all odds that he was really there, but no one was there.

Samantha got out of the tub and dried off. She picked up her clean clothes and got dressed. She decided that she wasn't ready to face anyone yet so she went to lay down on the bed. It didn't take her long to drift off to sleep.

She started dreaming... Her and Toby were sitting on the porch steps of the farm house that they grew up in, it was a beautiful day. The sun was bright and there were fluffy white clouds in the blue sky.

"Toby, why did you have to leave me, you said you wouldn't?" She asked him.

He smiled that sweet smile he reserved only for her, "Sammy, I didn't leave you. I told you I would always be by your side and I meant it."

Tears rolled down her face. "But you did. You died."

"Nothing can keep me from you, not even death." He said as he leaned over and kissed her lips softly.

She sunk down and put her head to his chest. "Toby, I want you back. I don't want to live without you."

"Oh, my sweet Sammy, I am with you." Holding her tightly.

Samantha wiped the tears from her face. "I will find a way to be with you again."

"Is that why you are releasing the Titans?" He asked.

"Not the only reason but if anyone can return you to me, they could."

Toby didn't respond to that, he knew the Titans could not help him return to her. Since he had died, he had seen many things that he never knew existed and learned even more.

"There is a way that I can come back to you." He said.

Samantha sat up and looked at him, "how? I will do anything."

BAM.

Samantha jumped out of the bed to see a crow had flown into her room and hit the wall, landing on the floor with a thud breaking its wing.

She picked the injured bird up and sat on the bed looking at it.

"You did that on purpose, didn't you?" She asked the creature.

The bird seemed to look at her in amusement but then looked away.

She tried to ignore the feeling that this was more than just a bird.

"You really should watch where you are flying." she said to the bird, thinking that it would turn and look at her but hoping it wouldn't. The bird continued to look towards the door.

As she stroked the bird's feathers, she saw the broken wing start to move. She heard the bones cracking and felt them as they were resetting themselves, she quickly sat the bird on the bed and backed away.

Within a few moments, the bird stretched both wings and looked at Samantha. It bowed its head and flew out of the window.

Samantha shut the windows and laid back down hoping to see Toby again, but the dream wouldn't come, instead she fell into a dreamless sleep.

After she had rested, Samantha found Gabby in the library. "Gabby, I have been looking for you. What are you doing in here?"

"After you got back, Hercules said that Hades wants the Shell of Judgement, I decided to come in here and do some research."

Samantha went to sit beside her friend on the padded bench.

"What did you find out?"

Gabby grabbed one of the books that she had lying open. "Look at this." She pointed to a symbol that Samantha had never seen before.

The symbol was in the shape of an angel but something bothered Samantha about it. "What is it?"

"That is the mark of Rhea." Gabby saw the look of confusion on Samantha's face. "Rhea is the wife of Kronos. Zeus' mother."

"Oh my."

"Now look here." She pulled another book out. "This is the Shell of Judgement."

The picture showed a pink shell with the same symbol on the middle of it.

"What would Hades want with it?"

Gabby shook her head, " I have no idea."

"Does the book say where we can find the shell?" Samantha asked.

"No. But it didn't have to tell me. Once I saw the picture I recognized it. It's on Mermaid Bay."

Samantha stood up. "Mermaid Bay? How are we going to get there?"

"Sammy, you are a Traveler. You can go wherever you want."

"Oh Yeah, but I don't know how to on my own yet." Samantha said.

Gabby took Samantha by the hand. "Yes, you do. It's the same as when we first came to the island. All you have to do is think of the place you wanna go and then go there. When do you plan on going?"

"As soon as I get the guys."

"No. Men are not allowed on Mermaid Bay." Gabby informed her. "But we could take Jade if you want. I'm sure Wayne would like for you and her to get to know each other."

"Yeah, that's a great idea. An all girl mission, no boys allowed." They were both laughing as they walked out of the library to find Jade.

Samantha and Gabby found Jade in the large dining room. Jade was sitting at the head of the table with four vampires sitting beside her, that Samantha had never saw before.

Jade looked up and smiled at the two girls. "Come on in." She said with a smile.

"We don't want to interrupt you. We can come back." Samantha said.

Jade shook her head. "Don't be silly."

"We can finish this later." Jade dismissed the vampires, who all seemed annoyed at having their meeting disrupted.

Once the door was pulled shut, Jade said with a smile, "Now, how can I help you?"

"You didn't have to stop your meeting. We could have waited." Samantha was sure that they had interrupted something very important.

Jade waved her hand, "it is nothing that the council can't discuss later. Tell me, what's going on?"

"Samantha wants to go to Mermaid Bay, I can go but the guys can't."

"So, you want me to go with you?" Jade asked.

"Yeah, if you're not too busy." Gabby answered. "Safety in numbers."

Jade looked at the girls, "when do we leave?"

"Right now." The two girls answered together.

Samantha stood in front of the fireplace with Jade on her left and Gabby on her right, Samantha pictured what Mermaid Bay would look like. Just as they were leaving Samantha saw Hercules and Vic come in the room. Both men ran towards them but were too late.

Samantha, Gabby and Jade appeared in the middle of a yensen. Even from here Samantha could see how beautiful this world was. She looked around her and all she could see was clear water and beautiful trees covered with pink flowers along the shore line.

CHAPTER 6

The sky was a magnificent shade of light purple with yellow clouds.

Samantha and Jade were so busy being amazed at the beautiful scene in front of them that they had not noticed Gabby taking her clothes off.

"Watch this." Gabby said as she dove into the water.

Samantha and Jade watched in astonishment as Gabby's legs were replaced by a gorgeous tail. There was a brilliant mix of light metallic blues pinks and greens. They watched as Gabby swam down deep and resurfaced by jumping out of the water into the air high enough to flip and dive back into the water without a splash.

"Gabby, you are beautiful. I have never saw anything so magical in my life." Samantha told her in complete awe.

Gabby's face turned a bright red. "Thank you Sammy."

Hercules traced the teleport trail to Mermaid Bay but was thrown back to Bella Isola by a great force. He and Vic then went to inform Wayne that Samantha had left and where she was going.

"Why didn't you stop her?"

"Jade went with her, they left too fast." Vic answered.

Wayne looked at Hercules, "why didn't you follow them?"

Hercules laughed, "you must not know that men, of any kind, can no longer step foot or fin on Mermaid Bay."

"How is it possible for them to have blocked you, a Traveler?"

"I assume they had help. The same kind of help Jade had to put a barrier here on the island."

Wayne turned away from them, "then they are on their own. I just hope they know what they are doing."

Jade and Samantha jumped into the water. Samantha expected the water to be cold but it was the perfect temperature. They swam to the edge of the lake and sat on the bank. Samantha was amazed when she realized that her clothes had dried the moment she had gotten out of the water.

"What about your clothes?" Samantha asked looking back at the small island.

"I won't need them in the village."

Samantha and Jade exchanged a strange look before they both shrugged their shoulders.

They followed Gabby through the woods. Samantha enjoyed watching the small animals running around, un-afraid of them. None of the animals that she saw here were like anything she had ever seen before.

First there was one that almost resembled a rabbit until she looked closer and saw that the only thing this animal had in common with a rabbit was it's fur. The face was elongated with pointed teeth and beady eyes. All the other animals were too fast to get a good look at.

It didn't take long before Gabby stopped.

At first Samantha thought Gabby had gotten lost because they had reached more water, this water looked like it went on forever. Then following Gabby's gaze, Samantha realized the whole village was under the water.

"How are we going to be able to be in the village? We can't breathe under water."

"Well, being a vampire, I don't need to breath. So the question is, how are you going to." Jade corrected with a smile.

"I just need to get my mother, she will give you something to help with that. I will be right back." she dove into the water and swam down towards the village.

It wasn't long before they saw two mermaids swimming back to the surface. They both pulled themselves out of the water and sat on the bank.

"Samantha, this is my mother, Isabel. Mother, this is Samantha Martin and Jade."

"I am so happy to meet you both. Gabby doesn't get to come home very often but when she does, all she talks about is you. I am so glad she has such a great friend." Isabel's tail was a mix between blue and purple. Her hair was the same shade of red as Gabby's.

"Awe, thank you. It's wonderful to meet you too!" Samantha replied.

Isabel handed Samantha what looked like a slug with small tentacles coming from its face. "This will allow you to breath underwater as long as you are welcome here."

"Um, what am I supposed to do with that?"

"This will go into your nose and enable you to breath underwater." Isabel explained.

Samantha cringed, "Up my nose?" she asked looking at Gabby.

"Yes, up your nose." Gabby laughed.

Samantha slowly put the slug like creature under her nose, it immediately started to slither it's way inside. Samantha expected it to hurt more then it did.

"It will only take a minute for it to get in place, then we can go to the village." Isabel said.

Samantha was surprised to find that the village was in an underwater air bubble. All the mermaids had legs and were walking around the village naked.

There were mermaids everywhere Samantha looked. Each one smiling and laughing. Samantha could tell that the mermaids were very happy people.

Samantha noticed that there were no children here and thought that was strange. There were at least a hundred mermaids and not one of them had a child with them.

The houses looked like small round hills that had walkways coming from each one and met in the middle of the village where a colorful statue of a beautiful mermaid stood.

She seemed to be watching over everyone with her golden eyes. Her long wavy blue hair flowing down her back as she sat on a rock with a serious look on her face.

"That is Madam Sirena. She is said to be the first of our kind." Gabby whispered to Samantha. "There is a myth that she still lives here, hidden somewhere. She disappeared after the first group of mermen found Mermaid Bay."

"How long ago was that?" Jade asked.

Gabby turned and looked at her wondering how she had heard them talking, then remembered Jade was a vampire, and so responded, "That was over a thousand years ago."

"No one has seen her since?" Samantha asked. "How could she still be alive?"

"I don't think she is, mermaids usually only live a few hundred years. Few have said that they saw her swimming around in the oceans, but I think that's just their way of keeping her alive." Gabby said. "Some even said that there are times when the statue disappears. They think that she sits there in plain sight making everyone think she is a statue."

Samantha turned and looked back at the statue, Madam Sirena now had a smile on her face, like she was mocking Gabby. Samantha thought it best not to mention that she saw the statue's face change.

They followed Isabel into one of the round hills. The houses were all under ground. Isabel's home had four stories to it. They had entered into the main floor, which had the sitting room and a small den.

They all sat down on the chairs that circled a small wooden table. Samantha looked around and saw two small windows that she had not noticed on the outside of the house, as she continued to look around she saw the only pictures were of Gabby and Samantha at the farmhouse or ones taken at school.

"Why are you really here?" Isabel asked not looking like the sweet kind woman who had just greeted them. "I know this is not just a social visit and I want the truth."

Samantha waited for Gabby to answer.

"Truth is, we need the Shell of Judgement." Gabby said quietly.

"What the hell do you want with that?" Isabel yelled.

"We need it for Hades. He made a deal with Samantha…"

"Made a deal?" She turned to Samantha. "Why would you make a deal with that creature?"

Samantha was almost afraid to answer, but decided she really had nothing to lose at that point. "I made a deal to release the Titans."

"The Titans! Oh, how I miss the days when they were in charge. Prometheus would bring the most wonderful gifts.

There was order on every planet. Kronos was a great leader, he had put a barrier up to keep anyone not full blooded mermaid from getting to Mermaid Bay.

With Zeus in charge the barrier was removed and the mermen returned. Wreaking havoc on our planet."

It only took Gabby a moment to understand what her mother was really saying, "I guess, you want the Titans back to keep all impure mermaids out as well?"

Isabel looked to her daughter, "what gave you that idea?"

"It's obvious that I am not welcome here, I'm only allowed two visits a year. With Kronos' return to power he will replace the barrier and I will not be able to return at all." Gabby was looking at the floor as she spoke, so disgusted with her mother that she couldn't bare to look at her.

"If he replaces the barrier and you can not return, I will leave Mermaid Bay. I would never choose anything over you." Isabel said firmly. "Besides, the barrier that is in place now is working perfectly."

Gabby looked at her mother and saw that she was telling the truth. Even though the other mermaids banished their children created by the mermen, her mother had always wanted Gabby with her as much as possible.

Gabby nodded in understanding.

"Will you help us?" Samantha asked.

"I will help you get the shell. But we must not be seen taking it. The punishment for stealing the shell is death." Isabel said to them.

"Where is it?" Gabby asked her mother.

"It's kept in the great hall. Which is guarded by Thyrus."

"I thought he was dead." Gabby said.

"No, he was dormant for a hundred years. We woke him when the shell returned." Isabel told them.

Samantha and Jade looked at each other then to Gabby.

Gabby saw the looks they were giving her and answered, "Thyrus is a dragon that has lived here before mermaids even existed."

"A dragon? I thought they were just a myth?" Jade asked.

Isabel leaned back in her chair. "Dragons exist on every planet, they hide in caves or underground very careful not to be seen by mortals. That is another change since Zeus took charge. The dragons use to fill the skies, until Zeus filled the mortals with fear of them. The mortals began hunting the dragons, so they started to hide."

"I know how the dragons feel, my kind also have to hide for fear of being hunted by mortals." Jade said.

Isabel took Jade's hand, "Kronos will put a stop to that."

Samantha asked Isabel, "Who has access to the shell?"

"No one. Anyone who touches it, is judged by Astrea, Goddess of Judgement. If judged bad you die instantly." Isabel answered. "No one is permitted to go near it for any reason."

"What if you're judged good?" Jade asked.

"No one has ever been judged good." Isabel shook her head. "I am afraid that all life has been corrupted since the beginning of time."

Samantha turned to Gabby, "If we can't touch it how are we going to be able to take it to Hades?"

"I don't know." Gabby said.

"What about a glove?" Jade asked.

Isabel turned to her. "Yes, that would work. Do you have one?"

"No." Jade answered. "But I do have this." She held up a piece of cloth.

"That just might work." Isabel said with a smile. "Do you know why Hades wants the shell?"

"No, I didn't ask and he didn't offer the information."

"Well whatever he wants it for can't be good. The shell of Judgement is a very powerful object."

The four of them started forming a plan to get past Thyrus and out of the village without being seen.

Isabel said she had a way to get past the dragon but getting out of the village would be difficult as there were mermaids who patrolled the village at night. They would need to be very quick and very quiet to pull this off.

Isabel showed them the rest of her house except the bottom floor which she explained was her private room. The second floor consisted of what might be called a bathroom. There was a large pool in the middle of the room.

As Samantha looked closer she saw what looked like eggs at the bottom, "what are those?"

"Those are my children. As you may have noticed, we do not flaunt our children in the open, they remain hidden until they mature." Isabel looked at Gabby, "well most do."

She then invited them into the kitchen on the third floor. After they had all eaten and it began to get dark they gathered in the sitting room back on the first floor.

Then they slowly made their way through the village towards the great hall. When they could see the building, Samantha was amazed that they had not been able to see it from the surface, it was enormous. It looked as though it were made out of marble. There were no windows and the door was made of some strange type of metal.

As they approached, Samantha heard a loud banging noise coming from inside the building. The closer they got the louder the noise became.

"Just how big is this dragon?" Samantha asked getting worried that someone else would hear all the noise.

"He's actually smaller than most dragons." Gabby replied quietly.

Samantha nodded her head even though she had never seen any other dragons to compare this one to. She had read about dragons and from what she had learned, she was not looking forward to coming face-to-face with this one.

Jade followed closely behind Samantha but did not say a word. Samantha looked back a few times to make sure Jade was still there, she walked so silently that Samantha couldn't hear her footsteps.

As they walked up the marble steps, something slammed into the door from the inside. Samantha hoped that the door would hold the beast in, looking closer she saw that the door didn't even have a dent.

"How are we going to get past Thyrus?" Samantha asked Isabel.

"Once he eats this, "She said holding a handful of seaweed out to show Samantha, "he will fall fast asleep and we will be able to enter safely."

"Seaweed, why would dragons eat seaweed, I thought they ate meat?" Jade asked.

Gabby started laughing, "Whoever told you the dragons ate meat? I've never saw a dragon that ate meat. Their favorite food is seaweed, even though it puts them to sleep. They rely on mermaids and other beings to get it for them since they can't go in the water."

"Well how would we know what it eats, we've never seen a dragon?" Samantha said.

Isabel turned and looked at the three girls. "Will you three be quiet? You are going to wake up the whole village. If anybody catches us trying to get into the Great Hall we will all be killed."

The girls fell silent as Isabel reached for the door, she slowly started to push the door open but stopped when Thyrus put his nose at the opening.

As the dragon breathed through its nose, out the door Samantha could smell a nasty odor. Isabel took the seaweed, reached inside the door and fed it to Thyrus, then she shut the door again.

"Now, we wait." She said looking at the girls.

"How did the mermaids get the dragon here if they can't be in the water?" Samantha whispered to Gabby.

"They have a machine that creates an air bubble around anything that they want. That's how they got Thyrus down here."

It took a long time for the dragon to fall asleep. Once all the thrashing and noise had stopped, Isabel carefully opened the door again and looked inside.

"All right I think it's safe now, I think he's asleep." She told them.

As she walked through the door, Samantha saw the dragon laying in the far corner fast asleep. Samantha held in her laughter as she looked at the tiny dragon.

Isabel took a torch off the wall and lit it. As the light reached the sleeping dragon, Samantha could see the wings and head of the beast.

"I thought dragons were bigger." Samantha said.

Isabel turned around, "don't let his size fool you, he may be small but he is just as powerful as the big dragons who left him behind."

They slowly walked around Thyrus to a door that had a mermaid carved into it. Isabel then pulled out a key shaped like a fish tail and opened the door. The smell that came from the room was worse than the dragon's breath.

Isabel then turned to Samantha, "You and Gabby must be the ones to go in. I will not risk being judged by the shell. Jade may not enter since she is a Vampire. Just make sure you do not touch it with your hand for you will be judged."

The two entered the room and at first thought it was empty. As Gabby used the torch to light up the darkest corners of the room they saw a table sitting against the back wall with something on top of it. As they continued walking they could see the shell sitting in the middle of the table.

As they got closer to it, it started to glow, by the time they reached the edge of the table the shell was radiating light so brightly that they had to look away.

As Samantha turned her head to the right she saw a man standing in the corner, half hidden in the shadows. She strained her eyes trying to see who it was, but when she blinked he was gone.

Gabby took the piece of cloth and wrapped it around her hand. She carefully picked the shell up, but when she turned to walk away she bumped into Samantha who was standing directly behind her still looking at the corner, both girls stumbled.

The shell slipped from Gabby's hand and out of reflex Samantha reached out and grabbed it with her right hand, knowing that she should have just let it fall to the floor.

The light that engulfed Samantha was a bright blue. She could still feel the shell in her hand but as hard as she tried, could not let go. The light continued to get brighter and brighter until she couldn't see anything but the bright blue glow.

Gabby's cries faded away and then Samantha could hear nothing.

Just when Samantha thought she could no longer stand the light, everything went black, and out of the blackness she heard a voice speak to her.

"Who are you?" The voice asked.

Samantha tried to move but was frozen. Then she tried to speak, no sound came out.

"You cannot speak. You cannot move. You cannot escape" The voice said.

'How am I to answer you if I cannot speak?' Samantha thought.

"I do not need to hear your voice to hear your answer. Who are you?"

'I am Samantha Martin, daughter of Athena.' Samantha answered.

"What are you? Where did you come from?"

Confused Samantha answered, "I am a Traveler, I come from Earth."

"Even you know that is a lie, however you do not know the true answer. No matter, you have touched the shell and so you will be judged accordingly."

"But it does matter." Samantha thought. 'You are a Goddess and should know who my parents are.'

'There are things even a Goddess can not know. You're mother held many secrets that no one else had ever found the answers to. Now you are ready to be judged Samantha Martin?"

At that question Samantha began to get very scared. She knew she was not perfect and was afraid to be judged badly. She wasn't ready to die, there were too many things she still had to do with her life.

'No I am not.' Samantha thought.

"You are holding the shell of judgement. If you did not want to be judged, why would you touch it?"

'I didn't mean to touch it. It was an accident.'

"Nothing is ever an accident. Everything is as it should be and happens as it should happen."

'So, I was supposed to be judged?' Samantha thought.

"Yes. What good have you done for your world?"

Samantha started to think of anything and everything that may be considered a good deed. She thought about the time that she had found the small kitten that had been attacked by a bigger animal. The kitten could hardly breathe.

Samantha had taken the kitten home and nursed it back to health.

"How did you saving that kitten help your world?" The voice asked.

'I don't know that it did.' Samantha thought. 'I don't know if anything I ever did helped my world.'

"Judgment is upon you. I have decided. You, Samantha Martin have been judged... good. You shall now have the knowledge of all those before you, who have failed judgement. Use it wisely."

Samantha fell to the floor crying. Gabby was by her side. " Are you alright?"

Samantha hugged Gabby tightly trying to get her emotions under control. The new knowledge that had been bestowed upon her started filling her head. It was almost too much for her to bear.

Images of the past flashed before her eyes. She saw a young girl crying, an old man dying and a creature sitting by his side.

She watched as images of what had to be other Travelers came and went through her mind. Different worlds and battles both won and lost. A thousand images past before her eyes every one of them jumbled with the last and the next.

After a few moments when Samantha's head had cleared up. She got to her feet.

"Yes. I am fine Gabby." Samantha answered.

"What happened? How did you survive?" Gabby asked. "Were you judged?"

Samantha nodded her head, "Yes. Believe it or not I was judged good".

At that Gabby smiled. "How was you judged? What happened?"

"I'm not sure all I know is that there was a voice that spoke to me and I... I." Samantha knew what she wanted to say but couldn't get the words out. "Guess I'm not supposed to tell you."

Gabby nodded her head in understanding. "Alright then. As long as you are alright let's get out of here."

The two girls walked out of the room, Isabel saw the shell in Samantha's hand. "How are you able to hold the shell?"

"I was judged." Samantha replied.

"And you survived.?" Isabel asked her.

Samantha nodded her head.

Thyrus shifted in his sleep.

"We better get out of here before he wakes up." Isabel said.

As they were exiting the Great Hall they heard a voice yell, "What are you doing in there?"

They turned and saw a woman with purple hair standing at the bottom of the steps looking up at them.

Isabel looked over her shoulder to the three girls, "Run." She said.

The four of them ran towards the closest edge of the village. Samantha and Jade had already started to swim to the surface. Samantha looked back just in time to see three mermaids grab ahold of Gabby.

Isabel had turned back to help her daughter.

Samantha watched in terror as a group of mermaids reached Gabby.

Gabby kicked her feet and screamed as they tied her to the post at the edge of the village. Isabel was fighting her way through to reach her daughter.

All of a sudden Samantha could no longer breathe underwater and knew that she was no longer welcome on Mermaid Bay. She fought against the water to reach the surface.

She could feel the water filling her lungs. Samantha felt a force slowly pushing her up through the water. She looked down and saw a silhouette of a man. She was almost to the surface when someone grabbed her arm and pulled her upward.

When Jade had seen Samantha struggling, she had jumped back into the water and pulled her to the surface.

Samantha coughed out the water onto the ground. "Gabby, Gabby, we have to go back." She cried.

"We can't go back. You would never make it, not being able to breathe underwater and it's too late, they already have her." Jade said.

Samantha looked back down under the water and saw the flickering of flames. Even though she did not want to admit it to herself, she knew that her best friend was now dead. Dead because she had helped Samantha.

Samantha laid on the bank crying. Jade did the best she could to console her.

Once again, Jade looked down in the water and saw no less than ten mermaids swimming up at them.

"We have to get out of here. They're coming." She told Samantha.

Samantha grabbed Jade's arm and disappeared.

Once back at Bella Isola, Jade told Hercules, Wayne and Vic what had happened. She told them about how they got past the dragon and how Samantha had got the shell. Then she they told them how the other mermaids had killed Gabby and her mother Isabel.

Samantha looked at Vic, "it's my fault. I should have never let her go with me, I should have gone alone."

"If you would have gone alone, they would have killed you." Hercules said.

Samantha looked at him with anger in her eyes, "but Gabby would be alive!" she yelled.

Vic wrapped his arms around her as she cried. "Shh, it's not your fault."

Seeing Samantha hurting was breaking Hercules' heart, he couldn't stand seeing her hurt so badly. He was sorry the moment he spoke the insensitive words to her. He never was good at knowing what to say in a situation like this. The fact that she had turned to Vic to comfort her, hurt even more.

No one noticed when Hercules had disappeared. They were all too busy trying to convince Samantha that Gabby's death was not her fault.

Vic held Samantha for a very long time before she finally stopped crying and fell asleep, he then carried her up to her room and laid her on the bed gently.

He couldn't stand the thought of leaving her, so he sat in the chair beside her bed the rest of the night. He didn't move until the sun was almost up and she started tossing around on the bed.

The moment Samantha had fallen asleep she was back at the farm house. Toby was sitting on the porch waiting for her.

"Toby!" Samantha ran to him, he stood up and took her into his arms.

"Samantha, my love. There was nothing you could do." He whispered in her ear.

"I should have went alone."

Toby started to laugh, "do you really think she would have let you?"

Samantha looked at him, "no I don't think she would have. But why did she have to die? Why not me?" she lowered her head.

"Don't you ever say that again!" Toby gently lifted her chin until he could look into her eyes. "You are all that matters right now. You must live."

"Why would I want to live when everyone I love dies helping me?"

"Sammy, you are more powerful and more important than you realize. You are the one that will save the universe and all those living. If you die the Forbidden will destroy every planet along with all other life."

Samantha started crying, "I don't want to go on without you and Gabby."

"What you want don't matter now. This is not about how you feel, it's about what you must do."

"To move on I must forget. I know what to do. I will remove the memories of Gabby dying so I don't know."

"And of me." Toby added.

"No! I never want to forget about you. I will find a way to…"

Toby and the farmhouse started to fade away.

"Continue your journey and all will be as it should be."

Samantha turned and saw Cy standing in front of the lake where she had met Poseidon.

"Cy, please tell me you are not dead?" She said walking over to him.

He smiled, "No Samantha. I'm not dead."

"Then how are you here?"

"That's not what's important. What is important is that you must continue the path you are on. Your father has waited a long time to see you."

"My father?" her eyes widen as what he said sunk in. "Cy do you know who he is? Or where I can find him?"

"Samantha finish the task you set out to do and things will fall into place for you."

Everything started to fade again, "no please don't go. I need to know who he is."

The next morning when Samantha awoke, she remembered everything from her dreams. She knew that she had to listen to Toby and Cy. She must continue on, no matter what happens.

She thought of how Toby had taken the bad memories from Gabby and placed them into a stone. She decided she would ask Hercules to take last night's events from her memory.

Samantha searched the castle looking for Hercules but couldn't find him anywhere. She asked everybody she saw if they had seen him, but nobody had.

Hercules had returned to Mount Olympus to speak with his father. He wanted a way to be able to enter Mermaid Bay.

"You must go to Tara, only she can open the protection spell." Zeus told him.

As Samantha sat eating breakfast she decided she could not just sit around, She had a mission to do. She had to get all the items to Hades to free the Titans and stop the Forbidden.

The undead blood was easy to get, for Jade offered it to her freely. Samantha knew Jade only gave her the blood because she felt bad about not being able to help Gabby. But no one could feel as bad about it than Samantha did.

Gabby was her best friend and Samantha had not been able to help her. Samantha knew that if she could understand and use her own powers more, she could have saved Gabby.

The tear of a ghost however, would be very hard to obtain.

Samantha wasn't even sure where to get a tear of a ghost. It wasn't until after she had finished picking at her breakfast that she remembered Ben was somewhere in the castle. He might know where to go to obtain the tear.

Ben had decided to stay in one of the 'rooms' on the lower level of the castle. Samantha went through the foyer and down the steps that led to the cells. She found Ben in the first cell on the left hand side.

"Why are you down here?" Samantha asked him.

Ben looked up at her and smiled, "guess I feel more comfortable underground." He laughed.

"I need your help." Samantha said.

"Anything for you." Ben replied.

"First, I need to know can you remove memories like Toby did?"

"Yes, all travelers have the powers to remove memories. What memories do you want removed?" Ben asked.

"I want the memories of the mermaids capturing Gabby taken away. I don't want to remember seeing her captured and killed." Samantha said with tears in her eyes.

Ben knew exactly how she felt.

A long time ago, Ben had made a request that Zeus allow him to visit Mount Olympus. Zeus had hesitated, he didn't want Hades son to take anything from there that could help Hades escape the prison that Zeus had trapped him in.

After Ben had sworn an oath of silence that stopped him from telling Hades anything that he may learn on Mount Olympus, he was allowed a place there.

Before Toby had been sent to be her guard, Ben and Toby had been best friends. Once Toby had left and started his life as a young child, he had forgotten who Ben was.

He remembered the time on Mount Olympus when he and Toby had been watching the mortals on Alpha One. Toby was fascinated by them since he was never allowed to visit there. He had found it amazing how the mortals would make promises and vows to each other only to break them, also how they could be so cruel and kill one another for such petty reasons.

Toby had resolved to help the mortals as much as he could from Mount Olympus. Eventually by doing this he gained Zeus' permission to visit Alpha One for short periods of time to help the mortals he felt needed him the most.

Every now and then, Toby would help one get through a hard time. If they had lost a loved one to Death, he would visit them at night when they were asleep and help ease their minds.

He also took pity on the mortal children, Toby saw how small and defenseless they were. He placed protection on every mortal child. If one would become sick, he would heal them.

Ben however, thought the mortals where a lower life-form that did not have a clue. He watched as they scrambled around the planet, not caring who they hurt or what they destroyed.

They had polluted the air and the seas with all their machines, gasses and garbage. He had never seen one mortal that he thought deserved the life they had.

Ben did not agree with Toby that the mortals deserved the help of the Gods in any way.

It was Toby who convinced him that mortals were doing the best they could with the knowledge they had. Toby had always said that the Gods and Demigods were blessed with expanded knowledge, which made them seem as though they were better, even though they were not.

After Toby had convinced Ben, he started to help his friend in protecting the mortals and their children.

Thinking of Toby he said, "I will help you Samantha. Do you have a stone?"

"No, no, I don't have a stone. Does it have to be a special stone or will any stone do?" Samantha asked.

"Any stone will do." Ben answered. "However, it has to be a stone of your choosing."

While Samantha was on her way up the stairs, Ben saw an opportunity. He went to the farm house and retrieved a stone that he had hidden there a few years ago. He then returned just outside the castle and placed the stone where he knew Samantha would find it. He disappeared just as Samantha had opened the castle door.

Samantha looked around for the perfect stone. When she saw one that had beautiful purple and green swirls, she picked it up. Something about this stone was familiar to her but she couldn't figure out why.

She took the stone back down to Ben. He held the stone against her forehead and removed all memories of Gabby. When he got done he looked at her, "now, how do you feel about Gabby dying?"

"Gabby who?" Samantha asked.

Ben smiled. "You said you needed my help. What can I help you with?"

Samantha thought for a moment then replied, "I need to find a ghost tear, but don't know where to find one."

"Mondo Del Fantasma is the only world where ghosts reside." Ben told her.

"How do I get there? "

"Why not ask Hercules to help you?" He snapped at her. Ben had tried to keep his jealousy at bay, he wanted to be a good guy. Someone who deserved Samantha.

"Look, if you don't want to help me then just say so." Samantha said.

"If you only knew the truth, things would be different." Ben said under his breath.

"What do you mean?" Samantha took a step towards him.

He backed away, "Look, I do want to help you, but I don't want to be the last one you come to for help."

Samantha was realizing that everything she did, said, or didn't do affected those around her. She had been so busy in her own head, with her own problems, that she failed to see the ones trying to help her were the ones she had been pushing away.

She knew there was something Ben wanted to tell her, but for whatever reason he wouldn't, or couldn't.

"Ben, I am so sorry. I didn't mean to make you feel like I didn't need your help, because I do. We have only known each other a short while. Hell, I didn't even know that you were a Demigod or that I was for that matter until recently."

He sighed, "I understand that Samantha, but now that you do know please understand that I want to help you and be there for you, if only you would let me."

Samantha took his hand. "Ben, I do need your help. Please will you help me?"

"I will help you. I just have one condition."

"Anything." she said slowly pulling her hand out of his.

He held her hand firmly, "Don't forget about me once this mission is done. Don't put me on the back burner again."

Samantha smiled, she was sure he would ask something big of her. "I promise I will never do that to you again."

Ben sighed and said, "then let's go get that tear."

CHAPTER 7

Without another word, he tightened his grip on her hand and they disappeared.

They arrived at Mondo Del Fantasma a few moments later. As Samantha looked around all she could see in the darkness was headstones and a bunch of creepy trees. The trees had no leaves on them, each one looked dead.

As Samantha looked out at the headstones, she saw what looked like mist floating up from random ones. She knew without knowing how, that they were the ghosts of the planet.

They watched as mist came out of the headstone directly in front of them, it approached them, stopping just in front of them.

"What do you want?" the ghost said taking the form of a man.

"Marcus, we need your help." Ben said.

The ghost laughed, "don't you always?"

Ben didn't laugh but smiled, " yeah, I suppose I do. This time you won't be helping just me, it will help you as well."

"What help do you think I need?" Marcus asked.

"There is a Forbidden that is alive and terrorizing planets. We have a way to stop it, but we need your help. If you do not help, it will eventually work its way here." Ben said.

"A Forbidden, are you sure? The Titans killed all of them centuries ago."

Ben shook his head, "they must have missed one."

"That isn't like them, they were always very thorough at whatever they did."

"Yeah they weren't this time." Samantha stated.

Marcus looked at her, "and you are?" he asked.

"I am Samantha Martin."

"Athena's daughter? I never thought I would ever get to meet you. It is a great honor to make your acquaintance." Marcus said bowing down.

"How do you know who I am?"

"Everyone knows who you and your sisters are by name, well anyone that is important."

"Have you ever met my sisters?"

Marcus shook his head. " No, but I did know your mother. I was shocked when I heard what happened to her. I was very sorry to hear about her departure. She was a good woman, and a good friend."

"Do you know who my father is?" Samantha asked.

"No. I don't think anybody knew who your father was or is. Is this why you have come here?"

Samantha looked at Ben.

"No." Ben answered. "We need to collect a tear from a ghost."

"A tear?" Marcus asked. "From a ghost? I don't see how that's possible. How can we produce a tear, if we can't take solid form?"

"So it's impossible then?" Samantha said throwing her hands up.

Ben gently took her arms and turned her to face him. "Nothing is impossible. We will figure this out."

Samantha looked over Ben's shoulder and saw a dark figure walking slowly towards them. As the figure got closer, Samantha could see that it was a young girl.

"I thought all the people here were ghosts?" Samantha whispered to Ben.

Ben turned around and saw the girl as well. "The only way anyone else could be here is if a Traveler brought them here, but I don't see why any of them would have done that."

Samantha turned to ask Marcus about the girl, but he had already disappeared.

Samantha saw the girl's face as she got closer. Where her eyes should have been was only sunken skin. Samantha's heart went out to the girl.

'Why would somebody desert this young girl on a world like this?' Samantha thought to herself.

The girl stopped a few feet in front of Samantha. "Zeus banished me here for helping the Giant Argos."

"Argos? The giant who helped Hera?" Ben asked. " That would make you Cassandra?"

"Yes, I see you have heard of me. Ben, son of Hades. I know why you are here." She said turning towards Samantha. "I can help you obtain what you need."

"How?" Samantha asked.

"You, Samantha Martin, daughter of Athena, have the power to make a ghost return to a physical being. You will need to use your powers to make Selena physical again." Cassandra said.

"How do you know what I need?"

"Cassandra is a seer. She sees things before they happen. She even sees what you will need before you know you need it." Ben answered.

"What else do you see?" Samantha asked Cassandra.

Cassandra held her hands up in front of her face, palms facing away from her. She moved her hands from side to side as if searching for something.

"I foresee four men, all of which love you in their own way. One loves you for your power, another is mystified by the power you hold over him. The last two of them have pure intentions and loves you truly. I also see those lost to you, will be returned." Cassandra lowered her hands.

Samantha pondered on what Cassandra had said, but only for a moment before asking, "Where do I find Selena?"

"Selena was taken to the Underworld for trying to escape." Cassandra said.

"So the one I need to make physical is in the Underworld?" Samantha asked. "Hades has had her this whole time?"

Cassandra nodded her head. "Yes. However, when you find her she will seem to already be in solid form. That is only an illusion of the Underworld. You will have to bring her back here, and once she returns she will regain her ghostly form.

You will have to use your powers to perform what needs to be done and get the tear you need."

Samantha looked at Ben. "We should take her with us, she could be of great use." Then to Cassandra she said, "will you come with us and help?"

"I would gladly help you, daughter of Athena." Cassandra replied.

"My father will not like this."

"He made a deal with us, why should he care how we get all of what he asked, as long as we get it?" Samantha asked.

"He would not like us taking a soul out of the Underworld. Because, the souls give him power." Ben replied. "Taking even one away will decrease his powers."

Samantha shook her head. "Well he will just have to get over it. It's the only way that we can get what he asked. If there was another way to get the tear we would, but there isn't."

"Alright, but we better ask him before taking Selena out of the Underworld."

"Okay, we will get his permission." Samantha lied, then to Cassandra, Samantha said, "give me your hand."

The moment Cassandra's hand firmly held Samantha's, they teleported to the Underworld.

Same as before, Ben pulled out a dagger and cut his hand to drip the blood on the hidden door, but the door didn't open.

"Are you sure this is the right place?" Samantha asked him. Then seeing the look he gave her she added, "Of course you know. But why isn't the door opening?"

"He knows why we are here and has sealed the door." Cassandra said, "Samantha you can open it. Concentrate."

Samantha looked at the ground and a mantra came to her, "Consenti Immissione." She repeated it three times and the door opened.

They descended down the dark staircase, the torches did not light on their own, Ben lit them as they went. When they reached the bottom Cerberus was not there, instead a different creature stood before them.

It had a long thin body, pointed tail and five long necks, each one with the head of a snake.

One of the heads came at Ben snapping its jaw shut just inches in front of his face. Ben jumped backwards just as a second one came at him.

The three of them backed onto the steps, as one of the heads came at them. Luckily for them the snakehead was too big to fit in the opening.

"Why would that thing attack you?" Samantha asked.

"That is Hydra my father's favorite pet. Even I have never seen it before." Ben answered. "He is trying to stop us from freeing Selena."

Samantha wished she had a sword to kill the beast. Even before she had finished thinking it, a sword appeared in her hand. She looked down at it and saw it had a gold handle with a purple gem shaped as a diamond in the center. The iron blade gave off a gleaming glow of silver light.

"Have you ever used a sword before?" Ben asked not surprised that she now held a sword.

Samantha looked at him. "No, have you?"

"Yes, fencing was part of my training."

Samantha was about to hand the sword over to him when Cassandra stopped her. "It has to be you."

Samantha swallowed hard and looked to the opening. Hydra had backed off, but was laying only a few feet away, all five heads watching them.

When Samantha stepped down onto the lower step, Hydra raised two of its heads. Samantha froze where she was and after a few moments the two heads laid back down.

Samantha stepped down one more step, three heads raised this time. After a short time they laid down again too.

When she stepped down on the bottom step Hydra did not move.

Just as she was prepared to step out into the cavern Ben said, "do you know how to kill it?"

"Yes, cut off the center head, right where the neck meets the body." Samantha said amazing herself that she had known that.

Ben looked amazed as well, but didn't say anything.

Samantha took a deep breath and stepped off the last step and out into the cavern. All five of Hydra's heads raised up high, hissing and snapping their jaws.

Samantha held the sword up high just as all five heads started snapping at her. She swung the sword cutting two heads off only to see four heads replacing the two.

"You have to cut off the right head or it will keep multiplying." Ben yelled.

Samantha wanted to turn and look at Ben and say, 'I know that' but didn't have time. It was hard enough for her to keep away from all the sharp teeth biting at her.

She continued to swing the sword cutting off head after head. Her arms had grown very tired but she knew if she stopped, she would die.

By the time Samantha had cut off the center head, Hydra had grown over thirty heads.

Once Hydra was dead, the blade of the sword disappeared leaving only the handle, making it small enough for Samantha to tuck it into her back pocket. Ben and Cassandra stepped out into the cavern.

Ben went to Samantha, gave her a quick hug and then gently pushed her sweat drenched hair back off of her face and neck.

Samantha was surprised when Ben showed such tenderness towards her. There was something that felt right about Ben being so close to her, something that she had not noticed until now.

"Which way do we go to find your father?" she asked as she tried to compose herself.

Ben looked around. "I'm not sure. It seems that my father has decided to reorganize the Underworld."

"Reorganize? Why would he reorganize the Underworld?"

"He knows we are coming. As much as he wants to get freed of this place, he still does not want the Titans or Selena freed." Cassandra answered.

"What's the deal with Selena? Why does Hades want her so bad?"

"She is being punished for trying to escape Mondo Del Fantasma with Marcus. They would have made it if Hercules wouldn't have showed up and took her away."

"Hercules took her? Why would he do that?"

Ben had decided that he would hold his tongue when it came to

Hercules, but now he felt Samantha needed the truth. "Hercules took her as a favor to my father. That's one thing they agreed on."

"What one thing?" Samantha asked.

"If they couldn't have the ones they love, no one should."

"That's horrible." Then a thought hit Samantha, "when did this happen?"

"Fifteen years ago." Cassandra replied. "Being forced to be separated from you changed Hercules' whole perspective on life. He no longer cared to help people, he was consumed with hatred that Toby was chosen to protect you and he wasn't."

"We better get going." Ben interrupted as he came off the steps holding a torch.

Samantha rolled her eyes, "let's try this way," she said frustrated that she had not gotten all the answers she wanted.

They headed down the tunnel, Ben took the lead with the torch he had taken from the staircase.

Samantha followed behind Ben thinking about why Hercules would damn anyone to this place. She had never seen that side of him when she looked into his eyes. She thought Hercules was someone that would help people no matter what he was going through.

They only had to walk for a short while before Samantha ran into Ben as he stopped.

"Sorry," she said.

Ben didn't say a word, he just smiled at her.

They stood there looking around and saw that they were in a cavern that was bigger than Hades' throne room. In the distance they could hear screams and cries of pain coming from the other side. Samantha could see a red glow of what she could only describe to be a hell fire glow.

As Samantha stared at the light in the distance she felt drawn to it. A strange feeling came over her that she should go forward.

Samantha started to walk forward, going towards the light when Cassandra grabbed her arm and said, "you don't want to go any further."

Samantha turned with the others to go back down the tunnel but, looked over her shoulder for one last look at the red glow in the distance.

She saw a man standing in the center, close enough that she could tell it was Cy. He raised his hand beckoning her to follow him. Samantha once again started towards the light.

"Samantha, let's go." Ben called to her.

She glanced at him and when she looked back Cy was gone. She followed Ben back through the tunnel.

Once they made it back to the cavern where Hydra's body still laid, Samantha said to Cassandra, "which way should we go? If you are truly a seer then you could see which path is the correct one."

Cassandra put her hands up once more, this time taking longer than few minutes. Then she pointed down a tunnel that was submerged in total darkness.

"Are you sure that's the right one?" Ben asked.

Samantha turned and looked at him.

"Okay." He said tossing his hands up.

They started down the tunnel but, stopped when they heard a scream.

Samantha ran back to the cavern and saw that Cerberus had returned and was growling at someone that he had trapped against the wall.

Samantha was about to help when she saw Hercules enter the cavern from the steps.

He jumped and brought a sharp sword down slicing off all three of Cerberus heads.

It was then that Samantha saw a girl cowering on the ground. She walked over and the girl looked up.

"Sammy!" The girl cried getting up and hugging Samantha.

Samantha stood there waiting for the girl to let her go. She looked at Hercules and he smiled.

"Sammy, I am so happy to see you." The girl said.

"Who are you?" Samantha asked her.

Hercules' smile faded. He looked at Ben, realizing that Ben must have done something.

Ben was furious that Hercules had killed his pet and even madder that he was even here.

Before anyone knew what happened, Hercules and Ben ran towards each other. Hercules had Ben on the ground holding him down.

"What did you do?"

"I did what she asked. She said Gabby was dead and didn't want to remember." Ben answered.

Hercules released Ben and approached Samantha. "Where is the stone?"

"What stone?"

"The stone that Ben used to wipe your memory." Hercules said.

Samantha looked even more confused.

"So, she don't even know who I am?" Gabby asked.

Hercules shook his head then attacked Ben again, this time swinging his fist and hitting Ben in the face.

Samantha hurried over to pull Hercules back. "We have bigger problems right now. You two need to stop."

Hercules backed off, Samantha looked around and noticed that Cassandra wasn't there. She went back to the tunnel they had seen the fire in and called Cassandra's name.

When there was no answer, Samantha turned back to the others. "Whatever is going on with the two of you, can wait. We have to find Cassandra."

They all followed Samantha as she started walking down the same tunnel.

When they came to a Y in the path, Samantha turned to Ben.

"This wasn't here earlier. Now what do we do?"

"I don't know. Every other time I was here, I was invited by my father." Ben answered. "It's like he is intentionally trying to stop us, or at least make it harder on us."

"Why would he do that, when he is the one that sent us on this mission?" Hercules asked.

Ben shrugged his shoulders, "I don't know why he does half the stuff he does."

"Hades!" Samantha yelled. "Why are you doing this? We have two out of the three things you asked for. If you help, we can get the final one and be done with this."

Samantha didn't think he would answer so she sat down on the ground. "I don't know what we are going to do."

"We could split up and check both tunnels." Ben suggested.

"That would be the easiest thing." Hercules surprisingly agreed. "Me and Samantha will go left, you two go right."

"Why would Samantha go with you?" Ben asked, stepping up so they were face to face.

"Because I said so." Hercules answered simply.

Ben pushed Hercules' chest, Hercules didn't budge. Ben tried again with the same result.

Hercules found it funny that Ben was actually trying to push him backwards.

"You would dare push me?" He laughed. "Well, 'try' to push me."

Ben looked around and saw the two girls were watching in silence. Embarrassed that he couldn't move Hercules, Ben swung and punched Hercules in the jaw.

Hercules still didn't move until he swung back. This time when his fist connected to Ben's face, Ben fell backwards.

"Like I said, Samantha goes with me." Hercules said. He grabbed Samantha's hand and started walking towards the left tunnel.

Samantha looked over her shoulder at Ben with an apologetic look. At this point she would rather not be near Hercules but if she would have said so the fighting would have continued.

Gabby helped Ben to his feet. "Why doesn't Samantha know who I am?"

As Ben got to his feet he answered, "She thought you were dead, so she asked me to take away the memories of you being captured and killed. I knew that if she remembered who you were she would ask where you were. So, I removed all memories of you."

"You erased me from her memory? Everything?"

"Yes, but she can retrieve them. They are in the stone. She just needs to want them back." He told her. "I hid the stone so no one can use it against her. There are more than just memories of you hidden in that stone."

"We better check the tunnel." She said turning her back on him and walking into the tunnel.

After Samantha was sure that Ben and Gabby couldn't hear them she stopped Hercules, "What was that all about?"

"He wants you all to himself. Don't you see that?" He said.

"And you don't?" She retorted.

"That's not the same. I...I care for you a great deal, he only wants you for your powers."

"Why do you want me? You showed me visions from when I was a baby and what you think is our future. Have you been just waiting for me to grow up?" She asked.

"Yes, I have been." He answered. "When you were little and I held you, the vision just came to me. After that I never wanted to be away from you again. I watched over you as much as I could and over the years the other visions would just come at random."

"What really happened to Toby?" She asked.

Hercules looked into her eyes, "I told you what I knew. When I got there he was already dead."

"Okay." She said as she turned to walk away.

Hercules grabbed her arm and turned her back to face him. "You don't believe me, you think I killed him, don't you?"

"Well it makes sense. You want me and he was in the way."

Hercules dropped his hands to his sides. "I can't believe you think I would do something like that. He was no threat to me. Eventually you would have seen that we belong together."

She shook her head, "That's only your opinion."

They walked in silence for a long while until they heard a woman scream.

They ran through the tunnel and came to a cliff that dropped down so far they couldn't see the bottom.

Looking around, Samantha saw on the other side of the canyon a woman being whipped by three giant men. Each one of them held a long leather strap and were taking turns inflicting pain.

The woman cried out again and again.

Samantha couldn't bear to see such punishment, "Leave her alone!" She screamed.

All three giants and the woman turned to look at them.

When Hercules saw the woman's face he whispered, "Mother?" He frantically looked around to find a way to reach her.

Samantha heard what Hercules had said and was trying to help find a way to get to the other side. She gazed down into the pit, her inner wisdom took hold. Samantha, as if in a trance, used her powers to pull rocks up from the bottom of the pit.

Hercules watched as the rocks started forming a bridge that extended to the other side.

Once the bridge was almost solid he looked at her in awe, before running across the bridge. Samantha followed close behind him and then ran past him.

The giants saw them coming and stood shoulder to shoulder waiting for them. Once Hercules and Samantha got closer the giants started charging at them.

Samantha pulled out her sword, when she held it up the blade appeared. She waited for the giant to get close enough then stabbed the sword deep into his foot. The giant fell to his knees and she jumped into the air bringing the sword down in one swift motion, cutting off his head. The giant body fell off the side of the bridge into the pit leaving the head behind.

Samantha turned to the next giant. The giant raised his hand and swung slamming Samantha into the wall. Samantha got to her feet and ran at the giant.

He swung again and missed as Samantha slid on her knees under his huge arm and drove her sword into the his chest.

Meanwhile, Hercules was still fighting with the last giant. Samantha ran to the woman, and untied her hands. The woman quickly hugged Samantha.

"Thank you so much. Please help my son?" The woman begged.

Samantha looked back to see Hercules being pinned to the ground by the giant. From behind the giant, she jumped up and stuck her sword through the back of the giants neck.

Hercules rolled out of the way just as the giant landed hard on the bridge.

The bridge that Samantha had built, started to crack and fall away. Samantha and Hercules jumped, as the last bit of bridge fell from under their feet.

Hercules then ran to his mother. "Are you alright?"

"Yes, I'm fine my son."

"Have you been here the whole time?" He asked.

"No not the whole time. For a while Zeus held true to his word and I was allowed to remain on Mount Olympus. It was Hera that grew jealous and sent me to the Underworld. I have been here since then."

Hercules had known that Hera had always hated him and his mother, but never thought that she would go so far as to banish his mother to the Underworld.

"You are coming with us," Samantha said.

Hercules had almost forgotten Samantha was there. "Samantha this is my mother, Alcemene. Mother, This is Samantha, Athena's daughter."

"Athena? Your mother was a kind-hearted Goddess. She helped me many times. I was so sorry to hear when she was killed. Was the one responsible ever caught?" She asked.

"No, we're still working on it." Samantha said. "But, I am very happy to meet you Al... Al."

"You may call me Alice, it was what Athena called me when I was in hiding from Zeus. Plus, Alcemene is very hard to pronounce to the modern-day people."

"Alice, yes much easier to pronounce." Samantha said with a laugh.

Alice turned and look at Hercules. "What are you doing here in the Underworld?"

"If I tell you, you have to promise not to get mad." Hercules said.

"How can I promise not to get mad if I do not know what I'm not getting mad about?" She questioned.

"We are honoring the deal we made with Hades."

"Why in Zeus' name would you make a deal with Hades? What good could possibly come of that?"

Hercules and Samantha quickly explained about the Forbidden and how they needed the help of the Titans. "Since he has the key to free the Titans, we had to make a deal with him to get the key." Hercules told her.

Once they had finished telling her everything they felt was important, she said, "then my son I will help you."

"No mother I must get you to safety. I don't want you involved in any of this." Hercules said.

Alice looked to Samantha hoping she would disagree, but found that Samantha agreed with Hercules.

"Where would I go, that I would be safe from Hera?"

Samantha turned to Hercules, "we could take her to Bella Isola." She suggested.

"That would probably be the safest place for her. Hera wouldn't dare start a fight with the vampires. She would know that would anger Zeus and she would be punished." Hercules said.

"Can you take her now and come back?" Samantha asked Hercules.

"No, no one can teleport out of the Underworld, I would have to take her to the surface first. Then I risk not being able to find you when I come back."

"So I will go with you for now." Alice said.

With no other choice, Hercules agreed. They turned to face the wall that had three tunnels that lead from the canyon.

"Which way should we go?" Samantha asked.

Before Hercules could answer her, Alice said, "the left one takes you to Hades throne room, the right one takes you deeper into the Underworld, and the middle one takes you to an underground ocean."

"I think we should take the right one then." Hercules said.

"If Hades is the one who took Cassandra, he would have taken her to his throne room to draw us in." Samantha said.

"What makes you think that?" Hercules asked.

"Think about it, for whatever reason he sent us on this mission but, now he is trying to slow us down by taking Cassandra. He doesn't want us to reach Selena." Samantha noticed Hercules flinched at the mention of Selena's name and that told her he remembered what he had done to her. "He must know that she is the one we came for."

"Why would she be so important to him that he would rather us fail then get what he wants?" Hercules said trying not to let on that he knew Selena.

"I don't know."

Meanwhile, Ben and Gabby were having problems of their own. Instead of watching where they were going, they had been talking and looking at each other when the path had suddenly sloped downward.

They fell into a sticky spider web, Ben pulled out his knife and started to cut at the web viciously.

Gabby watched as he cut at the web, "slow down, you get more work accomplished if you take your time and do it right."

Without stopping, he nodded his head indicating for her to look behind her.

Gabby turned her head and saw a massive spider making its way to them. "Never mind, hurry up and get us out of here!"

Now freed, Gabby faced Arachne, Hades giant pet spider that fed on anyone who had the misfortune to fall into her web. Ben was now separated from Gabby with Arachne between them.

He knew that the little knife that he held was no match for her.

If Arachne had been a male, Gabby could have used her hypnotic song to subdue the creature. But since Arachne was female Gabby's song would not work on her.

The giant spider jumped at Gabby, huge fangs dripping with venom ready to bite.

Gabby rolled out of the way as Arachne landed in the same area Gabby had been standing.

Figuring that he had to do something to help Gabby, Ben took his little knife and jumped on Arachne's back, again and again he stabbed the spider in the back of the head. Green blood oozed out of the cuts but the knife was too small to do any real damage.

Gabby picked up a big stone and threw it at Arachne, hitting her just above her left eye. The spider reared up and Ben fell off landing hard on his back. Arachne stepped backward away from Gabby. Her back leg came down in the middle of Ben's chest.

Ben screamed in agony.

Arachne lifted her leg and left Ben lying on the ground bleeding. He tried to get up but the pain was too intense for him.

Samantha felt a stabbing pain in her chest and dropped to her knees.

Hercules knelt down beside her, "Samantha, what's wrong?"

The pain only lasted a few seconds before it was gone. Samantha stood up. "I don't know what that was but it's gone now."

Hercules was still worried as they continued on their way.

Gabby wanted to run to Ben's side and help, but Arachne had turned her attention back to Gabby now. Just as Gabby had accepted her fate, there was a bright green light and Arachne rolled over pulled her legs in and died.

Once the light had faded Gabby saw a woman at Ben's side. She slowly approached her.

"Ben." Gabby said.

"Gabby, I'm sorry." Ben said taking his last breath.

"If only I had been here sooner, my son would still be alive." The woman said with tears rolling down her face.

"Your Ben's mother?"

"Yes, I am Persephone. Queen of the Underworld. I knew Hades was up to something. I never thought he would allow our son to die." She cried.

Gabby didn't reply to that, she was too busy thinking that Ben's father was Hades and if this was his mother, Ben wasn't a Traveler after all.

Just as Gabby was about to ask her about it, Persephone stood up.

Gabby hadn't realized how tall Persephone was until she stood upright. Gabby barely came up to her shoulders.

"You should not be in the Underworld." Persephone said to Gabby. "If you do not leave soon you will become trapped here."

"I did not come alone with Ben." Gabby informed her.

"Who else is here?"

"Hercules and Samantha, we separated when the tunnels split into two paths."

"Samantha Who?"

"Samantha Martin." Gabby answered.

"Athena's daughter?"

"Yes."

Persephone looked very worried. "We need to find them. They need to leave here now."

She held out her hand and Gabby took ahold of her. They disappeared and reappeared just behind Hercules, Alice, and Samantha.

"Sammy." Gabby said.

The three of them spun around at the sound of Gabby's voice.

"Gabby, where is Ben?" Hercules asked. Then he recognized Persephone. "What are you doing here? You haven't left your chambers in a thousand years."

"I would have stayed there a thousand more but I could feel my son in distress. However, I was too late."

"You mean, Ben is dead?" Hercules asked.

Samantha could feel something inside her break. Her right hand came up across her chest, now she knew what that pain was. Samantha had felt Ben dying. She wondered why she had not felt it when Toby had died.

"Yes Arachne killed him. Hades will pay for the loss of my son." Persephone said. "What is your business here Hercules?"

Hercules explained to Persephone why they were in the Underworld and about the deal that Hades had made them. He told her how they had to find Selena and why.

"Selena? I know where she is, I can help you get to her." Persephone said.

"What about Cassandra? I know Hades has her." Samantha said.

"If Hades has her, he would have her in the cell behind his throne room. Once we find Selena then I will go collect Cassandra."

They all followed Persephone down the tunnel and into a cavern filled with cages, each cage was different. The cages were randomly hanging from the ceiling, spaced far enough apart that the captor inside could not reach the others.

Persephone navigated between the cages until she reached one that held a beautiful woman with black hair.

"Selena." Persephone said.

"Persephone is that you?" Selena asked.

"Why were you put into this cage?"

"We do not have time for this right now." Samantha said.

Persephone unlocked the cage, Selena put her feet to the floor but fell as she tried to stand up. Hercules reached out and grabbed her before she hit the floor.

She looked up to see his face, pushing him away she said, "Get away from me you bastard."

Without letting her go Hercules replied, "you can be mad at me but I was just doing what needed done at the time."

Samantha quickly went to help Selena, "I got her." she told Hercules.

Hercules then let go of Selena and backed away.

"Not that I am not thankful, but why did you free me?" Selena asked.

"We don't have time for that either, we need to get out of here before Hades comes up with some other way to stop us." Hercules said.

They all agreed with him. They were amazed that they made it back to the steps that led to the surface without any obstacles. Persephone told them to wait for her at the top of the steps, as she went to get Cassandra.

It wasn't long before Persephone returned with Cassandra by her side.

Persephone looked at Hercules, "go now! Hades already knows she is gone and he is furious."

"What will happen to you?" Samantha asked.

"Don't worry about me I will be alright." Persephone said with a smile.

"No you will not." Cassandra told Persephone.

Samantha looked at Cassandra, "what makes you say that? Did you see something?"

"I saw her fate. I know what Hades is going to do to her for helping us. It won't be pleasant."

"We can't just allow him to hurt her," Samantha said looking at Hercules.

"There's not much we can do about that now, Samantha. We have to leave," he replied.

In that moment Samantha saw just how uncaring Hercules could be. He was willing to allow Persephone to an unknown fate just to save himself. Samantha looked into his eyes and saw no remorse in leaving her here to possibly die at the hands of Hades.

"Hercules is right, there is too much at stake. You must gather what he has asked and stop the Forbidden." Persephone said. She pulled Samantha aside, "I know you are looking for your father and your sisters, I do not know where they are but I do know they are not in this dimension."

"What do you mean this dimension? I thought each world was a different dimension." Samantha said.

"That would be what you would think because that's all Zeus knows. He thinks he controls all that there is, but he is wrong. Your mother found a way to cross into unknown dimensions. Ones that Zeus himself has never even heard of."

There was a loud scream that echoed up from the bottom of the steps and out to the surface. Persephone turn and quickly descended the steps. Samantha took a step to follow but stopped as the secret door closed behind her.

"Samantha we really have to go. Persephone has accepted her fate." Cassandra said.

The five of them disappeared and returned to Mondo Del Fantasma.

When they appeared Marcus was there as if he was waiting for them the whole time.

Samantha looked over at Selena, and saw the way she looked at Marcus. Selena was no longer in a solid form but now a thick mist.

Samantha could only guess that in the Underworld, Selena had to be a solid form in order to be tortured. Now that she had to return to the Ghost World she returned to her ghost form.

Selena turned to face Samantha, "can you please tell me why you freed me?"

"I need to turn you into a physical form again." Samantha said.

"Why would you need me in a physical form? Do you realize that when I become physical I will once again be alive?" Selena asked.

"I didn't think of that, but that would make sense." Samantha said.

"The only way you can make me physical is if I agree and I will only agree if you make Marcus physical as well."

Samantha looked to see what Hercules thought. He nodded his approval.

The two ghosts got side by side in front of Samantha.

Samantha then held her hands out in front of her with one in front of each of the ghosts. "Fare fisica." She repeated the mantra over and over, even though she had no idea how she knew what she was doing.

Hercules saw that with every time Samantha repeated the phrase the ghosts became more and more solid.

It only took a little while before both ghosts were completely solid and physical.

Samantha had just brought two people back to life, she realized that all she had to do was find Toby's ghost and perform the same ritual on him.

Selena and Marcus looked at each other. Tears formed in Selena's eyes as she hugged Marcus tightly.

"I have missed you so." Marcus said to her.

As a tear rolled down Selena's cheek, Hercules pulled out a small vial and caught the tear as it fell from her face. He put a small cork in the top of the bottle and handed it to Samantha.

"We have everything that Hades asked for. Now we must go back to the Underworld and free the Titans." Samantha said.

"No, we must take my mother to Bella Isola before going back to the Underworld." Hercules said.

They took Alice to the island and explained to Jade what was going on. Jade swore an oath to protect Alice at all cost.

Hercules had tried to talk Cassandra into staying at the castle as well.

"I am connected to Samantha now. Anywhere she goes I must go with her." Cassandra said.

"Why don't you stay behind?" Samantha asked him.

Hercules frowned at her, "You can not go and face Hades alone."

Samantha nodded, she didn't feel like arguing. She just wanted to free the Titans and get on with finding her sisters and Father.

Once that was settled the three of them left for the Underworld, leaving Gabby behind.

Everything seemed different on the Underworld now.

The hidden door was opened but there was no sound coming from within. They entered the Underworld to find the first cavern was completely empty. There were no monsters or creatures to fight and instead of multiple tunnels there was only one that led off of the cavern.

They followed it until they reached Hades throne room. Hades was sitting on his throne as if he had been waiting for them to return.

Samantha had all of the items in a pouch that hung around her neck.

She looked up at Hades and asked, "How can you sit there so calmly when your son died only a few hours ago?"

Hades shrugged his shoulders, "Ben made his own choices."

Samantha was shocked that Hades didn't care that his son was dead. But then she thought of Persephone and asked, "Where is Persephone? What did you do to her?"

Hades smiled, "Have you obtained all three items?"

"Yes, but before I give you the items I want to see the key." Samantha said accepting that Hades wasn't going to answer her questions.

"Silly girl, you think the key is a physical key?" Hades mocked.

"I don't understand," Samantha said. "You said if we brought you what you asked for you would give us the key to free the Titans."

"Oh, I should have specified that I would tell you what the key is. I do not have the key, only you do. You've had it the whole time." Hades started to laugh.

"Enough of your trickery." Hercules said to Hades. "Your riddles and lies are over. Tell us where or what that key is."

Hades sat quiet for a moment. "The key is your blood." he said to her.

"My blood is the key to freeing the Titans?" She questioned.

"Yes, You have but to go down the stairs to the entrance, a few drops of your blood smeared on the door, that should be sufficient. The door will open, but beware, the Titans are not the only creatures trapped in there,"

Hercules turned and looked at Samantha, "he's telling the truth. My father locked away a lot of fierce creatures before the Titans."

"What kind of creatures?" Samantha asked.

"Creatures from your worst nightmares." Hades laughed. "Things you could only imagine but never would never want to face."

"We don't have a choice, the Titans are the only ones who can defeat the Forbidden. We have to release them." Samantha said.

"Where is the door?" Hercules asked Hades.

"Just behind me, down the steps there will be a door with a dragon carved into it. Now give me what is mine." Hades demanded.

Samantha removed the strap from her neck, and tossed the pouch to Hades.

Samantha and Cassandra started walking around the throne when they heard Hercules say, "this better not be a trick."

"What need would I have to trick you now? You have made it possible for me to leave the Underworld."

Hercules then followed Samantha and Cassandra around the throne and down the steps. It didn't take long for them to reach the door with the carving on it.

It was then Samantha realized that she did not have a knife to draw blood from her hand, she still had her sword but wasn't sure if the blade was sharp enough.

Without a word, Cassandra grabbed Samantha's hand and scratched a deep cut on her palm.

Samantha smeared blood down the door and at once the door clicked and opened just a crack.

Samantha reached for the door but before she touched it, the door swung open with such force that the three of them were knocked backwards onto the steps.

Samantha hit her head off of the steps and could feel her hair getting wet with blood. She wasn't sure if she imagined the dark shadows that flew over her or if they had been real.

Once all was quiet, Hercules rolled towards Samantha putting his arm over her, "are you alright?"

"Yes I'm fine." She answered pushing his arm away and getting to her feet.

Hercules and Cassandra both stood up. Samantha was at the doorway looking in.

Hercules and Cassandra could see nothing but black. It looked as though everything that was in the door had already escaped.

"Are you Kronos?" Samantha said into the darkness.

It was then that Hercules and Cassandra realized that they just could not see what Samantha could see.

"No I am not Kronos. I am Oceanus. You must be a descendant of Poseidon. For he is the only one who could open the door. I was so hoping to see him once again."

Oceanus was about ten feet tall with golden skin and sea blue hair that touched the floor.

"He is my Grandfather." Samantha replied.

Just then another voice sounded from behind Oceanus. "Why would you speak to a descendant of one of those who trapped us here?"

Then all of a sudden there were many voices arguing inside the door.

Hercules was still looking confused at who Samantha was speaking to. He focused on the door and as he stared at it he could hear noise that he couldn't hear before. Then he could make out voices, voices all jumbled together as if they were fighting.

"Enough!" A deep voice yelled over all the others. They all fell silent.

The dark room suddenly lit up and Samantha could clearly see the Titans gathered in the center.

She had never imagined them to be so enormous. Each one was over eight foot tall. The biggest of the Titans walked towards her, the rest stumbled to move out of his way.

He was at least fifteen foot tall with white hair and gray eyes. Once he was at the door, he knelt down on one knee and said to Samantha, "you have freed us, but in doing so, have released thousands of others that will need stopped. The only thing worse than what you have released was the Forbidden."

Samantha knew this had to be Kronos, "That is why we had to release you. The Forbidden is threatening all worlds."

"Impossible, we destroyed all the Forbidden before we were trapped." Kronos said.

"You are mistaken. There is one remaining."

Kronos turned and looked at the rest of the Titans. "Is there any here who did not do as they were told?"

Not one of the Titans moved a muscle.

"Speak now or you shall all feel my wrath."

The smallest of the Titans stepped forward, "my Lord, I am very sorry to have failed you," she said.

"Theia, you did more than fail me. Do you not remember the destruction the Forbidden had caused?" Kronos asked her.

"I do, my Lord."

In a bright flash, Theia fell to the floor.

"This is what happens to those who fail the universe. Without order we have nothing. I am that order." Kronos said. "If any disagree speak now."

The rest of the Titans fell to their knees and bowed in front of Kronos.

Kronos then turned back to Samantha, "And you, are you willing to do as you are told and obey my laws?"

Hercules stepped in front of Samantha, "we do not need to follow your laws. We are the Travelers."

Kronos waved his hand and Hercules mouth snap shut. "I see we have a son of Zeus here. He was always a mouthy one too. Silence should do you some good." He looked back at Samantha waiting for an answer.

"If you say we must obey your laws, then I will shut the door now and never return."

"Oceanus, Tethys come speak to your descendant." Kronos said.

Oceanus stood up and walked towards Samantha followed by Tethys.

Samantha noticed that none of the Titans tried to go through the door. Even Kronos was careful not to cross the threshold.

"My child, Kronos is right. We must have order and he is the highest order." Oceanus said.

"All due respect, you have been locked away for a very long time. Everything has changed, everything is different." Samantha said. "I give no respect to any God or being until it is earned."

"You follow Zeus, are you saying you respect Zeus?" Tethy said.

"Of course I do not respect Zeus, I do not follow Zeus and I do not trust Zeus. If I followed Zeus I would not be here to free you." Samantha said.

"Is he not the son of Zeus?" Oceanus asked pointing to Hercules.

"Yes he is Zeus' son, but if he could speak he could tell you himself that he, for the most part disagrees with his father."

Oceanus looked at Kronos, "I believe she's telling the truth."

Kronos waved his hand once more releasing Hercules' tongue. " Speak boy."

Hercules glanced at Samantha before saying, "I hold very little feeling for my father and my respect for him disappeared the day he separated me from Samantha."

"If what you say is true then release us and we will follow you. We owe our freedom to you. You shall be leader of the Titans, from this day forward." Kronos said.

"The door is open, what more can I do to free you?" Samantha asked Kronos.

"There is nothing more for you to do, he must set us free." Kronos looked at Hercules.

"What do you need me to do?"

Kronos smiled, "it was your father's blood that sealed us in here, it must be your father's blood that releases us."

"How is he supposed to get the blood of Zeus?" Samantha asked outraged.

Now all ten of the Titans laughed loudly.

"It is hard to believe that you are descendant to me." Oceanus said. " The son of Zeus carries Zeus' blood."

"There is no need to speak to her like that. Until recently she lived among the mortals not knowing who she was." Hercules informed Oceanus. "What exactly did my father do to imprison you here?"

Kronos pushed Oceanus back. "He sealed the doorway with his blood."

Hercules looked at Cassandra and held out his hand. "Would you please?" he asked her.

She took her long fingernail and made one straight cut across his hand. Blood started to ooze out of the cut. Hercules took his hand and wiped the blood the whole way around the doorway.

Kronos approach the door slowly and with one hand, he reached through the doorway.

The Titans then shrunk down in size to fit through the door. Samantha, Cassandra and Hercules started walking up the steps with the Titans following behind them.

Once they were back in Hades' throne room, Samantha noticed the things looked totally different. Hades was gone as was his throne. The lava was still there however, the gargoyles were now gone.

"Maybe we should get out of here." Samantha suggested.

"Themis, you will stay and restore the Underworld to order." Kronos said. "The rest of you come with me, we will destroy the Forbidden and return the dimension to what it once was."

"The dimension is fine the way it is." Samantha told Kronos. "We freed you. You are in our debt you said that you would follow me."

Kneeling down on one knee, Kronos bowed his head and said, "Yes, my queen."

"You will keep the Titans in line and under control. I will consider your suggestions. However, I am in charge now." Samantha said to Kronos.

Kronos nodded his head in understanding.

Samantha and Hercules led the way back to the surface of the Underworld. On the way they saw that all the people and creatures that Hades had been in charge of were now free and were trying to find a way to get off of the Underworld.

Once they reached the surface, Samantha looked around and felt bad for all the souls that would be trapped here unable to leave. She decided that she could not leave them on this dead planet.

Samantha turned to Kronos, "they cannot all be trapped here, yet they cannot go home. Do you have any suggestions of how to help them?"

"We could create a new world, a paradise, for those who have been Hades prisoners, unjustly. Those who do not deserve forgiveness, shall remain here under the watchful eye of Themis." Kronos replied.

"That sounds like a wonderful idea. What shall we name the new world?"

"That is up to you my queen."

"Nuovo Mondo." Hercules suggested.

"What does that mean?" Samantha asked.

"It means new world." Hercules replied.

Samantha smiled. "I love it. That will be the official name, however most won't be able to pronounce that. So we shall simply call it, The New World," then to Kronos she added, "let it be done."

Kronos put his hands together as if he held a ball. A bright light appeared with in his hands. He twisted and turned the light molding it just right until it became a solid ball. He then raised the ball high above his head, it rose out of his hands and disappeared into the sky.

"How will we know who deserves to go to the New World?" Hercules asked.

"Coeus." Kronos called out to the Titans.

Coeus stepped forward, "yes my Lord?"

"You shall be in charge of The New World. You will help Themis to sort all the souls on this planet. Those who are good shall go with you to The New World, the rest shall remain here."

Hercules thought about how his father had sent Hades to the Underworld, trapping him there. "Kronos? You do not mean for them to be trapped on the worlds they are in charge of, do you?"

"No. I would never trap my brothers and sisters in that way. Only the souls shall be trapped."

"Now that this is settled," Samantha said. "We must get back to the task at hand, killing the Forbidden."

PART 3

The Past

CHAPTER 8

Kronos and the other Titans left to hunt down the Forbidden. Samantha, Hercules and Cassandra returned to Bella Isola.

They were welcomed by numerous vampires and wolves alike. Wayne had brought the wolf packs together on the island to live alongside the vampires.

Now that she had a minute to think, she started to realize that she must be more powerful than anyone imagined. Kronos had bowed down to her. Samantha decided to look for an opportunity to try out her powers in any way she could.

When Samantha saw the wolves there she hoped that Cy would be among them. She was disappointed to find out that he had stayed behind at the farmhouse.

She saw Randy, Allen and James sitting around a small round wooden table playing cards with some of the vampires.

Everywhere she looked she saw that the vampires and wolves were getting along and having a good time. Some of them were playing games, others were just sitting around talking.

Samantha found Wayne and Jade in the library, they were sitting with some wolves and vampires that Samantha had never seen before. There was a map of the island laid out across the table.

"We could easily expand here," Jade was saying, "there would be plenty of room for all the wolves to come to the island and build."

"Darling, I don't think you realize how many wolves there are now." Wayne replied. "As big as that area is, it isn't big enough for them all."

"I could always expand the island, make more land. That way everyone would have room." Samantha interrupted speaking before she could stop herself.

"You can do that?" Wayne said in surprise.

She shrugged her shoulders, "I can try."

Samantha could feel something strange surge through her body. A sort of electric wave that if she was honest felt good. She turned and walked away from the room.

Jade looked at Wayne, "do you think she can do this?"

"It would take a lot of her energy, but yes I think she can."

Wayne and Jade stood up and started following after Samantha, all the vampires stood up and followed Jade to the east end of the island that dropped off forming a cliff.

Samantha stopped at the very edge and looked down at the water below. As she concentrated she could feel her mind's eye going down into and through the water. Once she could see the floor she used all her strength to start pulling it upward.

"I don't think this is going to work." Jade said to Wayne.

The ground started to shake, the water slammed against the side of the cliff.

Wayne and Jade watched in amazement as an extension of land slowly pushed up out of the ocean. With the new addition the island was now double the size it had been.

"That was amazing." Jade said to Samantha. "Thank you."

All the vampires were in awe as they stood there looking out over the new land. Until this moment they had not known why Jade had allowed the wolves and Demigods to stay on Bella Isola. Now they were happy to have such a powerful ally.

They headed back to the castle to start plans for building houses.

Samantha pulled Jade and Wayne aside and told them about the Titans.

Once she finished telling Wayne and Jade everything that had happened, Wayne explained to Samantha that some of the wolves were not happy about living with the ones that killed parts of their family.

"Allen has them ready to fight the vampires, if necessary." Wayne said.

"What can I do to help?" Samantha asked.

"Can you take the wolves back to Mondo Del Lupo? That way we can avoid a war between our people. Allen has them gathered on the beach, near the docks."

Samantha agreed and started walking towards the beach to find Allen and the other wolves that wanted to leave. They would be leaving Wayne's pack forever to join Wayne's brother on their home planet.

Wayne and Jade watched as she slowly walked towards the castle.

"Will she be alright?" Jade asked.

Wayne, still watching Samantha, replied, "I don't know. I know that had to take a lot for her. She never used that much power at one time. I'm worried what will happen once she realizes that she no longer needs me."

"My love, she will always need you. You are the only father that she has ever known."

Wayne had always secretly wanted children of his own. He had even thought about having a child with Jade, but when he had brought the subject up to her she hadn't even let him finish.

'Do you know what that could create? There has never been such a child born.' Wayne could still hear those words in his head. After that he had never spoke aloud about it again.

Samantha and Toby had been the closest he had come to having children of his own. Now that Toby was gone, Samantha was his only child.

Jade saw the look in his eyes, "You see her as your daughter, don't you?"

"She is the daughter I can never have. Her father will come for her."

Samantha found Allen and almost thirty of the wolves where Wayne said they would be.

She approached Allen, "Wayne sent me to take you all to Mondo Del Lupo."

"Thank you. I don't see how Wayne thought that we would agree to live with these parasites." Allen replied.

Samantha nodded her head and four of the wolves grabbed ahold of Samantha. It took her many trips to get all the wolves to Mondo Del Lupo.

Allen was in the last group to go. Once they were all gathered together he looked at Samantha, "Thank you for bringing us home. Will you stay and meet Hawk?"

"Who's Hawk?"

"Wayne's eldest brother."

"Sure, that would be nice."

Samantha walked beside Allen through a forest that was so thick that they had to walk in single file for a long time.

Once they reached the edge of the forest Samantha saw a beautiful village surrounded by a wall, tucked neatly in a valley between three mountains. They descended down the path and approached the gate.

"Who goes there?" A voice from above boomed out.

Allen looked up and replied, "Azar. Son of Jerick."

The gate swung open and Allen led the wolves through.

Samantha grabbed Allen's arm, "Azar?"

"Yes, you didn't think that Allen was my wolf name, did you?"

"I didn't realize you had different names." She said with a small laugh.

As they walked through the village, Samantha was amazed to see the craftsmanship of all the houses. Each one had a unique style to it, above each door was a symbol that Samantha knew was the crest of the family who lived inside.

They approached a house that had two wolves facing away from each other, howling at two different moons.

The door opened before they had stepped foot on the porch. The man that stepped out looked like a older and bigger Wayne. The same brown hair and brown eyes, yet a rough look about him that told Samantha that he had seen many wars and battles.

He walked to the edge of the porch and stopped. "Azar, your father will be pleased that you have returned home."

Allen bowed his head, "And are you happy that I have returned?"

Hawk smiled, "Of course I am. Where is Wayne?"

"He stayed behind on Alpha One with Jade."

"The woman from Non Morti?" Hawk said with a disgusted look on his face.

"Yes."

"Who is this?" Hawk smiled and pointed at Samantha.

"This is Samantha, Athena's daughter. She brought us home." Allen said.

As Allen spoke, Hawks smile faded and was replaced by a blank look. "Athena's daughter? Athena has no children." He looked to Allen and back to Samantha, "If you are Athena's daughter, who is your father?"

"I don't know who my father is. I only know that when I was three, he took my sisters and my mother was murdered."

"Murdered." Hawk repeated.

"Yes. Wayne and Jade have been helping me to find my sisters."

Hawk laughed, "And you trust her?"

Samantha wanted to hit him for being so arrogant but knew that if she did it could cause more problems that she didn't have the time for. "Yes I trust her. I can see that you don't but that's between you and her."

"Very true. Will you stay for the feast?"

"The feast?" Samantha questioned.

"You have brought my people home. We have waited for far too long to have them return. That calls for a celebration."

"Then I don't see how I can refuse."

Samantha had never seen a party like it. There was a fire higher than the houses, people were dancing around and drinking a mix of different alcohols. There was a stage for anyone who wanted to sing or play music. Samantha was surprised to see that the stage was never empty.

She watched as Allen and the others were welcomed back into the village.

As the night went on and the moon became full, the people around her started changing into wolves. Samantha looked around and saw that every wolf except for Hawk, was black or a dark grey.

Intrigued she watched as Hawk began to transform. She expected him to be the same as the others, maybe bigger. However he was a beautiful pure white.

Hawk looked at Samantha and held her gaze. She felt like she was drunk even though she hadn't drank any of the alcohol.

Samantha was still staring at Hawk, until there was a loud growl. She turned and saw four of the wolves biting at each other. She looked back at Hawk and saw him leap over a group of other wolves and land, without a sound in the middle of the fighting group.

He growled at each one of them, then stopped and looked at the smallest one. "You should not be here. You are still just a cub."

"But I wanted to see…"

"Go back to your mother!"

Samantha watched as the small wolf slowly walked away. Hawk started walking towards her. As he approached he transformed back into a man.

Samantha took a step back.

"I am sorry you had to see that. Please let me explain…"

"There is nothing to explain. The little one just wanted to join the party. I bet he is back with his mother already. The way you yelled at him." Samantha said with a smile.

"You understood what I said to him?"

"Yes," she answered.

"How could you understand? You are not a wolf."

"I don't know how but I did."

"Nobody, not even your mother could understand us when we took wolf form. So what is it about you that makes it where you can?"

"I told you, I don't know." Samantha repeated.

Hawk was slowly getting closer to her. She backed up until her back was against a wall.

"Who are you? Really?" He growled.

"I told you who I am."

"You lie! What are you?"

Samantha knew that it didn't matter what she said, he wasn't going to believe her. "You need to back away, now." she told him.

He leaned in closer, "You do not tell me what to do."

Samantha felt a shiver go through her body as he brushed his hand along her cheek.

"I won't tell you again to back off."

He started laughing.

Samantha felt the power surge through her and she pushed him back.

He flew through the air and landed beside the fire on all fours as a wolf. He growled and six other wolves joined him.

Allen ran over and stood in front of Samantha, "Please don't do this?" he begged Hawk.

"She isn't who you said she is." Hawk said in a growl.

"Yes she is. I have seen her powers. She is more powerful than even you can handle." Allen tried to explain.

"Trader."

"Trader."

All the wolves started to chant together as they surrounded Allen.

Samantha stepped forward and sent a blinding light towards the wolves. It engulfed all of them. When the light faded Hawk looked at Samantha. "I want you off this planet and take the trader with you."

Allen went to Samantha's side, "You made a really bad choice in making her an enemy."

Samantha didn't wait for Hawk to answer, She took Allen's hand and went back to Bella Isola.

"Allen, I am so sorry." Samantha said.

Allen shook his head, "You have nothing to apologize for. Hawk was out of line."

"Allen!" Wayne called as he walked towards them. "I thought you were going home?"

"I did. Hawk and I had a falling out." Allen said looking at Samantha.

"Samantha." Wayne said looking at her.

"Hawk didn't believe I am who I say I am. He really got upset when I could understand him in wolf form."

"You understand wolf?" Wayne asked.

"Yes. Then he backed me against a wall and I..."

"You did what you had to." Allen interrupted.

Wayne saw the pain in Samantha's eyes and was filled with rage. "Take me to him."

"Wayne, it isn't worth it," she said.

"Yes it is. He had no business threatening you in any way."

"Who threatened her?" Hercules asked from behind her.

"My brother." Wayne answered.

"Hawk?"

"Yes. I am trying to get Samantha to take me to him but she won't."

Hercules smiled, "I will take you. I'd love to see you kick his ass."

Wayne seeing the look on Samantha's face said, "I just want to talk to him."

"Just talk?" Samantha asked.

"Yes. Will you please take Allen to my pack? Find Drake and tell him that Allen is there is my place until I arrive?"

Samantha nodded her head.

"Hercules, let's go."

CHAPTER 9

Wayne and Hercules appeared just inside of the village gate. Wayne looked around and saw the fire burning. He started walking towards where he knew Hawk would be.

They made it halfway before an alarm sounded. Wayne didn't even look around, he just kept walking.

Hawk saw Wayne and Hercules and started walking a little bit faster, trying to stop them from reaching the party.

Once face to face Hawk said, "Wayne, you have no business here."

"You would be correct if you hadn't threatened Samantha." Wayne replied.

Hawk ignored him and addressed Hercules, "You are not welcome here. Leave this place now or…"

"Or what?" Hercules said stepping closer to Hawk.

Wayne put his hand on Hercules' chest and nudged him back, "easy, I got this."

Hercules gave him one nod and stood back.

"Hawk, you disrespected Athena's daughter. My daughter."

"You? You are the girl's father?" Hawk said in surprise.

Without thinking Wayne answered, "Yes."

Hawk drew his fist back and punched Wayne in the face. "How could you? You knew we were to be married. I guess your vampire whore wasn't enough for you."

Wayne took a step back and then jumped into the air, turning into a wolf, at Hawk.

Hawk flipped backwards and also turned. The two of them started growling at each other.

Wayne ran towards Hawk, baring his teeth. Hawk bit into the side of Wayne's neck and tossed him to the ground.

Samantha and Allen pulled on the long cord to ring the bell. The gate opened instantly. They were stopped by two guards.

"Let us pass." Allen told them.

"You can go no farther until Lars gives you permission."

"Lars is in charge? Good thing we are here." Allen said.

Samantha gave a small laugh and both guards looked at her.

"Allen, I see you made it back in one piece."

Samantha looked past Allen and saw a tall skinny man walking towards them with a big smile.

"Lars. How are you?"

"Walk with me." Lars said looking at Samantha.

The three of them started walking towards a small house that sat almost against the front fence. Samantha couldn't help but notice that this village looked very run down compared to Hawks village.

A lot of the houses here were missing boards, leaving gaping holes in the walls. The people of the village looked as though they had not had a decent meal in a very long time.

Lars stepped up onto the small rotting porch. Samantha reached out and tapped Allen on the arm.

"What happened here?" Samantha asked Allen.

"That's a very good question. Lars?"

Lars turned around to look at them, "I admit things haven't been the same since you and Wayne left. The other packs took over our hunting grounds and burned our fields. We have been left to starve."

"All the Alpha's allowed this to happen here?" Samantha asked.

"Yes. They have made us the village that time has forgotten. Every time I send out a hunting party, only one or two return."

Allen shook his head, "Why didn't you appeal to the Alpha's directly?"

"I tried. I was told if I ever returned they would kill me. I am not from the Alpha bloodline, therefore, can not ask them for help." Lars explained.

"Alpha bloodline?" Samantha asked.

Allen nodded, "since Rowtag and Nina passed on without naming an heir, each of their boys now carry the Alpha gene."

"Okay. I understand now. But things will be alright now that Wayne is coming back. Right?"

"Wayne is coming back?" Lars asked.

"He will be here, right after he gets done talking to Hawk." Allen answered.

"Speaking of Wayne. He is taking an awful long time." Samantha said. "I'm going to see what's keeping him."

Before either of them could say a word, Samantha disappeared.

Samantha appeared right beside Hercules, who was standing in a crowd watching as Wayne and Hawk fought. She could see blood coming from both of them as they continued to bite at each other.

"Why aren't you stopping this?" Samantha yelled at Hercules.

He shrugged his shoulders but didn't answer.

Samantha looked back at the two wolves and knew she had to stop the fight before one ended up dead.

She allowed the power to rise up, this time not holding back. She looked to the sky and felt the lightning forming in the sky. She raised her hand and pulled the lightning down hitting between the two wolves as they charged at each other once more.

Both Wayne and Hawk stopped and looked around. When Wayne saw Samantha he slowly walked over to her. He looked into her eyes and said, "I'm sorry. But this must end now."

Wayne turned and just as he jumped Samantha held him in the air. Not allowing him to attack his brother.

Hawk changed back to a man, he bowed down.

"Samantha, look." Hercules said.

She looked at Hawk and saw him on his knees, then looked around at the other wolves and saw that they had all knelt down.

She lowered Wayne as he turned. Once he was a man again he started to laugh.

"What's so funny?" Samantha asked.

"Look behind you."

She turned around and saw that Poseidon was standing behind her.

"Grandfather! What are you doing here?"

"I am here to stop this nonsense and to set things right on Mondo Del Lupo." Poseidon answered. "Who is in charge here?"

Hawk slowly stood up, "I am the Alpha of this village."

"So you are the one who has mistrust in my Granddaughter?"

"How was I supposed to know she was telling the truth?" Hawk asked.

"Who are you to question me or her? You threatened my Granddaughter and still believe you should be allowed to live. You are nothing."

Hawk looked as though he was about to say something, "You will hold your tongue and show respect!" Poseidon scolded.

"I am truly sorry." Hawk said getting back to his knees. "How can I make it up to you?"

"You can start by apologizing to my Granddaughter." Poseidon said.

Hawk looked at Samantha, "I am very sorry."

Samantha nodded her acceptance.

"You will travel to Wayne's village and make amends with them. You will help rebuild the village and clear out their fields, plant new crops and restore the village." Poseidon commanded.

"Yes, my Lord."

Poseidon then turned to Wayne. "What plans do you have?"

"I am going to go back to Bella Isola and marry Jade." Wayne answered.

"Wrong! You may return to her, however, you must return to take charge of your pack. You shall have six months on Alpha One, then six months here." Poseidon said.

Wayne didn't like the sound of that. Six months away from Jade seemed to be too much, but he knew better than to argue with a God.

When Poseidon was satisfied that Wayne had nothing to say he continued, "You will also produce an heir within two years or you will be trapped on this planet for the rest of your days. You will not turn your back on your own people."

Wayne nodded. He would have to try to find a way around this dilemma but for now he remained silent.

"Samantha. A word if you please?" Poseidon addressed her.

"Yes, Grandfather."

She followed him out of the village. Once the gates shut he said, "How are things coming along?"

"Everything is fine." Samantha said. "Why are you forcing Wayne to have a child?"

"Simply because he can not walk away from those who need him. They are his people. If he isn't willing to be here then it is his responsibility to produce an heir that will."

"But he can not have a child with Jade."

"He can, he just has to convince her that it is for the best. The child will be raised here and when it is old enough, will take charge of the pack," he said.

Samantha wasn't sure what to say about that so instead she said, "I better get back. I am sure Kronos will find the Forbidden soon."

"I will see you soon, Granddaughter." Poseidon said as he disappeared.

Samantha went back inside to get Wayne. They went to Wayne's village and his heart broke. Now he understood why Poseidon was so insistent on having an Alpha here. His beautiful village was nearly destroyed.

He decided that he would talk to Jade about them moving to the home that he had built for them a mile from his village. That way he could be here and still be with her.

After spending a few hours talking to his pack, Wayne went back to Bella Isola with Samantha and Hercules.

The moment they appeared Jade and Cassandra came towards them.

"Where have you been?" Jade asked Wayne.

"I will explain everything but not here." He answered looking around at the Vampires that had started to crowd around them.

The pair started walking down the hall until Samantha called out, "Jade, where is Vic?"

Jade told her, "He kept trying to find a way to get to you, so I confined him to the castle."

Samantha started searching every room until she found him in an empty room. He was standing with his back to the door. She stood there wondering if she should just turn and leave but decided that she couldn't do that to him.

She slowly entered the room, when she got within arm's length of him, he quickly turned and grabbed ahold of her shoulders.

It only took him but a moment to realize who he had grabbed a hold of.

"Samantha?" He hugged her tightly. "You're finally home."

"You're kind of hurting me." She said with a laugh.

He loosened his grip but did not let her go. "I'm sorry. I have been so worried about you?"

"Well, you were worried for no reason," she said. " I have released the Titans, they are searching the dimension for the Forbidden. I see things around here are much better?"

"They are now that you are here," he said touching her cheek.

She could feel the blood rush to her face and knew her face had turned red.

Vic pulled her close and kissed her lips.

Samantha allowed him to kiss her even though she felt that it wasn't right.

Once Vic had broken the kiss, Samantha remembered what Cassandra had said. 'One is mystified by your powers.' Samantha started to realize that Vic only thought that he was in love with her.

She pulled out of his embrace to stand out of his reach.

When he took a step forward she put her hand up, "Please don't? I need to try something."

He stepped back and stood there waiting.

Samantha wasn't sure how she had to use her powers on him, but now thinking back she realized that he had fallen in love with her the moment he had looked into her eyes.

Staring into his eyes now she searched his soul. What she found broke her heart in two. She saw that he was truly in love with Jade.

Samantha knew that Jade would never leave Wayne to be with Vic. How could she put him through such pain? Yet, how could she keep him in a reality that was not his.

No matter what Samantha did Vic would be in pain.

After a long while, Samantha had decided to remove the memories that Vic held loving Jade. She would not remove all memories of Jade only the ones that included the two of them being intimate.

"Vic, I want you to go out and choose a stone and bring it back here for me." Samantha said to him.

He ran from the room without a word and returned a few seconds later. He handed her a gray stone which she took and placed to his forehead.

She carefully went through every memory and was careful not to remove anything that he may need to remember later.

All of Vic's memories flashed before Samantha.

She saw the first time Vic had seen Jade, he was mesmerized by her. He had followed her to a dark corner in a small village. Jade bit him on the neck, blood ran down into his shirt. When Jade pulled back, Vic looked into her eyes and dropped to his knees.

"My Queen."

Samantha could feel the love that Jade had created and knew that she had only been trying to recreate the feeling she had with Wayne. Jade had never realized that she had recreated Wayne's love for her, Vic truly felt that love.

Samantha carefully removed the memories of the feelings, but left the event.

Samantha was now standing in a strange room watching as Jade yelled at Vic.

"It was a mistake, changing you. You will never be him."

Vic had not said a word, he just hung his head in shame.

Samantha saw Jade apologize and Vic forgiving her many times, over many years. Until one day, Jade had ordered Vic to find Wayne.

"I thought you would do, but you are nothing like Wayne." She had said. "The only way I can be happy is for you to find him and bring him to me."

With tears in his eyes, Vic replied, "I have tried to make you happy. Do I not do all that you ask?"

"You do. That is part of the problem, you must obey. Wayne is my one and only true love. I was wrong changing you to take his place."

The memories started to change faster and faster.

Samantha watched as Vic and the Hunters killed off numerous wolves. Vic had started searching for Wayne but wanted him dead. All of the wolves were loyal to Wayne right up to the last breath they took.

Samantha removed the hatred that Vic held for Wayne and the wolves.

Once all memories were stored in the stone, Samantha took Vic by the hands and pulled all her power away from him.

"How do you feel?" She asked him.

"I'm not sure." Vic said shaking his head.

"I accidentally influenced your feelings towards me. Now that I know how to control them, I will never do that again," she promised.

Vic nodded his head, "thank you for that, but it wasn't such a bad feeling, being in love with you." He said with a smile.

Samantha's face once again turned red. For the first time she was seeing the real Vic. The Vic that was in control of his own feelings and thoughts. Samantha had released him in more ways than she had known.

Vic reached out and touched her cheek, "I may not be in love with you right now but you're still very cute when you blush." He joked taking her hand in his.

Samantha was glad to see that he was not angry with her for accidentally using her powers on him. However, the way he was looking at her and the way he had put his hand against her cheek told her that on some level he did have feelings for her.

Just as Samantha was about to turn to leave, Hercules walked into the room.

"Okay, enough is enough. Samantha you do not belong with a Vampire." He stated as he saw the two of them still holding hands.

"Hercules, this is not what you think." Samantha said letting go of Vic's hand. "I did not realize until just a moment ago that he was under the influence of my powers."

Hercules started to laugh, "So, you no longer love her?"

"I don't think I ever really did love her."

Hercules walked over to Samantha and taking her hand said, "Samantha do you see now that we are meant to be together?"

"At this point I don't see anything. All I know is that we need to make sure the Forbidden is destroyed and that the dimensions are safe." She replied slowly pulling her hand away from his.

Vic then excused himself from the room and disappeared.

"You still believe that I killed Toby, don't you?" Hercules said once Vic was gone.

"I think that it's too much of a coincidence. I mean, he left to take the wolves home, you followed. When you came back he was dead. The two of you were at odds over me from the very beginning. He was the only one standing between us," she told him.

"I can't believe you would think I would sink that low. As I told you before, I knew eventually you would see that we belong together, whether he was there or not.

I would have never killed him, simply because you would have never forgiven me." Hercules explained.

Samantha tried to see the truth in his eyes but something was blocking her. She wasn't sure if she should believe him or not, so she said, "let's handle the Forbidden and find my sisters and father. After that if you are still by my side I will know if you're telling me the truth or not."

"Fair enough." Hercules said. "We need to go check in with Kronos now. He sent for us."

"Okay."

It didn't take long for Hercules and Samantha to locate Kronos. Lucky for them the Forbidden, so far, had only destroyed a few moons and smaller planets that had no life on them.

Kronos and the other Titans had gone to Non Morti, the original home of the vampires. There were still vampires and a mix of other creatures living among the planet.

"Kronos we are here. How can we help?" Samantha said.

"We believe this is where the Forbidden plans to attack next." Kronos informed her. "It has already destroyed moons and small planets."

"How do we stop it?" asked Hercules.

"We do not. You shall stay out of our way. For you are no match for a Forbidden." Kronos then turned to Samantha, "However, with your powers I do not see why you even needed us here."

Samantha looked at Kronos in confusion. "If Hercules is not strong enough to kill a Forbidden, how would I be able to?"

Instead of answering, Kronos laughed.

"Why are you laughing at me?" Samantha asked.

"I laugh, not at you but because you know not where you came from. You know not the power you hold." Kronos answered.

Before Samantha could ask Kronos anything further there was a loud roar coming from the skies.

Samantha looked up and saw a creature swooping down towards them. At first she thought it was a dragon, but soon realized that the creature coming towards them was much worse than a dragon.

As it landed in front of them, Samantha saw the creature had no eyes and that its body was more of a fluid then a solid. At first Samantha thought the creature had no mouth, until the Forbidden let out an ear-splitting roar.

Rows and rows of razor sharp teeth lined the Forbiddens mouth. Samantha was so startled that she stumbled backward. Once again Hercules stopped her from hitting the ground.

"Seems you're always catching me." Samantha laughed.

Hercules smiled, "I will always be here to catch you. But, I don't think this is the time or the place for this conversation."

Samantha steadied herself and said, "later then."

Samantha was having a hard time controlling her emotions. She knew that she loved Ben and Toby, even if she was mad at Toby right now.

There was something that kept pulling her towards Hercules, something she didn't understand.

"Prepare yourselves," Kronos said.

Samantha turned back just in time to see the Forbidden launch itself at one of the Titans. As she ran forward to help, she saw that the creature had Oceanus down on the ground.

Oceanus swung his fists, hitting the Forbidden repeatedly in the head. Samantha saw that Oceanus' hits did not affect the creature one bit.

Samantha was afraid that the creature would kill her great-grandfather, she could feel the power rising inside her once again.

As the fear took over, Samantha screamed towards the sky. Then turned her face towards the Forbidden, a blinding light shot from Samantha's hands hitting the Forbidden just below its neck.

The Forbidden screamed in pain and flew away.

Samantha fell to her knees drained and tired. After a few moments, she looked around to see Hercules and all the Titans were staring at her.

Kronos was the only one smiling.

"What am I?" She screamed at him.

Still smiling Kronos answered, "You must discover that for yourself."

"You know who my father is, don't you?" she asked walking towards him, then stopping a few feet in front of him.

"I do. Once you are ready you will find the truth." Kronos told her.

"Why can't you just tell me who he is? Is he the one who killed my mother?" Tears fell from Samantha's eyes.

Kronos approached Samantha, "I regret not being able to help you. However much I want to, I can not."

"Other than killing the Forbidden, what use do I have for you?" Samantha said, as she dried her face.

Kronos hesitated for a moment before answering, "You do not need me to kill the Forbidden, however I am the only one who knows where to find your father and how to get to him."

"Take me to him, now." Samantha demanded.

"I can not, only a single being may pass through the barriers." Kronos said.

"What barriers? There is no where that the Travelers can not go," said Hercules.

At that Kronos laughed, "You know only what your father knows, boy. Zeus had no idea of the greater things beyond our dimension. Even he could not imagine what is out there, hidden past the barriers because he could never go there."

"My father knows all that is, was or will be." Hercules said, now unsure of himself.

"Enough of this. We still need to stop the Forbidden." Samantha said. "Where would it go now that it's hurt?"

Kronos shook his head. "It will hide well. Where that may be, I do not know."

"Will it return here?" Samantha asked.

"Yes. This planet was the intended victim, it will return." Kronos answered.

"Then, we shall stay here and wait until it returns."

Kronos and the other Titans gathered together and started whispering to each other.

Samantha had sat down against a tree, as she leaned back she saw Hercules was standing over her.

"What are you doing?" she asked. It was hard for her to see his face clearly since the only light was from the three moons reflecting the sunlight.

He knelt down, "You said that we would have a conversation about…"

"You always catching me. Yeah I remember." Now she was happy it was so dark, so he couldn't see her face turning red.

He could tell that he made her nervous and smiled. He lifted his leg over her and sat down beside her, casually putting his arm around her shoulders.

"Do you believe me? I mean about Toby."

She wasn't sure if she did or not but answered, "Yes. I do believe you and I'm sorry I thought you were capable of something so terrible."

"I understand why you thought I would have. I sometimes forget that even though I know you, you hardly know me. In time that will change and you will see what I see, we are meant to be together."

"Maybe," she said yawning.

Hercules looked over at her, she looked tired. "Why don't you try to get some sleep? I'll wake you up if anything happens."

It didn't take long for Samantha to fall asleep when she laid down. She didn't realize how tired she had been and how long it has been since she had slept.

Once asleep she had terrifying and wonderful dreams, she saw Toby trapped in a chair, held down with ropes. She was in a room that she did not recognize and he was across the room from her.

Samantha could see blood dripping from his arms where the ropes had dug into his skin. She ran towards him, wanting to release him.

She tried as hard as she could to reach him. She ran as fast as she could but the faster she ran the farther away she got from him.

She screamed his name and kept running. She watched as the room faded away and Toby disappeared into nothingness.

The nightmare ended, and now she was back at the lake by the farm sitting under the tree. She looked around and was surprised to see that Toby was sitting beside her.

He had on the same cowboy hat he had always worn. He turned to look at her with that familiar smile that Samantha had missed so much.

"I love you Samantha," Toby said as he leaned forward to kiss her.

"I love ..." Samantha screamed as Toby turned into a creature with purple skin and a round mouth filled with small sharp teeth. Drool ran down dripping off the creature's chin. It growled and snarled at her.

She pushed the creature backwards as she got to her feet. She started to run towards the farmhouse but fell to the ground when the creature's tongue caught her by the ankles.

She lay there helpless as it slowly crawled over her and opened its mouth to bite into her. Samantha felt the slimy drool land on her face.

She tried to use her powers to free herself and found that her powers did not work. She screamed as the creature lowered its mouth over her face.

Hercules knew something wasn't right by the way Samantha kept tossing and moaning in her sleep.

When she screamed he rolled her over and began trying to wake her up. As hard as he tried, she remained asleep.

Samantha's mind felt as though it was unraveling. Her dreams were changing so fast it was hard for her to keep up.

The dreams ranged from her being in Toby's arms happy and safe to watching Toby die the next moment.

She knew she was asleep but yet couldn't control her own actions.

She had wanted to fight the creature but ran instead. No matter what Samantha wanted to do, in this dream world, she did the opposite.

She had lost all control of her own self.

Suddenly she heard Hercules' voice calling her name over and over.

"Hercules, Hercules where are you?" She cried out.

Everything in her mind went black, she couldn't see anything at all. She heard Hercules saying her name in the darkness. She tried her hardest to create some type of light hoping she would find Hercules and be taken from these dreams.

She was afraid of what she might see next or that this was the end. Perhaps the Forbidden had come back and Samantha lay dying on the ground. She knew that these thoughts were just her fear making more out of it than what it really was.

Hercules was still trying to wake Samantha up when Kronos approached him. "She will not wake, she is under the influence of the Oneiroi."

"The Oneiroi have not been seen for hundreds of years." Hercules said.

"That is because they were trapped in Tartarus, when the door opened, they were released." Kronos told him.

Hercules looked back at Samantha, she was saying his name. He wanted so badly to be able to reach her and pull her out of the dreams.

Hercules had once faced one of the Oneiroi centuries ago, it had gone by the name Phobetor. He could remember the nightmares that had taken over his mind. Phobetor was one of the spirits of nightmares who took the shape of any animal it chose.

Hercules could still remember the gruesome creature he had faced while trapped. He still felt the beast's horns as it had rammed into him.

He had tried to run, which he had never done before, but no matter how fast he ran the beast caught him.

Hercules hoped that Samantha wasn't facing anything like he had.

He had faced not only the creature but not being able to stop his mother from being killed by a dragon with two heads.

He didn't know how long he had been trapped but he did know that if he wouldn't have woken up when he did, he would have lost his mind.

Now he was afraid that Samantha faced the same torture he had.

It had been Zeus that freed Hercules from the nightmares. However, Hercules knew that Zeus would not help now.

Kronos knelt down beside Samantha, he placed his hand across her forehead searching her mind.

"Leave her be. I have her now," a familiar voice said inside Kronos' head.

It didn't take much time for Kronos to place where he knew that voice, it was Samantha's father.

"Can you pull her out of this?" Hercules asked.

Kronos shook his head but didn't say a word. He knew he could easily pull her out but he wouldn't go against Bee.

He had found out a long time ago that no one could win against Bee. He was a far more powerful being than even Kronos.

Bee had been the one to split the original dimensions and allow Kronos to take charge of this one.

Kronos remembered the last time he had spoken to Bee. No one in this dimension had ever laid eyes on him, he spoke inside one's head.

Bee had told him that one day his daughter would come to him for help. Kronos was to help her but not do any of the work for her. Bee said he wanted her to prove how powerful she could be to herself.

CHAPTER 10

Samantha had relaxed into a peaceful dream.

She looked around and saw the farmhouse but instead of Toby waiting for her, Ben was there.

She hardly recognized him. His brown hair was combed back neatly and his grey eyes sparkled.

As she approached the porch, Ben stood up.

Ben and the farmhouse disappeared and now her mother and Toby were at her side. She was now in a beautiful forest facing a magnificent waterfall.

As she looked through the water she saw a man standing on the other side.

"Mother who is that?" she asked looking at Athena.

Athena turned and looked in the direction of the waterfall. "He is your father Samantha." She said gently.

"My father?" Samantha turned back to look at the man, she couldn't see his face but there was something very familiar about the way he stood there. Samantha felt as though she had seen him before, if only in a dream.

"Father, I have been looking for you." Samantha called out.

"My sweet daughter, I am always here." He said as he stepped through the water.

Samantha saw that he was standing on nothing but the water. His black boots touched the surface, not sinking at all. His clothes were dry despite the fact that he had just walked through a waterfall.

Looking at her father she realized that her hair was not only the same color but it also had the same waves in it.

"Father, how are you always here, when I've been searching for you?" She asked.

He continued walking across the water until he reached the shore and stood in front of her.

"You may not see me but I am there, always there beside you, always there watching you, and always there protecting you. Kronos is the key." He said. "Now wake up my child."

Before she could ask what he meant she was pulled from the dream and found herself laying in Hercules arms.

She looked up at him with tears in her eyes and said, "I saw him. I saw my father."

"That wasn't your father, you were trapped in your dreams, and most of the time you were tossing and turning and crying out. I was afraid that you would be trapped forever." Hercules replied.

She wrapped her arms around his neck and hugged him tightly. "I wasn't trapped. Well at first I was but then my father..." she trailed off thinking about her father.

Hercules helped her to her feet. "You saw him? Are you sure that it was really your father?"

"Yes, it was him."

"I told you, when you were ready for the truth, you would find the truth. Your father has come to you as a sign. A sign that you are on the correct path." Kronos said.

Samantha looked at Kronos, "You are the key." She whispered.

"What?" Hercules asked. "What do you mean the key? Key for what?"

There was a loud bang as lightning hit the ground. They all turned to see that Zeus was now standing there.

Zeus looked at Kronos, "Hello father."

"Zeus!" Kronos said with anger in his voice. "Why have you come here, boy?"

"I am here to stop the corruption of my son as well as Athena's daughter." Zeus replied.

Kronos threw his head back in laughter. "The only corruption came from you. You know not what these children face. You only care what you may gain from them. You will never gain the power you seek."

"You know nothing of what I seek," Zeus said walking towards Kronos.

As Zeus approached Kronos everyone that was nearby scattered out of the way, even the other Titans backed off. Samantha and Hercules were the only two that did not move.

"You seek the power of the three girls. You have finally realized that they are stronger beings than you or I. The power you seek will never be yours to control. Her father would never allow that." Kronos said.

"Her father? What does that coward have to do with anything?" Zeus replied.

Kronos shook his head and sighed, "you still do not understand. You have not changed one bit, you yourself are still just a child."

"I am not a child, I am Zeus king of Gods! You will respect me!" Zeus said as he shot a lightning bolt from his hand, hitting Kronos in the chest.

Kronos flew backwards but landed on his feet. "You will regret crossing me again."

"Stop!"

There was a tornado swirling blue and black.

"Hades, you dare to face me?" Kronos said.

"I am not here to face you father. I am here to make peace."

Zeus watched in amazement as Kronos' face softened.

Hades bowed down at his father's feet. "Forgive me Father for betraying you."

"Hades you coward!" Zeus exclaimed, "how dare you turn your back on me?"

Hades stood up to face Zeus, "I should have never helped you trap our Father."

"He tried to kill us. Remember, He ate us!" Zeus reminded him. "If it were not for me, we would still be in his stomach."

"Is that what you thought?" Kronos asked. "You thought I ate you out of anger, to kill you?"

"The prophecy was clear. I was to overthrow you, so you tried to kill me and all of your children." Zeus said.

"No my son, I was hiding you and your siblings from a much worse fate. I have to assume you have never heard the full prophecy. For it said, 'The youngest shall overthrow the father but in doing so shall seal his own fate, a fate worse than death.' I do not believe that you understood in full what that meant. All you heard was the part that you shall overthrow me." Kronos said.

"You lie! The prophecy said overthrowing you would give me more power." Zeus replied.

"No Zeus, You were lied to, but not from our father. Carnus lied, following orders given to her by Gaia, who wanted Oceanus in charge. She used us to get what she wanted.

She didn't realize that we would defeat all the Titans and trap them. Gaia only wanted Zeus out of the way." Hades said.

Kronos looked at Oceanus, "Did you have knowledge of this?"

"No, brother I swear." Oceanus said.

"No one knew except for Gaia and Carnus." Hades informed them. "I only found out after Carnus died and entered the Underworld. There she told me about how Gaia had promised her eternal life if she lied about the prophecy."

"It seems as though Gaia had lied to everyone." Oceanus said.

Samantha and Hercules had been listening to the conversation. She was sure they were ready to see an ultimate battle. However, it seemed as though this dysfunctional family had found a common enemy that had orchestrated the downfall of the Golden Age.

"So, what's going to happen now?" Samantha asked.

"Now we move forward and fix this dimension." Kronos replied. "I have been watching all the worlds. I found not the beautiful worlds they once were but worlds that have been destroyed by all the different mortals and immortals alike, and now the Forbidden."

"First, we need to destroy the Forbidden." Oceanus said. "Then we shall go in search of Gaia."

"The Forbidden will be here soon." Hades informed them, looking to the sky.

Within moments they heard the now-familiar screeching. The

Forbidden swooped down slamming into Tethys and knocking her to the ground. The creature sunk its teeth deep into her neck.

Oceanus grabbed the creature and threw it backwards, Samantha quickly gathered her powers and once again shot a bright light at the creature as it opened its mouth and lunged towards Tethys once more. Samantha, now more sure of herself than ever before, she felt the power grow and the white light turned to purple.

There was a loud screech as the Forbidden lay on the ground dying.

Once it stopped moving, Kronos pulled a jar from his robes and started to scoop up the black goo that had been the fierce creature..

Samantha couldn't see how it would fit in such a small jar until she noticed that it started to vanish as Kronos scooped up as much as he could before the rest disappeared.

The citizens came running and cheering as Kronos put a lid on the jar. As they approached Kronos they dropped to their knees showing their respect.

Kronos turned to Samantha, "It is not over. This is a female who has already given birth." He whispered to her.

Samantha gasped, "How many more are there?"

"There is no way to know. They never had a chance to reproduce before we destroyed what we thought was all of them. The Forbidden were to be an army, so I would assume she could have had a hundred or more offspring, each of which in turn could produce a hundred more."

"Wow, how are we going to stop that many?" Samantha asked.

Kronos shook his head, "They were not meant to be stopped. They will devour every planet."

"Together, we will stop them and this time, get them all." Zeus declared looking at his father.

Kronos nodded his head in agreement.

Samantha decided it would be better for her and Hercules to return to Bella Isola while the Titans and Gods searched for the rest of the Forbidden.

The moment they returned Cassandra approached Samantha, "Why did you leave without taking me with you? I have been going out of my mind trying to see you."

"What do you mean trying to see me?" Samantha asked.

"When a Seer is connected to someone, we should be able to find where you are at any time no matter where you are." Cassandra said. "You disappeared completely."

"I'm sorry. It won't happen again. I didn't mean to worry anyone, I was with Hercules and the Titans." Samantha replied.

Gabby walked into the room, "Samantha, I'm so happy your back."

Samantha allowed Gabby to give her a quick hug before excusing herself. Samantha went to her room to take a hot bath.

Meanwhile, Hercules was busy searching Ben's room for the stone that contained Samantha's memories. He came across a notebook and out of curiosity opened it.

The first page contained Samantha's name written at different angles and in different languages all over. The second page was more like a diary. Everything that Ben had written in the notebook had something to do with Samantha and her sisters.

Hercules started reading and decided he would read the whole thing to try to figure out what Ben was really up to. It wasn't until the last page that Hercules jumped to his feet and ran to find Samantha.

He was amazed that he hadn't realized that Ben and Samantha had a history.

In his hurry, he didn't knock on Samantha's door, he burst in the room, "Samantha, you have to read this."

Samantha sat up on the bed, "What is it? What's wrong?" Samantha asked.

"I was looking for the stone in Ben's room, but instead I found this." He said holding out the notebook and pointing to the last page.

Samantha took the book and started to read silently, until she reached the part that read,

> I have been trying to find a way to get back
> into Samantha's life, only to fail. It was my
> own fault that I lost her. No matter how hard

> I try, Toby is always there to keep me away
> from her. But, today I have found someone
> who can help me, her sister Saina.
> Saina came to me needing help. I am going with her to
> somewhere she claims is a different dimension. I will
> update all information upon my return.

"You know what this means?" Samantha asked Hercules.

Hercules smiled, "Yes, your sister has been to this dimension. She already knows about you, so she may be here looking for you right now."

"Where did you find this?"

"Under Ben's bed." Hercules said.

Samantha got up and walked from the room taking the book with her.

"Where are you going?" Hercules asked.

"To see if there are any more books." She called over her shoulder.

Hercules followed after her, back down to Ben's room. Together they searched the whole room and found three more notebooks that Ben had filled.

She read through them quickly. Two contained different information about Samantha and a past that Samantha didn't remember or that Ben had made up, the third one must have been when he had returned.

Samantha sat down on the bed with Hercules by her side, and started to read the notebook. Half way through the book Samantha came to the final entry, dated the day before he showed up at the castle.

> I returned today with Saina. I saw worlds that I never
> imagined possible. She showed me things that I could
> have never even dreamed of.
> She has made me realize that anything is possible.
> But we must go our separate ways now that she has no
> further use for me.
> Samantha if you are reading this then I am dead. I hope
> you know how sorry I am. I didn't know what she was
> going to do or what she had planned.
> You are the one that I loved.

I hid your stone in your favorite hiding spot. It holds more
memories than just the ones of Gabby. I am so sorry I
failed you.

Samantha re-read what Ben had wrote over and over. For some reason
reading it broke her heart.

"I have to go home to get the stone." She told Hercules.

"Okay. Do you want me to come with you?" He asked. Even though
Ben was gone, Hercules couldn't help being jealous. He clearly had the
relationship with Samantha that Hercules had always hoped for.

"If you want to, you can but I need Uncle Wayne to go," She replied
before walking out of the room and up the stairs.

Hercules followed after her.

Samantha found Wayne in the dining room eating dinner alone with
Jade. As soon as Wayne looked at Samantha's face, he knew something
was wrong.

Samantha had not entered the room but stood in the doorway looking
at her uncle. Wayne excused himself from the table and walked around the
corner with Samantha.

"What's wrong, hun?" He asked.

Samantha tried to hold the tears back but couldn't. "I need to go home.
There's something I need to find."

He wrapped his arms around her as he had done a thousand times
wishing he could take all her pain away so she could be happy.

"Samantha what happened? Why the need to go home?" He asked
gently.

"Ben hid something, something I need. We found this notebook," she
held the notebook up, still opened to the last page with the note to her on it.

Wayne read the note and looked at Samantha, "I was wondering if he
had told you the truth before he died. It seems even though he didn't, he
made sure you knew."

"What do you know about this? Are you hiding more things from me?"

"This wasn't my secret to tell. Let's go home, get the stone and then
you will understand it all."

Wayne walked back into the dining room to let Jade know he would be returning just as Hercules approached Samantha.

"As soon as he comes back out we are going to leave." Samantha said. "Can you please go find Cassandra and tell her that we are leaving and that if she wants to come with, come now?"

Hercules nodded once and walked down the hall in search of Cassandra. He wasn't happy about helping her, he already knew what the stone held. Hercules realized that was why Ben took all the memories of Gabby.

Ben had counted on Hercules making sure that Samantha retrieved all the memories of Gabby.

Once Samantha retrieved them, all the memories of Ben would be returned to her as well.

Five minutes later the four of them went back to the only home that Samantha had ever known.

Samantha looked around, the house was untouched. She saw Wayne's truck, the front end was smashed in. The barn had been burned down to the ground.

The front door of the house opened and Terry walked out onto the porch.

"Terry, what are you doing here?" Wayne asked him.

"A few of us decided to stay behind, in case the black eyed guys came back. So far, all has been quiet."

"That's good. I still haven't got a full list of those we lost."

Terry pulled a sheet of paper from his pocket.

Wayne started looking down the list, he saw the names Jasmine, Sissy and Toby close to the bottom. He wasn't sure if Samantha knew about the two girls but now was not the time for that.

Samantha reached over to take the paper, Wayne pulled it back and stuffed it in his coat pocket. "Don't you have something you need to do?"

"Yeah, I'll be right back," Samantha said walking towards the lake. When she noticed that Wayne had not moved she said, "Are you coming with me?"

Wayne nodded and caught up with her.

They walked in silence to the lake. Once there, Samantha looked out over the water, remembering the last time she had been here. This is where she had first met Poseidon, the night she had learned who her mother really was.

"You know I came here a lot and still don't know what the name of this lake is." Samantha said.

Wayne smiled, "This is Lake Athena. When your mother would bring you girls here, she would come sit by the lake to relax. It was her favorite place."

"So, you named it after her?" Samantha asked.

"Of course I did. She would sit here for hours and hours," he told her.

"Why did you need me to come with you?"

"Because you're the only one I trust enough to be here with me. I don't know what all memories are in that stone, plus I need you to give me a boost," she laughed pointing up into the tree.

He lifted her up high enough so she could grab a hold of the branch and climb on top of it. He watched as she reached into the tree and pulled out a small purple and green stone.

She looked down at him and smiled. As she started to lower herself he reached up to help her down.

They sat beside the lake and she placed the stone to her temple.

She saw the day the new kid had sat beside her in fifth grade math. Even at ten years old she knew there was something special about him.

Samantha now remembered the day he had asked her to be his girlfriend. He was wearing a blue t-shirt with blue jeans that had a hole in the knee of them.

Ben had quickly become the most popular kid at school. Samantha was surprised he asked her out at the beginning of sixth grade, she had done her best to remain invisible.

After that day, Samantha and Ben had been together most of the time, in and out of school.

He had changed his class schedule to match hers so they shared every class through the day. After school he would walk her home and they would sit by the lake doing homework together.

They had shared their first kiss by the lake on her thirteenth birthday.

She was at a party, a party that she hadn't remembered going to. She turned and looked around her, Ben was standing beside her. She looked down at her hand and found that their hands were entwined together.

As she looked back at Ben, he smiled, leaned over and kissed her lips. They had danced most of the night, just the two of them.

Samantha was back at the lake but now it was dark. She was laying on her back looking up at the sky. Once again Ben was at her side, instead of him looking at the sky he was looking at her.

There was something in the way he looked at her, like she was the only one in his universe.

As she stared into his eyes all the feelings that had been locked inside the stone came rushing back.

Everything that she was feeling told her that she had been in love with Ben. She had only been a young girl, even at the age of fourteen, she knew that he was the one.

Everything changed and now she was sitting at a desk at school. Ben sat two seats to her right.

As she looked at him, he was looking at the new girl that had just walked in. He had spent the whole class looking at the new girl, not looking at Samantha once.

For the first time Samantha was jealous.

After school she tried to avoid Ben by catching up with Toby. Ben followed the two of them home. He stopped her just as she reached the door.

"What's going on Sammy?" Ben had asked.

Samantha had tried to hide the tears, but when he turned her around and saw that she was crying he pulled her into his arms.

"Samantha no matter what it is you can tell me. Please?" He begged.

"I saw you," she cried, "I saw you looking at her. I saw the way you looked at her."

Ben shook his head, "I looked at who? There is no one but you."

"Ben, I saw you looking at her, the new girl. You looked at her the same way you look at me." Samantha said pulling away from him.

"I didn't look at her in any way." He tried to explain but she had already turned and slammed the door in his face.

The memory jumped to the next day, Toby had already gone to school and when Samantha got to the front doors she saw a crowd gathered around. She pushed her way to the center and found Ben and Toby arguing.

"Stay away from her," Toby had said, "I told you if you hurt her I would step in. She spent all of last night crying into her pillow because of you."

"I didn't do anything, it isn't what she thinks. I would never hurt her on purpose and I don't see what this has to do with you." Ben replied.

Toby took a step forward, "You know everything to do with her, has to do with me. Or have you forgotten why I'm here?"

Ben looked around at the crowd, as soon as he saw Samantha he walked over to her. Toby followed close behind him ready to attack if Ben did the wrong thing.

He took her hand and gently kissed the back of it. "I'm so sorry if I have hurt you. I didn't mean to. I love you." He turned and walked away before she had time to reply.

Now she was remembering her and Toby at the lake. He had bet her he could find a more unique stone than she could.

He acted so surprised when she had pulled the purple and green swirled Stone from the lake. She handed him the stone as they sat down on the bank.

She now remembered that Toby held the stone to her head and from then on she did not remember Ben except as another student at school.

Samantha looked at Wayne tears falling from her eyes, "Toby did this, it was Toby who took my memories."

"Why would he do such a thing?" Wayne asked.

"He thought that Ben had hurt me so he erased him. Uncle Wayne, I loved Ben and he loved me. I was only fourteen. We could have worked it out, we could have been together," She cried.

Wayne pulled her to him in a tight hug. "Baby I'm so sorry," he said. "Toby was doing what he thought best. He was trying to protect you. He didn't think about how you would feel about it. In all honesty, I think he used that as an excuse to get Ben out of your life. He was so jealous of Ben and you. Toby loved you even when you were both children. He could not stand to see you with another guy."

Samantha took a deep breath and wiped the tears from her face, "There is no excuse for what Toby did. He stole part of my life that I can never get back. I can't even tell Ben how sorry I am."

"I wasn't trying to make an excuse for what Toby did. I was simply explaining why I think he did it." Wayne explained.

They sat quietly for a long time, Samantha lost in her own memories. She had flashes of different moments she had shared with Ben. The more that came to the surface, the more painful it became.

He was gone now. She would never be able to tell him how she still felt. She started thinking about how he had said he didn't want to be the last one she turned to, she didn't fully understand why he would say that. Now she knew, He wanted to be the only guy in her life. He really had loved her.

As she sat there, every moment of Gabby returned to her as well. All the birthday parties, dances and even the day Samantha had cried over losing Ben. Gabby was always by her side when Samantha needed her.

"Samantha, We have to go." Wayne said pulling her to her feet.

She looked around and saw a dozen men coming towards them.

Samantha recognized the closest one, it was Kappas the one who had kidnapped her.

As he approached her, Wayne stepped in front of her. "Not another step or I will rip your throat out again."

"Easy dog," Kappas replied stopping where he was. "This has nothing to do with you."

"You're wrong there," Hercules said from behind Samantha.

When Samantha turned around she saw that not only Hercules but also Kevin was standing behind her.

She could see that she was one of the luckiest people alive to have people willing to fight to protect her.

"You want her, you have to go through us," Said Kevin, as he and Hercules stepped forward to stand on either side of her.

Wayne smiled, "You should turn and run now while you still have the chance."

Kappas laughed, "We still have you outnumbered. So, if I were you I would not be so cocky."

There was growling in the distance as six wolves ran towards them. Kappas turned and saw the wolves, "Attack!" he commanded.

Kappas went right for Wayne. Wayne jumped and when he landed in front of Kappas he was a wolf. Growling he went for Kappas' throat, but was thrown backwards.

As he landed on his back he struggled to get to his feet. Kappas was already on top of him before he could get up.

Samantha was facing two of the black eyes, but they seemed like they really didn't want to fight her. She tried to use her powers but nothing happened.

Hercules was having the same problem, he hit one of them as hard as he could but there was no damage and the black eyes just stood there.

Kevin was having fun. He shot different spells at the black eyes. But even his powers were no match for the black eyed guys.

Just as Kappas was about to break Wayne's neck, everyone except Samantha, Hercules and Kevin, froze in place.

"My, my. What is going on here?" Said a woman dressed in a long black dress.

"I know you." Kevin said.

"I should hope so. It's been such a long time, Kevin," she replied.

"How do I know you?" he asked.

The woman laughed and answered, "I gave you your powers."

"Hecate," Kevin whispered.

"Yes, it's been three hundred years since I last saw you," she replied, "I see you have used my gifts for good, unlike others who turn the power to suit their own needs."

Kevin bowed down at Hecate's feet, "My lady."

She smiled with appreciation, "Stand, my boy. You have more work to do before you are done today. However, you can not win this battle," She said looking at the three of them, "These creatures are not from this dimension, they neutralize the powers of the Travelers."

"So what do we do?" Hercules asked.

"She has the power. She is not a Traveler," Hecate said pointing at Samantha.

"If I have the power, why can't I use it?" Samantha asked.

"Your powers are connected to your emotions. You can not use your powers because you feel too much sadness right now. Learn to control your emotions and you will control your powers." Then to Kevin she added, "I will not allow you to lose this battle. If I do not help, you will die and I can't have that."

Samantha watched as Hecate pulled a blue and green swirled stone from her dress.

"As long as you possess this stone your powers will be tenfold of what they were." She said handing the stone to Kevin.

As soon as the stone touched his hand sparks flew up. Kevin's eyes glowed a bright white.

Hecate disappeared, Kevin stood looking at the stone.

Samantha knew that time would continue on soon and saw that Wayne was on the ground with Kappa ready to kill him.

She walked over and pulled Wayne, still a wolf, out and far enough away that he would have time to get on his feet.

Just as time continued on, Kevin held up his hands and a shower of blue and green sparks cascaded down on them all. All of the black eyes screamed in pain. One by one they disappeared in a puff of black smoke.

Samantha knew that the black eyes were not dead but had gone back to where they had come from.

Samantha watched as the wolves turned back into humans. She knew Terry, Crystal and Jen but she didn't know the other three. Wayne, back to his human form, approached Samantha with the other six following close behind him.

"Samantha, you remember Terry, Crystal and Jen?" he said to her, "and this is Frank, Mike and Shawn."

Samantha nodded her head, "it's nice to meet you all."

As the group walked back to the house Kevin was still holding the stone that Hecate had given him. Samantha took her own stone out of her pocket, the colors were different but the markings were exactly the same.

For some reason she knew that the stones were connected in some way. The question was how were they connected and why would Hecate give that one to Kevin.

All of a sudden, she was standing in the middle of a cave. There were six men all dressed in maroon and gold robes gathered around a small table where three stones were placed in a line.

A purple and green stone was on the left, a blue and green in the middle and a red and green was on the right.

The men stood in a circle around the stones. "We must hide these. The prophecy says, three babes, born of not only a Goddess but also of Iblis, shall come to possess these stones and destroy the world as we know it."

The others nodded in agreement but said nothing.

The man that had spoken, laid three golden cloths on the table. Gently he placed the stones separately on the cloths. He wrapped each one carefully and securely tied it with a string.

Another of the men sat a wooden box on the table. They placed the stones inside the box and sealed it with wax.

The box was placed in a hole in the wall cave. A third man stepped forward, waved his hand and the hole closed.

As the hole shut, the first man said, "We, the brotherhood shall protect the stones until the end of our days as will our children after us."

Samantha saw a shadow on the wall and in the next moment a big black bird came swooping into the cave. The men ducked as it flew over their heads to perch on the table.

There was a bright flash of white light that came from nowhere, Samantha looked away until it faded.

When she looked at where the light had been she saw her father sitting on the edge of the table where the bird had landed.

"You really think that I don't know what you are doing here?" He said with a grin.

Samantha's father laughed as he watched them trip over each other to get away from him. Then he said, "You think you can protect what belongs to me? I can take them anytime I want."

The one that had used magic to seal the wall, stood as he gathered his courage, "they no longer belong to you, they were given to us by your father to protect them from you and your spawn."

"We shall see about that," Samantha's father replied.

"Samantha, you alright?" Wayne said standing over her.

Samantha wasn't sure what just happened, but knew there was some meaning to it that she just didn't understand yet.

"Yes, I'm fine. What happened?" she asked.

"You passed out. What do you remember?" Kevin asked her.

"Not much," Samantha lied, "I was just walking and then I woke up with Wayne standing over me."

She wasn't sure why she had lied to them, she just knew that she couldn't tell them what she had just seen.

Hercules stood off to the side not speaking at all. When Samantha looked at him she expected to see concern but only saw suspicion. He turned his back and walked away.

Wayne and Kevin helped Samantha to her feet, "hat's his problem?" Kevin asked.

"No idea." Wayne replied.

They walked back to the farmhouse and expected Hercules to be waiting.

When they saw he wasn't, Samantha looked at Cassandra, "Did Hercules come back here?"

"No. Why? What happened?" She asked looking at Wayne's side.

Wayne looked down and saw his shirt was soaked in blood. Now that he saw the blood, he could feel the gash that went up his side.

He slowly pulled his shirt up, when Samantha saw the cut she walked over to look closer.

She saw that the cut wasn't as deep as it appeared to be but he would need stitches.

Samantha looked up at Wayne and saw that his face had gone white, "Uncle Wayne, are you alright?"

Instead of answering he fell to the ground.

"I don't understand, he isn't cut bad. What's wrong with him?" Samantha cried.

"Those creatures are not from our dimension."

Everyone turned to find Poseidon standing a few feet away.

All the wolves gasped at the sight of him.

"Grandfather, can you help him?" Samantha asked.

Poseidon shook his head, "I can not. However, you can."

"How..."

Samantha remembered the bird with the broken wing. She realized that the bird had not healed himself, she had done it.

She looked back to Wayne, "I don't know what I am doing."

"Yes you do hun. You just have to try." Wayne said.

Samantha shook her head, "I don't want to make it worse. Maybe I can get Kronos."

"There is no time, Samantha," Cassandra was standing beside her now, "You must do it now."

Everything faded before Wayne's eyes.

He was home. The familiar green hills of Mondo Del Lupo were a sight like no other. His house now stood before him. He had missed this place for far too long.

He walked up the wooden steps and noticed how the third one creaked when he stepped on it. He had been meaning to fix it before he left for the war, along with numerous other things.

He had wanted the house ready for when Jade was to move in with him.

When Wayne had passed out Samantha quickly tried to muster up the power to heal him. No matter how hard she tried, she couldn't.

"You need to stop feeling so much."

Samantha turned and saw Cy walking towards them.

Samantha just stared at him for a long moment before turning and looking at her uncle.

Cy stopped behind Samantha, put his hand on her shoulder, "You can do this, Sammy."

Samantha could feel Cy's hand on her shoulder and felt her power start to grow. She closed her eyes and focused on the poison running through Wayne's veins.

Once she located it, she focused on slowly pulling it back out of his body.

Cy knew that if he removed his hand Samantha would lose her focus so he remained as still as he could. When he saw the color return to Wayne's face, Cy removed his hand.

Samantha opened her eyes and looked at Wayne's face. His eyes slowly opened.

"Samantha," he whispered before passing out again.

Samantha turned to thank Cy, but he was gone. She looked at Terry, "Where did Cy go?"

"Cy?" Terry looked around confused, "Cy hasn't been here since the black eyes attacked the farm."

"He was just here," Samantha said.

"No one but us have been here, Samantha."

She turned and looked back at Wayne, his breathing was steady and she knew that he needed rest. She decided to take him back to the castle.

When they arrived, Kronos, Zeus and Hades were waiting for them.

"Samantha you need to come with us," Kronos said.

"To where?" She asked him.

Hades took a step closer to her, "Who are you to question us girl?"

Zeus grabbed Hades by the arm and pulled him backwards. "Easy brother."

"Enough of this," Kronos said looking at the two of them, then to Samantha, "We need your help. The Forbidden, as we suspected, laid over a thousand eggs which have already hatched."

"A thousand eggs? How could one Forbidden have so many offspring at a time? Why would you make such a creature?" Samantha said to Kronos.

"Does it matter right now why he made them? Shouldn't we be more concerned with destroying them?" Hades asked.

Samantha hesitated for just a moment then replied, "You're right. What do you need me to do?"

"Come with us and we will explain it," Zeus said.

Before anyone had time to stop them Kronos, Zeus, Hades and Samantha were gone.

PART 4

Saina

CHAPTER 11

Samantha looked around to see nothing but destruction. Whatever planet Kronos had taken her to was completely destroyed. Decrepit old buildings surrounded them, in the distance Samantha could hear screams and screeches.

"What's going on? What's all the noise over that way?" Samantha asked Kronos.

"We have called all the Travelers to help battle the Forbidden. For the first time in all the histories the Titans, the Gods and the Demigods will fight side-by-side," he replied.

Samantha looked around confused, "If the fighting is going on over there, why are we here?"

"We are here because of her," Hades said.

Samantha looked in the direction he was pointing. In the distance she saw a girl standing between two buildings.

The girl slowly walked towards Samantha but stopped when she was close enough for them to clearly see each other.

Samantha looked at her in disbelief, it was like looking in a mirror. The two girls were identical.

She knew that this had to be either Saina or Sandra, but either way this girl was her sister.

Ever since Samantha had found out that she was a triplet she had longed for the day to meet her sisters, however now that one stood before her she had no idea what to do or say.

"Samantha, go to your sister." Kronos said in a soft voice.

Samantha slowly started walking then stopped and turned around, "Where did you find her?" she asked Hades.

"I did not, she found us," he answered.

"How is that possible?"

"Just go to her," Zeus said.

Samantha continued walking towards her sister.

They stood facing each other for a long moment before Samantha was pulled into a hug.

"I have finally found you."

Samantha hugged her sister but felt a weird surge pass through her body. She let go to look at her sister again this time she realized that however much they looked alike on the outside, they were totally different.

"Which one are you?" Samantha asked.

"I am Saina, you are Samantha," she replied.

"Saina." Samantha repeated with a forced smile remembering what Ben had wrote in his journal. "Where have you been?"

Saina shook her head, "That's not important right now." Then looking past Samantha she said, "We need to stop those creatures before they completely destroy this world."

Kronos came forward, "Unfortunately, the Titans are ineffective. We were trapped too long. It will take time for our powers to be restored."

"So what are we going to do?" Saina and Samantha asked in unison.

"The two of you must stop them," Zeus answered. "We have kept them busy here but our numbers are diminishing."

The girls looked at each other, Samantha could feel the power coming from her sister. Even though Samantha didn't trust Saina, Samantha knew that together they could do anything. The girls nodded, turned and were in the middle of the battle.

Samantha heard Kronos calling out to the Gods and Travelers to fall back.

Samantha and Saina now stood in the middle of a swarming army of Forbiddens' alone. She was amazed when Saina spun and lifted herself over ten feet high and then shot red fireballs at the creatures.

Samantha stayed on the ground and began pulling lightning bolts down hitting every Forbidden she could.

Just as Samantha started to have fun, a Forbidden slammed into Saina, both slammed to the ground.

Samantha felt the stone in her pocket getting hotter as she ran to her sister's side. The Forbidden that had knocked Saina down, now launched itself at her. Reflectively Samantha held out her hands and shut her eyes.

She heard a loud pop and opened her eyes. She saw a pile of dust lying in front of her. Samantha realized that she had used her powers even though she didn't try to.

"Thanks sis," Saina said getting to her feet dusting her jeans off. "How many do you think are left?"

"I don't know, too many," Samantha replied as she watched a group of Forbidden land a few yards away from them. The creatures crawled along the ground like a group of cats stalking their prey.

"We need something more than my fire and your lightning," Saina said to her.

Samantha held her hand out, "Take my hand."

Saina didn't hesitate, she grabbed her sister's hand and with the other hand held the stone tightly. Immediately there was a blast of red and purple smoke that made a circle around the two of them and pulsated outward. As the smoke touched each of the Forbidden on the ground, they disappeared in a cloud of dust.

The creatures flying above their heads started swooping down at the girls. Samantha and Saina ducked to avoid the sharp claws.

"What are we going to do now?" Samantha looked at Saina with concern in her eyes.

"Take my hands," Saina said holding her hands out to Samantha. "Now concentrate, release the power from within you."

Samantha felt the power growing inside her she could also feel the power coming from her sister, feeling the force of their powers connecting she looked at her sister's face and saw Saina's eyes, there was a brilliant white light coming from them and for a moment she wondered if her eyes were doing the same

As the power grew stronger and stronger both Samantha and Saina looked to the skies.

Still holding her sister's hands, Samantha could feel the power spilling out. Even though she could still see the Forbidden clearly she could now see beams of purple and red light disintegrated every creature they touched.

One by one the Forbidden disappeared until the skies were clear.

The beams of light faded and the girls both fell to the ground. Kronos, Zeus and Hades followed by numerous other Gods, Titans, and Demigods approached Samantha and Saina.

"Are you okay?" A Traveler that Samantha did not recognize at first asked as he held out his hand to help her up.

Samantha looked up and couldn't believe her eyes. Toby was staring back at her with the same cowboy hat on and the same smile that he always had when he looked at her.

"Toby?" Samantha whispered just before she sank into darkness her mind and body completely drained.

As Samantha came to, she heard voices yelling, she tried to focus and clear her head so she could understand what they were saying.

"Where the hell were you?" Samantha heard Wayne yelling at someone.

Then to her surprise Hercules voice answered back, "I was where I needed to be and as you can see she is fine."

"I don't think fine is appropriate. She has been unconscious the last four days" Gabby said.

Samantha slowly got up and saw that she was back at the castle. Someone must have brought her here for Jade to watch over her. She looked around the room and realized that she was in the study connected directly into the foyer.

She slowly opened the door and saw Wayne, Hercules, Gabby and Jade standing at the bottom of the steps.

"Where is he?" Samantha asked.

They all turned to look at her but only Wayne replied, "Where is who?" He said as he walked towards her.

"Toby. I saw him. Why wouldn't he be here when I woke up?"

Wayne froze where he was, not sure what to say to her.

Hercules rushed forward and put his arms around her. She immediately pushed him away. "Don't touch me!" she said.

He looked at her with bitterness in his eyes, "We need to talk," he said grabbing her hand.

Before Samantha knew what had happened, she was in the middle of nowhere alone with Hercules. Samantha did the best she could to ignore the fact that Hercules had just kidnapped her.

"I have nothing to say to you," she said with contempt.

"Well you may have nothing to say to me but I have a lot to say to you. Like the fact you cannot let go of Toby. He is dead. Do you not understand what that means?" He said still holding on to her arm.

"But he isn't dead," she replied.

Hercules shook his head in disbelief. "I don't understand what your obsession with Toby is. Even if he did come back, he is not the one for you Samantha. You belong with me."

"I'm sorry, but no I don't. There was a short time where I could see a future with you. That was until I realized it has been Toby's all along. Toby was there to protect me, comfort me and love me for all of my life."

Hercules let go of her and turned his back. "It was supposed to be me."

Samantha reached out and touched his arm. "But it wasn't you Hercules. You had a choice, you said it yourself, you could have came for me at anytime but you didn't. I've spent all my life lost and afraid, the only real thing I ever had was Toby."

"So you feel you owe him for being there and doing his job?" Hercules asked.

"No, I don't owe him and he wasn't just doing a job. Toby cared for me when everyone else forgot me," she replied.

Hercules spun around and grabbed her by both arms, "You will be mine maybe not right now but someday you will be mine."

"Never!" she said pushing him backwards. She disappeared and returned to the castle.

Wayne was sitting on a bench waiting for her to come back. As soon as she appeared he ran to her. "Are you okay? He didn't hurt you did he?"

Samantha gave a small laugh as she said, "Uncle Wayne I don't think he could hurt me if he wanted to."

Wayne pulled her into a tight hug.

"There you are. I was starting to worry," Saina said coming down the stairs.

"Saina, you're here?" Samantha said as her sister gave her a quick hug.

"Where else would I be? I don't know where Sandra is and I'm not about to lose the one sister I have found."

"Speaking of which," Wayne said, "how did you two find each other?"

Samantha wasn't quite sure how to answer that since Saina was the one who found her. She looked to her sister waiting for an answer.

"I guess it was just luck," Saina said.

"Luck?" Samantha questioned.

"Well yeah, I don't know how else to explain it."

Samantha started thinking about how Kronos had come for her help. When she got there Saina was already there and now looking back she realized none of the Forbidden really attacked them.

"How did we destroy all of the Forbidden without a scratch?" Samantha asked her sister.

Saina looked shocked at the question. "I don't know what you mean?"

"Nothing. Never mind, it doesn't matter. I'm just happy that no one was hurt." Samantha said. Then turning towards Wayne she added, "I'm still a little tired. I'm going to go lie down for a nap."

Without waiting for a response, Samantha walked up the steps down the hall and into her room. Once the door was shut she turned the lock.

Samantha sat down on the edge of the bed closed her eyes and tried with all her might to clear her head.

She didn't know how long she sat there before the image of the same waterfall where she had met her father in a dream came into focus. Once again her mother and Toby were there.

"Mother, Toby," she cried.

"Samantha my darling, what has happened?" Athena asked hugging her daughter tightly.

"It's Saina," Samantha started.

Athena pulled back just enough to look at her daughter, "Saina? What about her?"

"I found her. Well, more accurately she found me. But mother something's wrong."

"What do you mean by something's wrong?"

Samantha used the back of her hand to wipe a tear away. "When I touched her, I could feel something, something evil. I'm not sure if she truly is Saina or something else entirely."

Athena guided Samantha to a boulder along the water's edge. As they sat down together Athena said, "Unfortunately she is your sister but you are correct in thinking something evil is within her, however the evil is not foreign, it is a part of her. It is who she is, what she is. Samantha do not trust her."

"How could she be my sister and yet still be evil? Am I evil?" Samantha asked.

"No my darling, you are not evil," Athena said.

"How could we be so much alike yet completely different? I don't understand, Mother."

"You were raised with love and understanding. With protection and a family. I am so thankful that Wayne took you in and raised you as if you were his own. Saina wasn't so lucky. Do you want me to explain everything to you?" Athena asked.

"Yes Mother, I need to know the truth," Samantha replied.

Athena had waited all these years just for the chance to be with her daughter and to be able to tell her daughter the whole truth about everything.

"You do know about Zeus and the ultimatum that he had given me?"

Samantha nodded her head, "Yes."

"The night I left my body, your father had come for you girls. I guess he couldn't take all three at one time, so he grabbed the closest two.

When he went through the portal with your sisters I grabbed you and called Wayne for help, but before he had got there one of your father's servants came for you.

I tried to fight him off and if I would have had my powers I may have succeeded. I failed. Hercules got there just in time, just as Kappas approached the portal Hercules pulled you from his grasp.

Not long after your father had your sisters, Saina was taken away from him by his father and given to the last remaining Titan." Athena paused giving Samantha time to absorb and question everything she had just told her.

"Who is my father?" Samantha asked.

"Your father is a very powerful being from the first Dimension. I don't think I ever truly knew who he was or even his real name. All I knew him by was the name Bee," Athena told her.

"So Saina was raised by a Titan? I thought all the Titans had been locked up."

Athena nodded, "All but one. She is the most vicious, the most cruel evil being that I had ever come across. She mostly goes by the name Lilith."

She took a moment to think about that and then said, "That's why I got a weird feeling when I touched her. She's not evil, she was just raised evil." Samantha stated.

"No being or creature is born evil. Evil is created by circumstance. And in this case Lilith needed a powerful source to take over the dimension that she has been a prisoner in for so long."

"All right, Wayne raised me, Lilith raised Saina. What happened to Sandra?" Samantha asked her mother.

"Sandra was raised by your father. Samantha, do you understand? Sandra was raised good and pure. Saina was raised to be evil and dark. You learned to be both, good and evil. You have the potential for both, depending on what you decide."

Samantha was amazed that three identical people were so completely different. She was also confused, if Saina was raised to be evil why did she help defeat the Forbidden?

"Samantha, I must go now. However, I will return. Always remember I am with you. Enjoy your visit with Toby darling. I love you." Right before her eyes her mother disappeared.

Samantha had forgotten that Toby was there. She was so wrapped up in hearing everything her mother told her and everything she wanted to hear.

Now that it was just the two of them she went to him and collapsed into his arms.

"My sweet Sammy. Everything will be okay." He whispered in her ear.

Samantha started to cry, "You were there. I saw you just before I passed out."

"What do you mean? I can't leave this place," Toby told her.

"But I saw you," she said.

"I can only see you. I can never come to you, no matter how much I want to," Toby said.

"So when my mother said she always with me, she lied?"

"No," Toby said taking her hand. "She is a full Goddess, I am only a Demigod."

"Is there anyway I can bring you back?"

Toby shrugged his shoulders, "I don't know if you have enough power but I have heard a few have returned to the living."

Samantha could feel herself being pulled back to her body.

"Toby, Tell me how can I bring you back?"

"You have to find…."

CHAPTER 12

Samantha's eyes flew open, she was back in her room at the castle. She threw herself backward on the bed, "Why now? I only needed a few more seconds," she yelled out at no one.

The bedroom door flew open with a bang, Wayne followed by three vampires rushed into her room.

"What happened?" Wayne asked as he looked around the room to see who she had been yelling at.

Samantha had tears in her eyes, "Uncle Wayne, I think I can bring Toby back."

Wayne looked over his shoulder, "We're good here, thank you," he said dismissing them. They each nodded and pulled the door shut as they left the room.

Wayne walked over and sat beside Samantha on the bed. "Who told you that you could bring him back?"

"He did," she replied.

With confusion on his face Wayne asked, "How could he tell you anything? Samantha honey, Toby is gone. No one comes back from death."

She shook her head furiously, "He said I could bring him back but I have to find something."

"What do you have to find? If it is possible to bring him back I will do anything it takes to help you."

"That's just it, I don't know. I got pulled back before he told me what I had to find." Samantha's eyes lit up, "If I can bring Toby back I can bring my mother and Ben back."

Wayne knew what a bad idea bringing both Toby and Ben back was, but kept his opinion to himself. He could see the hope in her eyes and did not want to break her heart.

"Whatever it is that you need, I will help you," he told her.

"Uncle Wayne, can I ask you something?"

"Anything," he replied.

"What do you think about Saina?" she asked plainly.

"Well for one thing she does not know much about vampires or Wolves," he said.

"What do you mean?"

"She must not realize that almost everyone in this Castle can hear everything going on within the walls." When he saw the confusion on her face he added, "She walked out of a room speaking to someone, it was obvious that it was to be a private conversation. She was informing whoever she was speaking to that she had found you and was now inside the castle."

"Something about her has been bothering me and it was confirmed when I spoke to my mother," Samantha said.

Wayne sat up straighter, "Samantha, how is it that you've been speaking to your mother and Toby?"

She shrugged her shoulders, "I'm not sure but at times even though I'm here, I'm not here. I go to the waterfall and they're there."

"Waterfall? Do you know where it is?"

"I don't think it's anywhere. I've never physically been there. It's like my mind goes even though when my mother hugs me I can feel her touch." Samantha replied.

"Tell me a little more about this waterfall."

Samantha smiled, "It's the most beautiful place I have ever seen. The water is so crystal clear you can see right through it. The pool that the waterfall spills into is surrounded by trees that are every color and no color at the same time."

"How could trees be every color and no color at the same time?" Wayne asked.

"It depends on the way I look at them. Sometimes they seem full of colors like a rainbow but other times I can almost see through them. There is a boulder big enough for three people to sit on comfortably. The bottom of the pool is lined with the most beautiful rocks of every color."

Wayne was watching her face as she spoke about the waterfall and its surroundings. She seemed to be in awe just describing it.

"Have you wished you could go there and stay?" he asked.

She nodded her head, "Yes, but that was before I knew I could bring them back."

"Is Ben there too?"

"No, just Toby and my mother," Samantha said glancing over at Wayne. "You know where it is?"

Wayne stood up and walked across the room, "No I don't," he said before walking out the door.

Samantha jumped to her feet and opened the door to stop Wayne but he was already gone. She shut the door and turned to walk to the window. Before she made it halfway across the room there was a knock at the door.

"I'm glad you came back there's so much more I want to…" she started as she swung the door open and saw Vic standing there.

"I'm sorry I shouldn't be showing up at your room like this," he said.

Samantha took a step back and said, "It's fine come on in."

Vic entered the room just enough for the door to shut. He slowly pushed the door shut then whispered, "Can you take us somewhere no one can hear us talking?"

"Where do you…"

"Anywhere."

Samantha grabbed his hand and they disappeared.

Samantha went to the first place she thought of, the lake by the farm house.

Vic looked around. "Where are we?"

"The only place I ever felt at home. This is the lake I come to, it's like my hideaway."

They sat down on the bank. Samantha looked up at the sky. It was a clear summer night, the stars were twinkling in the sky. The air was warm and like always the crickets were chirping away.

Vic sat silent for a long time staring at the water.

"Why did you want to leave the castle?" Samantha asked.

"I didn't want Saina or Hercules hearing what I have to say to you," he answered.

"Why? What's so important that you want to hide from them?"

Vic looked at her, "Who is Cy?"

"Cy? Why would you ask about him?"

He didn't answer, he just looked at her.

"Cy is a wolf. He is a good guy."

"Are you sure about that?" Vic questioned.

"Well, I was until you said that. What do you know?" Samantha asked turning her legs so that she now faced him.

"Hercules thinks there is something between you and Cy. He told someone that you saw Cy at the farm house, when Wayne got hurt."

"I did."

"But no one else could see him?"

"No. I was the only one who saw him. I guess I just wished he was there and my mind played a trick on me."

"What really happened when you passed out? What did you see?"

Samantha wasn't sure how Vic had known about that but decided to tell him the truth. She felt as though she could really trust Vic.

"I saw my father," she whispered.

Vic's head snapped up to look at her, "What does your father look like?"

"Why?"

"Because I think I saw him this morning," He answered.

"How?"

Vic looked out over the water as he said, "He pulled me to him. I don't know, maybe it wasn't him. I'm sorry, I shouldn't have wasted your time."

Vic started to stand up, Samantha grabbed his hand, "Please tell me?"

He sat back down. "I was lying on my bed, thinking about you. All of a sudden I felt someone pulling me. But it hurt. I have not felt pain since I was turned. Not physical pain."

"What was different this time?"

"I think it was because he wasn't pulling me across the world but into a different dimension." Vic knew he sounded crazy but still hoped that Samantha would believe him.

"He isn't in this dimension, so that would make sense," She said.

Vic let out a sigh of relief that she didn't think he was just a lunatic. "He said that he knew I have feelings for you and that he could use that to help you."

"Help me, how?"

"You might not want to hear this," he said taking her hand.

"Please, I need to hear it."

"He told me to tell you to stop looking for a way to get Toby back."

Samantha pulled her hand away. "What! Never. I won't stop until I find a way to bring him back."

"Samantha, please."

She shook her head. "No."

"He just wants you happy. He knows how hurt you are, losing the two men you love..."

"Stop!" Samantha yelled at him.

"I'm sorry," Vic said standing up and walking under the willow tree. He knew she needed space right now. He hated to see her hurting. Ever since she had taken the spell off of him, he had felt like a ghost to her, watching her go off on missions with everyone but him.

Every day she had been at the castle he had fallen more and more in love with her. He knew that her father asking him to tell her this was his way of ensuring that Samantha would never be his.

Vic wanted her to be happy, no matter the cost he had to pay. He walked back over and sat down beside her.

"I just realized something," he said.

"What?" she snapped at him.

"Your father don't want you looking for a way, that means there is a way to be found."

Samantha looked at him, "So you think there is a way?"

"Yes and I'm going to help you find it. I'm going to help you get him back."

She hugged him tightly. "Thank you Vic."

She stood up, "Are you ready to go back?"

"Um, not just yet. There is one more thing your father said," he took an unnecessary breath and said, "he told me to keep Hercules away from you. And I see his point there, Hercules is a strange guy. He is always skipping out and hiding things."

"Like what?"

Vic ran his hand through his hair, "Like his kids."

Samantha's eyes grew wide, "His kids?"

"Yeah, have you met them?"

"Met them? I never even knew about them," she said. "Where are they?"

"That's just it, no one knows. Honestly I didn't know about them either, until your father told me."

Samantha had a feeling that Hercules had been hiding something from her, but she never imagined it was his children he had been hiding.

"Well, let's go ask him," Samantha said grabbing Vic's hand and disappearing.

Once back at the castle Vic looked at Samantha.

"It's okay. You go. He don't need to know where I heard it," she told him.

Vic smiled and walked down the hall towards the kitchen.

Samantha started looking for Hercules. She found him in the library.

"Oh, hey. Where have you been?" he asked when he saw her.

"Just off having a chat with a dear friend," Samantha sat down beside him. "I was thinking, you were right."

"About what?"

"Us being together. You were right." She moved closer to him and brushed her hand through his hair.

"Yeah?"

"Yeah, you are the one person who never lied to me or used me for anything." She leaned in closer, now she could feel his breath on her face. "You would never lie to me, would you?"

"Of course not." He placed one hand on her back and the other on her cheek. "Samantha, I love you."

"So, I'm the one you want to be with? The one you want to marry and have children with?" She asked softly.

"Yes. I want to marry you and of course I want children with you."

She smiled sweetly, "Am I the only one you have wanted kids with?"

"Yes," he replied but was sorry the moment she pushed him backwards.

"You already have children," she said standing up. "How dare you sit there and lie about your own children."

"I never said I don't have children, only that I never wanted children with anyone but you."

"Really?" Samantha turned to see a beautiful woman with short red hair standing in the doorway of the library. "So our boys were, what, a mistake?"

Samantha immediately realized that this woman was the mother of Hercules' children and she couldn't help but smile.

"Pala, what are you doing here?" Hercules asked, clearly trying to act innocent. He walked over to her and bent to kiss her cheek.

Pala pulled away, "You are a swine. I heard what you just said to her. I can't believe it took me two hundred years to see you for what you really are."

Hercules looked at Samantha, "You knew she was here?"

"No but this sure is funny. You have done all you could to stop me from being with anyone but you. All the while you had a woman...."

"Wife," Pala corrected.

Samantha felt rage rise in her stomach. "All this time you have been trying to be with me and you had a wife waiting for you!" Samantha yelled at him, her face had turned red with rage.

"Samantha it's not like that. I told her I didn't want to be with her."

"Oh, well that makes it all better," Samantha said sarcastically.

Hercules rushed over to Samantha, "I do love you. I should have told you about them, I know I messed up. Please forgive me?" He dropped to his knees.

Pala laughed, "Wow. You got him begging. It's your call, if you want him I will quietly leave."

Samantha looked down at Hercules, "No. I don't want him. He is a liar."

Hercules looked to the floor. "Sammy, please."

"How dare you!" Samantha pulled her hand back and slapped him across the face. "You don't get to call me Sammy, only people I care about get to call me that!" Samantha turned and walked out of the room.

She passed a lot of people on the way to her suite, but wasn't interested in talking to any of them at the moment.

Once in her room with the door securely shut and locked, she slid down her door allowing the tears to fall.

She looked at the ceiling, "Father, please help me?" She said quietly.

"My darling daughter, I can not."

Samantha looked towards the fire place and saw her father standing there.

"Father!" she cried as she went to him.

He wrapped her in his arms, "It's all fine now daughter. I am here."

"Why do you want me to stop trying to bring ..."

"Ben and Toby back," he finished. "I don't want you searching for them. They are not lost."

"I don't know what you mean."

"If I tell you a secret will you promise to not go off the handle and run out of here?" he said with a smile.

"Yes, I promise."

"Ben is not dead. He faked his death to get revenge on Hercules."

"He what?"

"That's not all." He took her by the hands, "Toby and your mother are not dead either."

Samantha pulled away from him, "You're lying."

"I am not."

Samantha had been so upset that she had not noticed that her father was wearing jeans and tennis shoes, instead of his normal black slacks and black dress shoes. She took a few steps backwards, "you are not my father."

Samantha watched as her father transformed into Saina.

"Saina? What are you doing?" Samantha asked.

"Trying to teach you sister."

"Teach me what?"

"Teach you that you need to stop with these stupid guys. Not one of them deserve you. Toby, Ben, Vic, Hercules. They are nothing compared to us, sister. We hold all the power."

"You don't know what you are talking about," Samantha said.

"Don't I? Toby took your memories of Ben. Ben took your memories of Gabby. Hercules hid his wife and kids from you and Vic, poor Vic was only interested because you used your powers on him."

"It was you, wasn't it?"

"What?"

"In the library. It was you. Was Hercules and Pala even there?"

Saina laughed, "Took you long enough. It was me by the lake too. You are so gullible. You believe anything and you leave your mind wide open. You really shouldn't do that. Anyone can just slip right in there."

Samantha felt like a fool. "How did you find Kronos?"

"Ah, you finally caught that. Well I have been waiting for the right time to come to you. Ever since Ben and I, well I will spare you the details." Saina gave Samantha a crazy smile, "Like the Titans made a mistake. I just can't believe that Kronos killed one of his own for nothing."

"What are you talking about?"

"In Tartarus, when you told him that there was a Forbidden that they had missed."

Samantha thought about Theia and how she had apologized to Kronos for failing him. "The Forbidden was destroyed before the Titans were locked away, weren't they?"

"Yes! Now you're getting it." Saina walked towards Samantha, "It was me, I created a copy of the Forbidden and sent it to you. It was suppose to kill you but then I realized that it was a good thing you survived, our powers combined are more powerful than even I had suspected."

"Why did you do all this? What did I ever do to you?"

"It's not what you did, it's what you have. You had a loving home, you had school and friends and Ben."

"That's it, isn't it? Ben," Samantha said, "You did all this for him.

It was you the whole time. The new girl in school, the one he looked at with love in his eyes. That's why he didn't know what I was talking about." Everything started to become so obvious to Samantha now. "You disguised me to look like someone else and you walked in looking like me."

"I am impressed. You finally figured it all out," Saina said. "He loved you so much that even after Toby took your memories and you had no idea that he loved you, he still didn't want me. I even created a whole new persona just for him."

"Sarah."

"Yeah, then when I saw you on your birthday, our birthday, you only had eyes for Toby. I thought that was it, that he would finally be free of you. But low and behold he came to you that night. He just couldn't move on. I showed him things that no one in this dimension knows exists but the whole time he wouldn't shut up about you."

"That's because no one can compare to Samantha, not even her twin." Samantha and Saina both looked to the door, Ben was standing with his arms across his chest.

"Ben!" Samantha said, "Is it really you?"

He nodded his head, "Yes and I can prove it. Ask me something only we know."

"Where did you hide the stone?"

Saina looked confused.

Ben smiled, "In your favorite place."

Samantha smiled as she walked over and wrapped her arms around him.

Saina screamed, "This isn't fair! Why her?"

Just then the door swung open Wayne, and Vic stood in the doorway.

"Ben get back," Samantha said. "All of you stay back. This is between me and my sister."

"Let's take this somewhere else," Saina said.

CHAPTER 13

Before Samantha could say a word they were back in the same town they had fought the Forbidden in.

"Saina why are you doing this?"

"Because I love him. I tried being you, being someone else. Hell, I even tried spelling him. But his love for you is too strong. Nothing I did made him love me."

Samantha felt sorry for her sister, "You can not make someone love you. You can't trick them into it. If you really love him you will stop all these childish games and be my sister. Let the rest work itself out."

"You still want me to be your sister?"

"Of course I do. I have been trying to find you. I don't want to fight you."

Saina had never felt wanted by anyone. She was told everyday how much of a burden she was. She never had anyone truly love her.

"Can I show you something?" Saina asked.

"Of course, sister." Samantha remembered what her mother had said about Saina being evil but she couldn't believe that her sister wasn't capable of good.

Saina reached out her hand hoping Samantha would trust her. When Samantha took her hand Saina smiled.

She opened her mind up to her sister, Samantha felt cold and isolated, she was inside a cage. Scared and more hungry than she had ever felt before.

A woman came to the cage door, "Have you learned your lesson yet?"

"Yes Ma'am."

"The next time you disobey me I won't be so lenient on you. When I tell you to kill someone you will do as you are told. If I wanted to do this alone I wouldn't have bothered with you. You belong to me and you better prove your worth or I will leave you to rot in this cage."

"I won't fail you again."

The woman smiled, "Good because I have the perfect job for you to prove to me that I haven't wasted my time with you. You will go to the third dimension and kill the son of Zeus."

"How will I know who he is?"

"Use your powers, stupid girl." The woman slapped her in the head. "You will go to what they call Alpha One and find him. I want him dead and you be back here before the next solar eclipse."

Samantha blinked and looked at Saina, "I am so sorry you had to live through all that. Things can be better if you let them."

"Can I ask you something?"

"Of course." Samantha replied with a smile.

"Have you seen mother?"

Samantha smiled, "Yes, but only in my dreams."

"Did she say anything about me?"

Samantha flinched just enough for Saina to notice.

"She told you that I am evil, didn't she?"

"Yes, but I'm sure that's only because she didn't have the chance to know you."

Saina wiped a tear from her face, "I saw her too but she wouldn't talk to me. I begged her to just acknowledge that I was there, but she wouldn't even look at me."

"Our mother would never do that. Are you sure someone wasn't blocking you from reaching out to her?"

Saina thought about that for a moment, "I never considered that, but now it makes sense. Lilith must have been stopping her from knowing I was there."

"Will you please come back with me?" Samantha asked.

"To the castle?"

"Yes."

"I don't think anyone wants me there."

Samantha shook her head, "If they tell you to leave then we will leave together."

Saina gave a small smile, "Really? You would leave your friends for me?"

"You are my sister. We belong together."

"Okay. I'm in."

While the two girls were gone, Hercules and Wayne took the time to question Ben about where he had been.

"How are you alive?" Hercules asked.

"My mother saved my life. When Arachne stepped on me, I was bleeding out pretty bad."

"Persephone is your mother?" Hercules questioned.

"Yes."

"So you are not a Traveler."

"No. I am not," Ben answered. "But Arachne's venom is life threatening to even Gods, So I really was dying. My mother pulled me from my body until she could heal it, then put me back together."

"Why did she lie then?" Gabby said walking into Samantha's room where the guys were waiting for Samantha to return.

Ben looked at Gabby and felt guilty for everything he had put her through. "She had to make everyone believe I was dead so no one realized that I am a God. Gabby, I am so sorry."

"Why is it such a big deal that you are a God?" Gabby asked.

"Because if Zeus knew that I am a God, he would have trapped me with my father. Hades lied to Zeus, telling him that I was his son and that Selena was my mother."

"If you are a God, then Samantha can not spell you," Hercules said. "You really love her, don't you?"

"Yes I do. But she can spell you, you are part mortal," Ben answered.

"Did she?"

"I don't think she meant to, she was so young when she did it that she probably don't remember."

"You were there," Wayne said. "The day I asked Zeus to let Samantha come back with me."

"Yes, I was the one who suggested Tobinus go in place of Hercules. I saw that she had already spelled him and I was afraid that he would get to close to her." Ben looked at Hercules, "I am sorry for that."

"No, I understand," Hercules said, even though he didn't.

Ben read Hercules' mind, "Tobinus was my best friend, we had a bond. He gave me permission to place a block on him so Samantha could not spell him. It was too late for me to place one on you, you were already spelled."

Hercules understood what Ben was saying but he didn't believe that Samantha at three years old had spelled him. Ben saw this in Hercules mind but decided to let it go. He knew when Samantha got back Hercules would talk to her about it.

"What about the journals? You said you were with Saina and that you were sorry, you didn't know what she was planning."

"I was with Saina for a short time and I didn't know what she was going to do. You must not have been around much since she showed up," he said looking at Hercules.

"Is Samantha alright?" Wayne asked.

Ben closed his eyes for a moment, "Yes, she is talking to Saina. They will work this out. After all they are sisters."

"What was Saina planning?" Hercules asked.

"It wasn't fair of me to put the blame on her like that, she was doing what she thought she had to until she met me and I told her about her sister and how you fit into it all."

"Ben just tell me."

Ben held up his hands, "She had orders to kill you, but she changed her mind when she saw you."

"Kill me? Why? I don't even know her."

"It wasn't about you, it was something your father did to someone. Saina had orders to kill Zeus' son."

"But once I saw you, I couldn't do it." Saina and Samantha had returned.

"Samantha," Ben said getting up and taking her in his arms.

Samantha held onto him as tight as she could, she never wanted to let him go. She looked up at him and he lowered his head to kiss her.

"Um, that's enough," Wayne said gently separating the pair.

Samantha laughed, "Uncle Wayne. Thank you." She said hugging him.

"For what?"

"For wanting me and always being there for me," Samantha replied.

"You are most welcome sweetheart," he said as he hugged her tightly.

Samantha looked around and saw Gabby, Hercules and Saina all looking at her.

Samantha saw that Saina and Gabby were smiling however, Hercules looked as though someone had punched him in the stomach and was ready to vomit. Samantha took a step towards Hercules, Ben reached out and caught her hand.

"May I speak with you, alone?"

Samantha glanced back at Hercules before nodding. Samantha and Ben disappeared.

Samantha looked around, the world that Ben had brought her to was even more beautiful than Bella Isola. There were multicolored flowers spread across a green field. Along one edge of the field was a forest, full and alive.

Samantha looked into the sky, White clouds crept across two suns that were almost side by side in the sky.

"Where are we?" Samantha asked.

Ben smiled, "This is the New World that you had Kronos create."

"It's beautiful."

Ben took Samantha by the hand, "Samantha, the reason I wanted to talk to you, Hercules…"

"I know, I feel so bad. I never wanted to hurt him."

"I know and you didn't. Not really," Ben said.

"Ben, I saw the look on his face," she replied.

"Samantha, when you were three, Hercules brought you and Wayne to Mount Olympus. Wayne begged to be allowed to keep you."

"He told me."

"Did he also tell you that while Hercules was holding you, you spelled him?" he asked.

"How? I was only a child."

Ben pulled her so close to him that she could feel his heart beating. "You are very powerful. Even as a child you used your powers, without knowing it. He has been under your spell for fifteen years. That's why he can't move on and let you go."

Samantha looked at the ground, "I didn't know."

Ben lifted her chin so she faced him. "Darling, how could you have known? You were so small. You had just lost your mother and sisters. Everything you ever knew was gone. You have to take the spell back. Free him. So that we can be together."

Ben bent his head down and kissed her forehead, her cheek and then his mouth found hers. The moment their lips met, the world started spinning. There was nothing but her and Ben. Everything else melted away.

Hercules now knew that he was under Samantha's spell, but it still hurt when she disappeared with Ben. He walked out of her room and went to his own room to be alone.

Wayne went to the hallway and said, "Jade?"

Within a few moments she was by his side. "I heard. It's wonderful that Ben is still alive."

"Yes, Ben being here will make everything easier for Samantha. But I must confess, I always wanted to see her and Toby together and happy." A single tear rolled down his cheek.

Jade put her arm around him and the two of them walked down the hall and disappeared into their room.

Saina and Gabby sat down at the small coffee table. Neither of them knowing what to say to each other.

Ben and Samantha had forgotten about everyone back at the castle, they were lying in the middle of the field watching the clouds float over them.

Samantha had not felt this content since the last time her and Ben had laid beside the lake watching the stars.

She closed her eyes and fell asleep.

The waterfall looked more beautiful than the other times she was here. She looked around and didn't see anyone. She climbed up on the boulder and sat down watching the water splashing as it fell.

"Sammy."

Samantha turned and saw Toby standing by the edge of the pool.

"Toby!" she ran to him.

He took her in his arms. "My sweet Sammy. What are you doing with Ben?"

She looked up at him and in that moment she remembered that Toby had been the one that took her memories of her and Ben being together.

"Why did you put my memories in the stone?"

"I took the memories because he couldn't see that he was being tricked. When that other girl walked into the room and he thought she was you, that showed me that he couldn't have loved you the way he should have. The way I do." He bent down and kissed her.

Samantha kissed him back. All she had wanted the last few weeks was to have Toby back. She didn't ever want to leave here.

"Can I stay here with you?" she whispered.

"No my love, you must go back."

"Then tell me how to bring you back. If we are meant to be together then let me bring you back."

"Samantha."

She looked back at the waterfall and saw her father standing there watching them.

"Father."

He walked towards them and Toby dropped his arms from around her and stepped backwards.

"Go!" he said to Toby.

Toby glanced at Samantha then disappeared.

"Father?"

"You must go back to the castle. Your sister is in grave danger as is all within the castle. I will take care of Toby, now go."

"But I…"

"GO!"

Samantha sat up so fast that Ben jumped.

"What's wrong?"

"We have to go. Now!"

Samantha tried to teleport into the castle but ended up on the new part of the island. She looked toward the castle and saw the bright glow of fire. She started running as fast as she could to reach her family and friends.

As she got closer she saw that the city surrounding the castle was completely engulfed in flames but the castle was untouched. She sighed with relief for just a moment.

Then she saw it, hovering above the castle was giant dragon. She stopped and was trying to figure out what to do when Ben caught up to her.

"What's going on?"

Samantha pointed to the sky.

As soon as Ben saw the dragon he started laughing.

"What are you laughing about?" Samantha asked looking at him.

"It's only a dragon, Sammy," Ben answered. Then he looked back at the castle and saw not only the one dragon but a total of nine dragons. "Oh."

"This is bad. What are we going to do?"

"Those are the nine keepers of the dimensions."

Samantha turned around and saw Kronos was standing directly behind them. The other Titans and Gods were all standing behind him.

"So what can we do?" Samantha asked.

Kronos knelt down in front of her, "My Queen, a great evil has entered our dimension. We await your command."

Samantha looked at Ben and then back at Kronos, "I don't know what to do."

"Yes you do," someone behind Kronos said.

Kronos stood up and stepped aside. Samantha's father walked forward. "You know what to do. You just have to trust in yourself."

Kronos once again dropped to his knees as did all the Titans. "My lord," Kronos said.

Bee looked at Kronos, "Thank you for accepting my daughter, in doing so you have helped reconnect the two dimensions." Then to Samantha he said, "The dragons are not attacking, they are guarding the castle. They are making sure no one escapes."

"Who is commanding them?" Samantha asked.

"Someone created from pure hate. Her name is Lilith," her father answered.

"The one who took Saina?"

"Yes. She is more powerful than any being from this dimension. She is here because Saina has failed her. She has demanded that they send Saina out of the castle so that Lilith can punish her. They have refused."

Knowing that Wayne and Jade were trying to protect her sister made Samantha happy. She knew that the standoff couldn't last forever and it was up to her to save everyone in the castle.

"Kronos, you and the Titans distract the dragons," Samantha commanded.

Kronos nodded, "Yes my Queen." He led the Titans closer to the castle.

"Zeus," Samantha called out. She looked through the crowd. "Where did Zeus go?"

Poseidon stepped forward, "He is gone."

Samantha looked around hoping that Poseidon was wrong even though she knew he wasn't.

She turned back to her father, "Can't you just go help them?"

"Yes, I could but what lesson would I be teaching you?"

"Lesson? Your daughter is in there!" Samantha yelled at him.

"Samantha, you have to understand, the only way for you to get stronger is to learn to use your powers. How will you learn if I fight your battle for you?" He replied in a soft voice.

Samantha was surprised that he had not so much as raised his voice to her. She understood what he was telling her. He wanted to see if she could handle the situation, without help from him.

"I will be here if I am needed," he said with a smile.

Samantha turned back to Poseidon, "Take the Gods, go to the other side of the castle. When you see the purple flash in the sky make your way into the castle."

Poseidon led the Gods away to await Samantha's signal.

There were a few dozen people left in front of her. She looked through them trying to figure out who all she had left. She saw that most of them gave off a blue glow the rest had a glow of green.

Samantha looked at Ben, "Do you see that?"

"See what?"

"The blue and green."

"No, I don't see anything blue or green."

Bee leaned in and whispered, "Only you can see that. It is how you will be able to tell who is what."

She looked at him and smiled.

"The blue are Travelers, the green are witches. Later you will see a multitude of colors to sort different beings out. Very handy little power."

Samantha hadn't known any witches were even there. She figured Kevin would show up at some point, now that she looked, she saw him standing in the front of the group. A beautiful mix of blue and green coming from him.

"Why..."

"You know the answers to all the questions you have. Stop asking for help and trust in yourself," her father told her.

Samantha looked back at Kevin and knew that he was not just a witch. "Kevin," she called then waited for him to look at her. She motioned for him to come forward.

Once he reached her, he knelt down.

"Kevin, please don't do that," she said with a smile.

Kevin stood up, "How may I serve you, my Queen."

"Kevin, I am not your Queen, I had hoped we were friends."

"You are the Queen of the Titans and so you are my Queen as well."

Samantha decided to just accept that everything was now different. She would lead her people and win this fight.

"You and the rest charge the castle on my signal. We don't know how many if any enemies are in there," she told Kevin.

Samantha closed her eyes and searched for Lilith in her mind. She found her standing on a mountain behind the castle. Samantha figured that Lilith had created the mountain since the island had been flat.

"I found her," Samantha whispered to Ben, "Let's go."

Samantha took Ben's hand and they disappeared.

Meanwhile inside the castle, Wayne and Jade were preparing for war. They knew that the dragons would not let anyone out. Saina had told them who was demanding her to leave the castle and what Lilith would do to everyone if she didn't go.

"I won't let her hurt any of you. I will do as she says," Saina said.

"I don't care what she does. If she wants you, she will have to go through us first," Wayne told her. Then he turned to Jade and nodded.

"Vampires, follow me. Wolves stay with Wayne," Jade called out as she headed down the hall towards the room at the end of the hall that had been locked since they had built the castle.

When the door opened, all the vampires gasped in surprise as the light fell on a scepter. The rest of the room was empty.

Jade walked over and picked up the scepter. Instantly the pink stone started to glow. Jade looked at Vic, "This will be our salvation." Then to all of them she added, "The castle is in ruins, after this we will all go home to Non Morti."

No one made a sound as Jade then walked through them all and up to the tallest tower. Vic and the other vampires followed her.

They watched in amazement as Jade held the scepter high above her head.

All nine dragons came towards the pink glow.

"Where did you get that scepter?" Vic asked.

"Athena gave it to me a long time ago. She said she got it from a different dimension."

Samantha and Ben appeared just behind Lilith.

Lilith turned and a silver ball flew at Samantha and Ben. Samantha moved to the side but Ben didn't move fast enough. Samantha watched as the ball hit him directly in the chest. He flew backwards landing on his back.

Samantha turned back to Lilith, "That was a big mistake."

Lilith laughed, "What are you going to do to me, girl?"

Samantha realized that Lilith thought she was Saina, "After all you have done, I will destroy you. You threaten the people I love. Held my sister captive after kidnapping her from our father."

"Samantha?" Lilith whispered in shock.

Samantha smiled, "Yep." She pulled lightning from the sky, formed it into a blue electric ball and threw it at Lilith.

Lilith spun around and disappeared just before the ball reached her.

Samantha went to Ben's side. His shirt had a black burn that covered his whole chest.

"Samantha."

"Ben, you will be alright. She's gone now."

She looked towards the castle and saw the nine dragons had gathered at the tower. As she looked closer she saw Jade holding something that was glowing. The dragons seemed to be drawn to the light.

Poseidon saw the dragons move away from the door. He looked to the sky but didn't see Samantha's signal. He decided that this might be his only chance to make it inside the castle.

He led the Gods into the castle. He found Wayne and the wolves were already transformed and ready to fight.

Wayne turned back into a man, "Where is Samantha?"

"She is outside. She went after the one that has been keeping all of you here."

Cassandra had been sitting on a chair in the study, watching everything that was happening with Samantha. She saw as Samantha's father appeared and then as the group split apart. She knew that Samantha wouldn't need to use any signal.

"It's over," Cassandra said as she saw Lilith disappear. "The dragons are leaving."

Saina didn't like being told to hide when everyone else was fighting to protect her but she did as Wayne said and had locked the door to the study. She had sat there waiting with Gabby until Cassandra said it was over.

Now she went to the door and opened it. The three girls walked out into the foyer.

Saina stopped when she saw Poseidon standing in front of Wayne.

"You left her to fight on her own," Wayne was saying.

"She is not on her own. Ben and her father are out there with her," Cassandra interrupted.

"Her father," Wayne repeated.

"My father is here?" Saina asked. "Why is he here?"

Poseidon looked at her then, "He came to help Samantha…"

"It's always about her! Why can't one person do something just for me?" Saina cried.

Poseidon took a step towards her, he reached out to touch her shoulder. He wanted to reassure her that her father had not just come for Samantha but before his hand reached her she disappeared.

Kevin was still watching for the signal when Bee appeared beside him. "You are needed inside the castle." Bee put his hand out and Kevin reached out and took it.

Samantha had teleported Ben into her suite. She laid him down on the bed then went to the bathroom for a cold rag.

When she came back into the room Ben was surrounded by people. Poseidon and Wayne stood at the foot of the bed. Cassandra and Gabby stood off to one side, Kevin and Bee was on the other side. All of them was looking down at Ben.

"What's going on?" Samantha asked.

Bee looked over at her, "Ben is dying."

"No, he just needs rest," she said as a tear rolled down her face.

"Kevin. Do it." Bee said.

He opened Ben's shirt to see how bad the damage was, he saw the black hole had gone through Ben's shirt and burned into his skin. Blood was oozing out in small streams. Kevin put his hand on Ben's forehead.

Ben arched his back and his eyes flew open.

Samantha started to run to Ben but Bee grabbed her. "This has to be done. It's the only way to get rid of the poison."

Samantha watched as Kevin did his magic. After a half hour had gone by, Kevin backed away and sat down on the chair by the fireplace. The black mark on Ben's chest was smaller but still there.

"I'm sorry. I can't save him," Kevin said.

Ben looked worse than he had before. His clothes were drenched in sweat and his face lit up with fever. Samantha sat on the bed beside him and held his hand. She tried to convince herself that he would wake up at any moment.

Everyone stayed in the room until the sun came up. Even Bee stayed, standing beside the bed near Samantha.

Samantha didn't even realize that they had left. She had not taken her eyes off of Ben's face all night. Now she realized they had all left, she laid down beside him and fell asleep.

After Bee left Samantha's room, he returned home. He knew he should have just saved Ben for his daughter's sake but he wasn't convinced that Ben deserved his daughter. Even though he did not raise Samantha he still felt the protectiveness for her.

What Samantha needed now was her mother but Bee wasn't ready to go that far yet.

Poseidon went back to Mount Olympus to look for Zeus. He found him and Hercules in the white meeting room.

"Why did you abandon us?" Poseidon asked.

Zeus looked at him with the same hatred that Poseidon had seen before when Zeus would speak of Hades.

"We didn't abandon anyone," Hercules answered. "That was not our fight."

"Of course it was. Samantha..."

"Samantha chose Ben. Now he is dying and she will be alone," Hercules interrupted.

"She will never be alone. Do you not see that? She has her father now."

At that Zeus turned his back on his brother. "He is nothing but a coward. He could have come for her at any moment but chose to leave her to be raised by the wolf."

"Well he has returned," Poseidon said. "That still does not explain why you left."

"My reasons are my own. I do not answer to you!" Zeus said.

"But you will answer to me!" Kronos said as he appeared in front of Zeus.

"I will not answer to you. I did what I did for my own reasons."

Kronos turned to Hercules, "And you, you left as well. Why?"

"My son does not answer to you," Zeus answered for Hercules.

"Do you not want Samantha to remove the spell she has you under?" Kronos asked Hercules, ignoring Zeus.

"No, I do not."

"Why not?" Kronos asked.

Hercules looked at Zeus before he said, "Because she is what I want. I do not believe that I only love her because of some stupid spell. She belongs with me."

Kronos looked from Hercules to Zeus, "You have put this nonsense in his head."

"My father put nothing in my head. I am the son of Zeus and she is the daughter of Athena, we are destined to be together."

Kronos shook his head, "I see you have made up your mind, so I will leave you to it."

Kronos disappeared to meet back up with the Titans on Bella Isola. They had all decided that they would all share the island for the time being.

Jade had been sitting in the library waiting for Wayne.

"What happened?" Jade asked as Wayne sat down beside her.

"Ben is dying."

"I know, I heard. What I am asking is how? Who did it?"

Wayne rubbed his face with his hands, "That is being handled. We need to talk about what we are going to do."

"About?"

Wayne looked at her, "About where we are going to live. Do we go to Non Morti or Mondo Del Lupo?"

"Mondo Del Lupo? Why would we go back there?" Jade asked.

Wayne knew he should have told her about what happened when he was there. He had been waiting for the right moment but now realized there was no 'right moment'.

He took her hand in his and then told her about his village.

When he was finished she smiled, "Your people need you. The answer is simple. We go to Mondo Del Lupo. You must restore the village."

Wayne had hoped she would say that but his hope faded when he realized, that meant there was no way he would convince her to have a child.

"Athena!" Bee called out into the darkness.

"What happened? Is Samantha alright?" Athena said as she walked out from the shadows.

"She is fine. It's Ben. He is dying."

"And you are going to let him die?" she questioned.

"If I let him die and she finds out that I could have saved him…"

"She will hate you forever," Athena finished for him.

"Yes. But if I save him, what am I teaching her?" he asked.

Athena shook her head, "Why do you feel the need to always be teaching her? She is our daughter. We must help her when we can."

"So, you believe that she belongs with Ben?"

"I don't know who she belongs with. That isn't for us to decide. That is her choice. You fought your father to be able to choose your own path. Why would you want to control hers?"

Bee knew that she was right and now knew what he had to do. "Thank you," he said to Athena before disappearing.

Cassandra and Gabby waited a few hours before knocking on Samantha's door.

Samantha was glad to see both of them when she opened the door.

Gabby saw that Ben looked worse than he had when they had left. She walked over to the bed, bent down and whispered, "You need to wake up. Samantha needs you."

"He isn't going to wake up any time soon," Cassandra said. "Samantha, Saina is gone. She has returned with Lilith."

"Where are they?" Samantha asked.

"They returned to the first dimension. That's as far as I can see from here."

"Can we follow them?" Gabby asked.

Cassandra shook her head, "Not all of us." She looked at Samantha and added, "but me and you can go."

"Let's go!"

PART 5

Lilith

CHAPTER 14

On her eighteenth birthday Lilith decreed that no one was to hunt in the Royal Forest. She hated to see the animals being killed off for sport.

A group of four men gathered together and planned on an execution of the Princess. They called themselves the Huntsmen.

They camped out in the woods and waited for her to take her daily ride. They were surprised to see that the princess was surrounded by six guards.

The Queen of Atlantis, Lilith's stepmother, had ordered that the Princess have extra protection. She knew that once Lilith had made her decree, numerous hunters would want her dead.

Eric signaled for the others to get into position. Joshua and Alex climbed up the two trees that were on either side of the path. Eric went into the woods to set the trap that would pull the horses legs out from under them. Then he made his way around to come up from behind the Princess.

John had missed Eric's signal and stood in the middle of the path, not sure what to do.

The guards saw John standing in the path and stopped the Princess from approaching him.

"He is just a lone man. He doesn't seem like he could hurt a thing," she told them.

"At the very least, he is trespassing and should be apprehended. Stay here Princess."

Four of the guards went forward towards the man. As they passed the two trees, Alex shot an arrow into the closest ones back then jumped down from the tree.

Joshua brought an ax down sinking it into the top of the guards head. He fell to the ground, jumped up and pulled a snake from his satchel. He threw the snake on the ground in front of the two remaining horses.

Joshua walked over to one of the guards lying on the ground and sunk his sword deep into the guards chest. Meanwhile, Alex used his dagger, stabbing the other guard in the stomach.

Lilith heard a noise coming from the woods behind her. She turned to look and saw a man coming towards them with a sword. Both guards turned and charged him.

Eric waited until the horses were close enough then he swung his sword slicing into both horses. The horses reared up throwing the guards to the ground.

Eric wasted no time in slicing their throats and then started towards the princess.

Lilith kicked her horse to get him to run pass the other three ruffians. Just when she thought she had gotten away she was thrown from the horse, landing hard on the ground.

She saw that the horse had been caught in a snare trap.

She looked back the path and saw the four men running towards her. She got up and started running away from the Huntsmen. Lilith, not looking where she was going, fell into a large pitfall. She landed on bones and leaves but unfortunately one of the wooden spikes impaled her left leg.

She held in her cries of pain the best she could. After a few moments she heard someone walking towards her.

John looked down into the pit and turned to call out to the others when the loose dirt gave way and he fell into the pit, landing on a spike. Lilith watched as John fell and the spike pierced through his body. He died instantly.

She tried to pull her leg free but the pain was so intense that she passed out.

When she woke up she was in a strange place. She looked around and saw that there was four beds and a small round table. Then she saw a fireplace with a fire burning and a big black pot hanging over it.

She slowly got up and went to the door to look out side. She saw nothing but trees.

Lilith walked around the outside of the cabin. There was a wood pile with an ax stuck in a log close by. The woods were very thick so she knew she was farther in the forest than she had ever gone before.

"What are you doing out here?" A voice said startling Lilith.

She turned around and saw a young girl that was covered in dirt, looking at her.

The girl swung a rope holding five dead squirrels to the ground.

Lilith quickly grabbed the ax, but couldn't pull it out of the log.

"There is no need to be frightened," the girl said taking a step closer. "My name is Katrina. This is my home. You are safe now, Princess."

"You know who I am?"

"Of course we know who you are."

"We?" Lilith looked around expecting to see a second person.

"My husband is the one who found and healed you. He will be back later."

Lilith looked down at her leg, there wasn't even a mark left from the spike that had been stuck through it. She looked back at Katrina, "How is this possible?"

"Anything is possible with Abraham. That is why we must live out here. Everyone from my village said he was unnatural and they tried to kill him."

"How long have you lived here?" Lilith asked.

Katrina picked the squirrels back up, "For three winters. We better get these into the pot if we want to eat tonight," she said as she walked into the cabin.

Lilith followed her into the house and watched as the young girl took a knife and stabbed into one of the squirrels. Then she cut it open and pulled the skin off. When Katrina started pulling the insides out, Lilith looked away. Katrina did the same with the other ones then put a stick through them.

Lilith waited as Katrina took the animals outside and then returned.

"I suppose you being this far out, you did not know about my decree to stop all hunting in this forest?" Lilith asked.

Katrina smiled, "How would we eat if we can not hunt? We never kill what we do not eat."

Lilith thought about how every meal she had at the castle had meat in it. She had never thought about where the meat had come from. Now she realized that her choice to stop hunting was making her people suffer.

"Katrina, can you show me the way back to my castle?"

"Of course, however I can only go halfway with you."

The two women set off through the woods. Lilith now knew that she had a lot more to learn before being crowned Queen. She had been trying to protect the animals and had not realized the negative impact on her people.

She wanted to be a great Queen, like her stepmother had been in the years since her father had passed away.

They came to a split in the path, "This is as far as I will go. Just follow the path and it will lead you to the castle," Katrina said pointing to the path on the right.

It didn't take Lilith long until she saw the opening that led to the royal gardens.

When she emerged from the forest, three guards approached her, "Your Highness, what are you doing out here without your guards?"

"We were attacked. My guards were all killed."

"Killed!" one of the guards repeated, "Go inform Angelo. Tell him to gather..."

"That will not be necessary. I have the matter well in hand," Lilith interrupted.

"Take the Princess to the Queen at once."

Lilith was escorted to the Queen's chambers. The Queen took one look at Lilith she ordered her own guards to leave the room.

Once alone, Lilith went to her stepmother and was embraced.

"Shh, hush now, child," the Queen said. "You are safe now."

"I made a mistake. This is my fault."

The Queen pulled back just enough to look at her stepdaughter, "How is it your fault that people are so cruel?"

"I made them be cruel. I decreed that no one shall hunt. I didn't realize that they need to hunt to survive. The men that attacked us, they were fighting for their livelihood."

The Queen nodded, "I understand. What would you have me do?"

Lilith looked at her, "I must change the decree to say that no one may hunt simply for sport."

The Queen rang a small bell and a guard came into the room. "Yes, your Majesty?"

"Gather the magistrate. We will be along shortly."

The guard turned and left the room.

"Go get changed and I shall meet you in the library," the Queen told her.

After seeing Katrina's home, Lilith felt that her room was just too much for any one person. As her servant brought water in for her to wash, she thought about how dirty Katrina had been.

She vowed to herself that one day her people would prosper and no one would go without in all the kingdom.

After meeting with the magistrate Lilith ordered her guards to find the three remaining men that had attacked her.

The guards searched for half a year before they found them in a pub. They had been retelling the story of how they had single handedly stopped the Princess' decree and how they had killed six royal guards.

Eric saw the guards watching him, "We need to get out of here," he said to the two others.

The three of them walked outside the pub but before they could mount their horses, the guards grabbed them and tied their hands. They were put on horses and taken to the castle.

The guards informed the Queen and Princess that they had apprehended the men and were on the way to the Great Hall.

Lilith sat beside the Queen and waited for them to enter.

The three men entered the room, walked to the front and bowed before them.

The Queen nodded to Lilith, giving her permission to address the men.

"How did you come to be in our kingdom?" she asked them.

Eric looked up, "Our brother banished us from Estonia."

"Why would he do such a thing?"

"He feared that one of us might kill him to take the throne," Eric replied.

Lilith stood up and walked down the three steps to stand in front of him. "You are a Prince?"

"Yes."

"Then why would you try to kill me over hunting?"

"We have traveled far and wide searching for a kingdom in need of a Prince. This is the last remaining kingdom that has an unwed Princess. When we first got here, I tried to enter the castle. I wanted to explain then, we were thrown out. We made ourselves a home in the hope that someday we would have the chance to meet with you," Eric explained.

"Then why try to kill me?"

"I apologize. We were not going to kill you, only your guards. It was the only way we could speak to you. They would have never allowed us near you."

Lilith glanced back at the Queen, "Shall we believe them?"

"I do not trust anyone who kills six of our guards." Then to Eric she asked, "When was it that you first came to the castle?"

"Ten winters, Your Majesty."

Lilith tried to hide how shocked she was, "That's when father died."

Ignoring Lilith the Queen continued, "Have you tried since then to enter the castle?"

"Yes, we were turned away each time, your Majesty," he replied.

"You wish to marry my step-daughter and become king to my people?"

Eric looked to each of his brothers then back at Lilith, "Only with your blessing, your Majesty."

The Queen sat quietly for a long time before saying, "You three will be our guests. Be warned, you will be watched very closely. If the day comes that the Princess chooses any of you, you will be welcomed with open arms."

"Thank you, your Majesty."

"Do not thank me yet, I still may decide to hang all three of you." Then turning to the guard standing on her right she added, "Show them to their quarters."

The guard nodded and ushered the men out the door.

Once alone Lilith asked, "If you do not trust them, why let them stay here?"

"Because, my dear, we keep our potential enemies close. They are here and so will be watched at all times. If they have any thoughts of betraying us we will find out faster with them here, with-in our walls."

Lilith nodded before taking her leave.

Years went by and the Queen grew very ill. The time was near for Lilith to take the crown. However, she was not able to do that until she was married.

She had grown very fond of Eric since he arrived. They had spent hours walking in the garden together, followed by at least three guards.

As Lilith sat by her step-mother's side, she decided that the time had come for her to make a choice. She kissed the Queen's forehead and left the room.

She found Eric sitting in the library, reading as he always did when he wasn't with her.

Lilith sat down beside him on the bench and placed her hands on her lap. "You know the Queen is dying."

He looked up at her with sadness in his eyes, "Yes, I wish there was something I could do to help."

"There is one thing you can do," she said.

"What would that be?"

She reached over and took his hand, "You can marry me."

They were married the next day and planned the coronation for the following week.

The day after the coronation, Lilith's step-mother took her last breath.

CHAPTER 15

As the years went on Lilith and Eric tried to produce an heir, with no luck.

Both of Eric's brothers had married and each had children of their own. Every time they would come to the castle Lilith could see more and more of her husband dying. She knew how badly he wanted a child.

She started to feel that it was her fault and so one night she stood outside on the balcony and looked to the stars, "I wish we could have a child."

Over the next year Lilith started to feel weaker and weaker. She was afraid she would die and never know the joy of having a child.

When she got so weak that she could no longer stand on her own, she called for the medicine man.

He told everyone to leave the room while he examined the Queen. After checking every part of her he said, "Carrying a child does make one weary, however, there is no reason you should not be able to walk on your own," he said as he packed his instruments into his bag.

"I am not with child," she said trying to hide her pain.

"You most certainly are with child. But I fear that you may have been poisoned."

"Poisoned?"

"Yes, that would explain why you have grown so weak," he answered.

Lilith thought about who in the castle would do such a thing to her. She had made the kingdom a wonderful place to live. All her people were happy and thriving.

Then a horrible thought crossed her mind, "Please do not speak of this with anyone."

He nodded his head as he opened the door.

As soon as the medicine man left, Eric went to Lilith's side. "Darling, what did he say?"

She watched as he struggled to look concerned, "He does not know what is causing my weakness." Then just to see his reaction she added, "but he is sure that I am dying."

As she had suspected, he hid his face by bending over and putting his head on the edge of the bed.

He stayed only a little while before excusing himself. Once he was gone she sent her maid to get Treville, the head of the royal guard.

She started to tell him what she suspected was going on, until he interrupted her, "Your people have turned on you, your Majesty. They have already burned part of the forest and now are camped out waiting to attack."

"Why would they attack?" she asked confused.

"I understand that you are not well. They do not. The people demand their Queen's attention."

She knew that over the year she had not looked after her people the same as she had in the past. She was no longer able to ride to each village to make sure all was well.

Lilith had sent the King and guards in her stead. This was the first she had heard of any problems in the kingdom.

"Why was this not brought to my attention before now?" she asked, doing her best to sit up on the bed.

Treville looked confused as he said, "You were notified on numerous occasions, your Majesty."

"I was?" she asked as she tried to remember being told about any of this. She could not remember one time. Then she realized that Treville must be helping her husband.

She couldn't figure out why they would want her dead. She put her hand over her stomach and felt something move.

"You are dismissed," she told Treville.

Alone once again, she used all her strength to pull herself to her feet and walk out onto the balcony.

Looking to the sky she quietly said, "Please help me." Her legs gave out and she fell to the floor.

"Why is a strong woman, like yourself, giving up so easily?"

Lilith looked up to see the most handsome man she had ever seen in her life looking down at her. He reached his hand down and she allowed him to help her stand.

"Who are you and how did you get in my chambers?" she asked.

"My name is Bee and I am not from this world. I can go any place I like," he replied in a gentle voice. "I am here to make your wish come true."

Lilith could feel her legs wanting to give out again so she started to take a step towards the bed.

Bee knew she was in pain, he blinked his eyes and she was sitting on the bed.

"How did you do that?" she asked.

He smiled, "I can do more than that. What is it you wish for more than anything else right now?"

"I wish to be healthy and have my child," she answered quickly.

Bee started to laugh, "That would not help. Your husband would still find a way to kill you. And what of your people? They have all turned their backs to you when you need them the most."

Lilith thought about what he was saying and decided that he was right. She had trusted Eric and he was now trying to kill her. Her people had turned on her, believing that she had given up on them. They should have known better than that.

She had always done what was right for her people. No matter the cost to her, the kingdom had come first.

Now here she sat dying as they attacked the royal guards and destroyed the beautiful kingdom that she worked so hard to build.

Lilith looked at Bee, "I want to make them all pay for what they have done."

Bee nodded, "I can help you with that. All you need to do is agree to be my friend and I can give you the power to exact your revenge on them all."

"You came to my aid when I needed it. You offer all that I ask, how could I refuse to be a friend to you?"

"Close your eyes," Bee told her.

Lilith could feel herself healing on the inside. Her strength was returning to her.

"Open your eyes."

She did as he said and felt a strange feeling come over her. She shivered even though she wasn't cold. "What did you do to me?"

"In order for me to heal you, you had to die first. Now we can be friends for all eternity."

Lilith placed her hand on her belly and felt nothing. "Where is my baby?"

"The boy has been sacrificed."

"You said I would have my wish. My wish was to have my child," she cried.

"Ah, but that wasn't your wish. You wished to get revenge on those who have wronged you. I have given you the power to do so," he said gesturing towards the looking glass.

She walked over to see her reflection looking back at her. Her hair was a smooth cascade of black, flowing down past her rear. She noticed that her skin looked much younger than she was.

As she looked at her face she saw that her eyes had turned black as the darkest night sky.

"What do we do now?" she asked.

"Now, you may do as you wished. You can make them all pay in any way you see fit. I must go for now. I will return tomorrow evening to hear what you have decided to do."

Right before her eyes Bee disappeared, leaving her alone with her thoughts. She laid down on the bed hoping that she would wake up and it was all just a dream.

She closed her eyes and fell asleep.

Lilith walked past the royal gardens and down the path that led to the forest. She hadn't been to see Katrina since she became ill. Everything in the woods looked different now.

She would had never before been this deep without guards along side her.

As she walked around the curve, that led to Katrina's small cabin, she saw that the cabin was not there. Lilith looked around, confused. She was sure she had gone the correct way.

"Katrina!" she called out.

"Lilith."

Lilith turned around and saw Katrina standing on the only path that led from here.

"Why have you come?" Katrina asked.

Lilith looked at the ground, "I needed a friend."

"Friend? Lilith, we can no longer be friends."

"What?" Lilith said looking at Katrina in shock. "Why can we not be friends?"

"You have made a deal and sold your soul! And for what? Revenge?" Katrina questioned.

"You do not understand, he was killing me. My people turned on me. I had no one. I was dying!"

"Lilith, you do not realize what you have condemned yourself to. An eternity of being alone, without even your own child to comfort you."

"My child? How did you know?"

Katrina looked away, "We know everything."

"Who are you? Really?" Lilith asked.

Katrina looked back at her and smiled. Then, as Lilith watched, Katrina vanished.

Lilith suddenly felt very afraid. The sunlight had lit up the woods, now darkness came making everything dark with black shadows everywhere she looked.

She started running down the path, hoping that she would not make a wrong turn.

She had a feeling that she was being watched. She stopped and looked around her, straining her eyes for the slightest movement.

When she heard a twig snap, Lilith started running again. Now she could hear someone or something running behind her.

She knew whatever was chasing her was getting closer. Lilith knew whatever it was, wasn't human. She could hear a low growl coming from it.

Lilith jumped up, out of the bed. She had been so sure that the dream was real but was happy to be back at her castle.

Lilith walked into her dressing chamber and took the sweat soaked gown off to replace it with a dry one. Then she walked out on the balcony. She looked out over the forest and saw a flickering light.

As she stared at the glow, she was amazed that it was getting closer. Slowly she could make out a group of voices and then she saw them. A group of men sat around the fire roasting meat and talking.

"Why did you come along, Fredrick? I knew your sister works at the castle. What happens if she gets killed?"

"It was her choice to stay at the castle. If she dies, so be it," the man that must be Fredrick answered. "What about Kobal? His son is in the royal guard."

A man the size of a bull stood up, "No matter who they are to us, if they stand by the King and Queen, they are our enemies."

Lilith blinked her eyes and she was back in her chambers. She couldn't believe what she had just heard. Those men were willing to kill their own family just to destroy her.

"They deserve it," a voice from behind her said.

Lilith didn't need to turn around. She knew that Bee had returned.

"You slept a whole day through. While you slept, those men positioned themselves to attack the castle," He told her.

"Why? Why are they attacking?"

"They are attacking because the King has put them all in poverty."

"What do you mean, poverty?" she asked.

Bee slowly walked towards her and took her by the hands. "Look, out there," he said pointing beyond the forest.

She looked and at first only saw trees. She focused harder and then she could see the closest village. Every home had been burned to the ground. All the crops in the field, gone.

"Who did this?" she asked.

"Your guards, on order from the King. He told them that he was carrying out your wishes. That you were the one that gave the order!"

"I would never…"

"No, however, they do believe that you did," he interrupted her.

"How can they believe I would give such orders? I did all that I could to make their villages happy. Maybe if I just talked to them…"

Bee shook his head, "They will not listen. You heard those men, they are out for blood."

"Then I shall have theirs before they have a chance," She declared.

Bee smiled, "And what of the King?"

"He shall die with the rest!"

"Lie on the bed. I will make sure that your maid comes in to find you," Bee told her.

"For what?" Lilith asked confused.

"She will find you dead and then we can work together to destroy them all."

"Why would she believe that I am dead? I am in perfect health."

"She will believe it because you are dead. You had to die to become what you are."

"And what, exactly am I?" she asked.

"You are my friend. What you are, has no name. You are the first of your kind. You shall never age, get sick nor die again," he told her.

Lilith had so many more questions but did as he asked. She laid down on the bed and shortly after, her maid came. Mary screamed when she saw the Queen lying dead.

She ran from the room to summon the King.

Lilith smiled to herself as she got up and followed Bee out the window to start her new existence and her revenge.

Bee took her to a dark cave and there they formed the perfect revenge.

"If the whole of my kingdom wishes me dead, then I shall not spare a single one. They must all die," she told Bee after he had told her of a plan against only the King.

"As you wish," he replied. "Let us get off this planet and go home."

She nodded her head and followed him out of the cave and to her surprise, up through the sky.

"Where are we?" she asked looking around.

"Home. This is where you will live from now on. Together we shall build a new kingdom."

"How will I…"

"You can do anything you wish."

"I wish to kill them all."

"Then do it," he told her.

"Can I sink all of them?"

"Sink them? Into the sea?" Bee smiled at the thought, "Yes, if that is what you want." He pointed at a rock basin filled with a strange liquid.

Lilith walked over and looked into it. She saw the kingdom like she was flying above it.

"Focus on what you want to do."

She did and was amazed to see the whole island kingdom shake and slowly sink. She watched as all the people scrambled around looking for a way to save themselves.

Lilith watched as the island disappeared into the water, killing every living thing.

She smiled knowing that everyone who had wanted her dead now laid at the bottom of the sea.

Lilith had joined Bee in many adventures over the centuries. They destroyed many evil people. Bee showed her different planets, some he said were even in different dimensions.

There were times that she would think back to how she once was and couldn't believe how naive she had been to think Eric was anything but a slug. She had gained so much knowledge through the years. She was no longer the child like Queen of a small island.

Lilith thought about Katrina a few times. She had tried asking Bee about her but he would either change the subject or tell her to stop worrying about someone so unimportant.

She wondered if Katrina had really left or if her dream was just that, a dream.

It was when Bee took her to Dimension three that she met Kronos, the Lord of the Titans. Bee had her pretend to be a Titan to get closer to them. She was to report everything back to Bee.

Over a thousand years passed with Lilith posing as Rhea the Titan. Then Kronos' son, Zeus had overthrown him and started capturing the Titans.

When she returned home, to escape capture, she found that Bee was gone. She found him on Earth and saw that he had fallen in love with the Goddess Athena. Lilith had always thought that Bee and herself would be together for all eternity.

She approached Bee and asked him why he betrayed her.

"I betrayed no one. You are my friend, no more than that," he told her.

"Friend? That's all I am to you? After all this time together, you toss me aside for her!" Lilith screamed. "You are no better than Eric!"

Before she knew what happened, Bee swung his fist, hitting her across the face. "You dare to speak to me in such a manner. I saved your life. I allowed your revenge. I offered you a friendship that would last an eternity."

"A friendship that I do not want. You will regret this. I promise you that," Lilith said before disappearing.

She watched from afar as Bee and Athena grew closer and closer. She heard the lies he told her and then watched as Athena grew to be afraid of Bee. She saw Athena flee back to the third dimension.

Lilith had been there when Zeus made Athena choose between her children and Mount Olympus. She was there when Athena had given birth to three daughters.

That's when she saw how she could make Bee pay for betraying her. Bee had successfully retrieved two of his children. As he prepared to return for the third, Lilith snuck inside, what was once her home, and grabbed one of the girls.

Bee turned and saw her disappearing with the child.

"You owe me this much," she said just before she was completely gone.

Lilith started calling the girl Thea but she would not answer to it. The only name she would respond to was Saina. So Lilith decided to just let it go.

The first few years were filled with the most wonderful moments. Lilith had taught Saina how to talk and every time Saina called her mama, it melted Lilith's heart. She loved the little girl as much as she would have loved her son if he had been born.

It was on Saina's tenth birthday that Saina turned on Lilith.

"You are not my mother!" Saina had yelled at her after Lilith told her she was too young to go to Earth alone.

Lilith was filled with rage, she grabbed Saina by the arm and put her into the cage that usually held prisoners that Lilith wanted to torture.

Saina sat quietly as a strange woman came to speak with Lilith.

"Lilith, you need to see that the things you do, are wrong," the woman said.

"Wrong? Was what they did to me not wrong? I lost everything that day, Katrina," Lilith replied.

"You only lost what you allowed to be taken."

"My kingdom had turned on me, they wanted me dead. My own husband poisoned me while I carried his child, which I lost as well."

"Lilith, it was not Eric that had poisoned you. It was Treville. He had poisoned the King as well. That is why when you told him that you had been poisoned, he put his head down. You had confirmed what he had known all along."

"It wasn't Eric?" Lilith said as she sat down. She had been so sure that she had been right. Bee had even confirmed it. Unless, Bee had lied to her.

"Eric loved you. He was fighting to restore the kingdom the way you wished it."

"Why did you abandon me? I came to you but the cabin was gone. Why did you say we could no longer be friends?"

"You sold your soul to Bee. I can not be involved with anything to do with him," Katrina said.

"Why? Please tell me? I need to know the truth."

Katrina sighed, "Bee is my husbands brother. Bee was thrown out of his home for disobeying their father. You made a deal with Bee and so we could no longer help you."

"Help me? How did you help me, other than pulling me from the ..."

"It was my husband and I who helped calm the hearts of your subjects and made the crops go on land that they otherwise would have never grown. We answered your prayers to have a child," Katrina told her.

"How could you do all that? Unless you are…"

"Yes, we are the same as Bee, only we did not turn our backs on our family. Once you made the deal, your soul became tainted. We were no longer allowed to help you. Now you must do the right thing and return the girl to Alpha One in the third dimension."

Lilith shook her head, "I can not do that, her mother is dead. Who would care for her?"

"There is a wolf from Mondo Del Lupo there. He is raising Samantha, the girl's sister. I'm sure he would gladly take in Saina," Katrina said.

"No!" Lilith exclaimed. "The girl stays with me. Allowing the girls to know each other is no punishment to Bee."

"Lilith, you sadden me. You are so wrapped up with revenge that you do not see the damage you do to yourself."

Katrina disappeared leaving Lilith to face Saina.

"How can you keep me from my sister?" Saina asked with tears in her eyes.

"Because you belong to me," Lilith replied.

Saina cried for hours that night before falling asleep.

Once Saina was sound asleep Lilith went to Alpha One and watched the wolf and the other girl. She saw how happy and protected Samantha was and decided that she would allow Saina to come be with her sister.

She returned home to find that Saina had destroyed the cage and was gone.

She looked everywhere for the girl over the next eight years but couldn't find her.

PART 6

The Sisters

CHAPTER 16

Samantha looked around at the strange world that her and Cassandra had just entered into. There were building reaching for the sky. Strange vehicles zoomed past them beeping their horns.

They saw some people holding weird thin plastic things to their ear, talking into them. Everyone around them seemed to be in a rush to get somewhere.

Samantha saw a teenage boy riding a flat board with wheels on the bottom. As he got closer she reached out and caught his arm. The board rolled a little way before stopping a few feet from them.

"Where are we?" Samantha asked him.

"Hey, let go!"

"Where are we?" she repeated.

"New York City," he answered as he pulled his arm out of her hold and went to pick up his board.

Samantha turned to Cassandra but before she could ask, Cassandra said, "This planet is called Earth. We are in the first dimension."

"Everything is so strange here," Samantha said as she watched a big sign change from one image to another. "Even the vehicles are different."

"Saina is not here," Cassandra told her. "But I think we should stay here a few days."

"A few days? If Saina left why would we stay?"

"Because your sister will be here the day after tomorrow," Cassandra replied.

Samantha rolled her eyes, "Why didn't you just say that she will be back?"

"Because Saina will not be back. You're other sister is coming."

"Sandra?"

"Yes. I suggest we find somewhere to stay and wait for her to arrive. There are things called hotels here but we need money from this world to pay for shelter."

Samantha held her hand out and a pile of strange paper appeared. She looked at it and started to laugh.

"What is so funny?" Cassandra asked.

"It is only paper with a crazy looking guy's picture on it."

"Paper money? I have never heard of such a thing. Are you sure you did that right?"

Samantha shrugged, even though she knew Cassandra couldn't see her. "Let's find out."

They walked down the street a little way before Samantha stopped Cassandra.

They were standing in front of what Samantha assumed was a store. The sign said Macy's and people were exiting carrying bags with the same name as the building.

They entered and walked around until they found where clothes were hanging on metal bars. Samantha picked each of them out a few shirts and jeans then went to the counter and watched in amazement as the woman ran the items over a red light.

The woman told Samantha what the total was and Samantha handed her some of the green paper. The woman smiled and handed her some coins back with a white piece of paper.

"What is this," Samantha asked the woman.

"You're receipt," the woman said still smiling.

Samantha looked at the paper and saw every item they had purchased listed with a price.

Samantha and Cassandra left the store and started looking for a hotel. After walking around for over an hour, Samantha stopped an old man and asked him where the closest hotel was.

He pointed her in the right direction before walking away without a thank you.

They found the Hilton hotel and went to the counter. The man there smiled at them, "Welcome to the Hilton. Would you like two singles or a double?"

"What?" Samantha asked.

"A double please," Cassandra answered.

The man nodded and pushed buttons on a plastic board with letters that weren't even in order. He reached down and produced a plastic card. Then he handed the card to Samantha, "Here is your key. You are in room 403." Samantha handed him some money but he handed it back.

"You don't pay until check out," he told them.

Samantha and Cassandra followed the room numbers to a staircase. On the second floor Samantha realized that the first number, '4', was the level the room must be on. They went up the stairs to the fourth floor, it didn't take them long to find their room.

Samantha figured out how to open the door with the plastic card and they went inside.

The room was painted a plain tan with a grey carpet. Each bed was made and had a picture hanging above it.

After they had taken bathes and slept, they decided to go find a place to eat. They found a place that served something called pizza. They both ordered a piece and decided they liked it. They ordered more to take back to their room with them.

The next two days they didn't leave their room except to pick up more pizza. On the third day Cassandra led Samantha to what they were told was a mall.

Samantha saw that a few of the people emitted a lite glow of color. Some red and purple, then she saw a group that were green. Samantha knew that the green glow indicated witches.

The two walked around looking in the store windows but stopped when Samantha saw a golden glow coming from a red headed girl with her back to them.

"That has to be her," Samantha said to Cassandra.

Cassandra nodded.

Samantha opened the door to the store and walked in. The red head turned around quickly and looked at Samantha.

They stood looking at each other for a long time before the girl started to walk towards Samantha.

Now face to face Samantha could tell the girl was her sister.

Sandra smiled, "Samantha?"

"Sandra?"

"I have waited a long time for you. I knew you would eventually come. Saina comes through here all the time. I figured that it was only a matter of time before you would too," Sandra said in a single breath.

"What happened to your hair?" Samantha asked with a laugh.

"I dyed it."

"Why would you want your hair dead?"

Sandra laughed, "I didn't kill it, I changed the color."

"Why?"

Sandra took Samantha by the arm and started walking towards the door. "Because too many people are looking for us. It helps me blend in."

They walked out the door and Samantha introduced Sandra to Cassandra, within a few seconds a man appeared at Sandra's side.

"This is Tony, my witch. He is the one that changed my hair."

Tony smiled as if pleased with himself.

For the first time Sandra stopped smiling, "Why are you here? Not that I am not happy to finally see you but…"

"We followed Saina and Lilith here. Cassandra saw that you would be along and so we waited."

"Lilith! So she found you and Saina?" Sandra asked.

"Yes, but how did you know that Saina was with us?"

"When Saina ran from Lilith eight years ago, our father searched for her but couldn't find her. Lilith told Kappas that Saina had went to live with you and the wolf," Sandra answered.

Samantha looked at her sister in confusion, "She just showed up a few weeks ago. She didn't live with us at all. I didn't even know the two of you existed until about a year ago."

"Then where was she the whole time?"

"She was with me."

Samantha and Sandra looked over at the same time and said, "Hades!"

"Yes, Saina spent the last eight years with me in the Underworld. She was very good at creating new pets for me. We became very close. She is the daughter I never had."

Sandra and Samantha looked at each other. Tony stepped forward so that he was between the two girls and Hades. He raised his hands and Samantha saw a glimmering mist drop down around them.

"You can hide but I will find you," Hades promised as he vanished.

Samantha looked at Tony, "You can fool Hades?"

He nodded.

"I don't think you going after Saina is a good idea. He will be watching very close to where you go next," Sandra told Samantha.

"Then we will just go home for now. Would you like to come meet everyone at the castle?"

"Castle? Like a real castle? I didn't think any of them survived."

"Maybe not in this dimension but in ours there is still one standing. It's full of wolves and vampires. With the occasional visit from the Gods and Titans."

Sandra jumped up and down, "Yes, yes."

Samantha took Cassandra and Sandra by the hand, "Tony hold on to my shoulder."

As soon as his hand touched her, they disappeared.

They appeared on the docks of Bella Isola. Samantha looked up at the castle. She could see that everyone had been busy rebuilding not only the castle but the whole island.

"Why did we teleport the whole way out here?" Sandra asked.

"Jade must have had Trisha put the barrier back up," Samantha replied.

They walked up to the castle, Samantha found it strange that they had not seen a single person. She pushed the castle doors open and entered the empty foyer.

Samantha looked at Cassandra, "Where is everyone?"

"Most of the wolves and vampires have gone to Mondo Del Lupo."

"Wayne!" Samantha called out.

"Samantha? Is that you?" Wayne yelled from up the stairs.

"Yes, Uncle Wayne."

"We are up here," He called.

The four of them ran up the steps and down the hall to Samantha's room. Ben was now sitting on the couch and Samantha wasted no time, she ran over and hugged him tightly.

"How?" she asked Wayne.

"Your father came back right after you left and healed him. He took everyone who wanted to go to Mondo Del Lupo and said he would return when you got back."

"He healed Ben?"

"Yeah." Then to Sandra he said, "What have you done to your hair?"

Sandra looked confused.

Samantha knew that Wayne thought that Sandra was Saina. "Uncle Wayne, this is Sandra."

"Sandra? Oh my. You three are so identical. Forgive my mistake," he said to Sandra.

"Samantha! Thank goodness you are home," Gabby said running to her friend.

Samantha hugged her back then asked, "Where is Kronos and the Titans?"

"My Queen," Kronos and the others appeared and knelt before her.

"Kronos, you have to stop that," she told him.

"My Queen?"

"That, calling me Queen and bowing to me. I know you follow me, you do not need to bow."

Kronos stood up, the other Titans following his lead.

"Much better," she said. "Kronos this is ..."

"Sandra. Your father will be pleased to see you," he said.

"Father is not here, is he?" Sandra asked.

"No, He is searching for Lilith and Saina. He believes they may have gone to the ninth dimension," Wayne answered.

The Titans all gasped.

"Is that bad?" Samantha asked.

"The ninth dimension is full of horrible creatures. If Lilith took Saina there it could only to be to kill her," Kronos replied.

Samantha stood up and walked over to Sandra, "If they are there, we need to go help our sister."

"You most certainly will not." Everyone turned and saw Bee standing in the doorway. "One of you being in danger is bad enough."

"Father," Sandra whispered.

"I will deal with you later, child. I have searched every way into dimension nine, nothing has gone through. Lilith must have taken Saina back to where ever she hid her for fifteen years."

"Father, Lilith did not have Saina for fifteen years, Saina ran from her eight years ago," Sandra said.

Bee looked furious at that news, "Where was she the last eight years?"

"She was with Hades on the Underworld," Samantha answered.

"Hades!" he said.

"She is not with him now," Sandra quickly added.

Once again they all turned towards the door, this time Cy stood there.

"Cy!" Samantha said going to hug him.

He put his hand up to stop her and looked at Bee.

Samantha looked from one to the other and then said, "Wait, you were working for my father?"

"Not for, with. It was my job to make sure you were taken care of and protected."

"Enough of this, I want my daughter back!" Bee said.

"I have an idea," Samantha said going back to Sandra. "Give me your hands."

Sandra held her hands out.

"Focus on Saina."

Both girls closed their eyes and started searching for their sister. They searched every dimension quickly starting in the first dimension. They made it to the fifth dimension before Sandra fell to the floor.

"Are you alright?" Samantha asked her.

"I'm fine, I haven't used my powers in a long time. That's why Tony goes with me everywhere."

"Tony. That's it!" Samantha exclaimed as she ran from the room.

Everyone exchanged confused looks.

Samantha ran down the hall and up the stairs that led to the tower. From here she could see the whole island. She looked towards the docks and yelled, "Kevin! I need you."

Within a minutes time she saw someone appear on the dock. She turned and ran down the stairs and back into her room.

"He's here. We will find Saina," she said as she darted back out of the room.

Just as she reached the foyer there was a knock on the door. She swung the doors open and hugged Kevin tightly, "Thank you for coming."

"Why am I here, Samantha?"

"Follow me."

She led him back upstairs where everyone was waiting to see what would happen next.

"Give me the stone," Samantha said to Kevin.

"What stone?"

"The stone that Hecate gave you on Alpha One."

"Oh, this one?" he said pulling out the blue and green swirled stone.

Samantha reached out and grabbed it. She handed it to Sandra.

As soon as the stone touched Sandra's hand she stood up. "Wow, what is happening?" she asked.

Samantha smiled, "It unlocks our powers." Samantha pulled her own stone out. "I assume that the red and green one belongs to Saina," she said looking at her father.

Sandra hugged Samantha, "Let's get our sister."

They both held their stone in their left hands and put their right hand over each others stone. The power was so intense that it only took a minute for them to locate Saina.

She was in a cave that had been enchanted to block every living creature from finding it. They were in the first dimension.

Sandra and Samantha smiled at each other as they opened their eyes.

"Did you find her?" Bee asked.

"Yes and we will bring her back," Samantha said as the two girls disappeared.

After the two girls left Bee looked at Wayne, "I will return soon. I have to go speak to someone."

Wayne nodded.

Meanwhile, Zeus and Hercules had stayed on Mount Olympus. They both wanted different things, Hercules wanted Samantha. Zeus wanted to regain his place as king of the Gods.

Zeus refused to take orders from Kronos or a girl. The only problem he couldn't figure out was how without the Gods on his side. He needed an ally.

"Father look," Hercules said pointing behind Zeus.

Zeus turned to find Hermes and most of the other Gods had returned. "We stand with you," Hermes told Zeus. "They are the reason my son is dead. I want them to pay for his death."

CHAPTER 17

Standing outside the cave, Samantha looked at Sandra, "Are you ready?"

"Sure, I mean we are more powerful than Lilith so there isn't anything to be afraid of," Sandra replied.

They slowly entered the cave but stopped when they heard Saina say, "You will stay in your cage until I see fit to release you."

"Please Saina, let me out. I'm sorry, I know I should have listened. I should have just let you go. But I couldn't. I love you too much."

"Love is nothing but a weakness. Weakness makes you vulnerable. Vulnerable gets you killed. You loved Eric and see where that got you. You actually believed that story my father told you."

Samantha and Sandra slowly made their way to the opening so they could see Saina and Lilith.

Saina continued, "You loved the child that grew in your belly. Where is he now?"

"Dead," Lilith whispered.

"Dead? See you are so gullible. He is not dead. He lives even as we speak."

"How is that possible?" Lilith asked getting to her knees.

"He has been paying for your stupidity since the day your perfect friend, Katrina took him from your womb. Destined to live and die just to live again."

Samantha had heard enough, she stepped out into the cave with Sandra behind her.

"Saina! What are you doing?" Samantha asked.

"Oh look, it's my sisters. Come to rescue me, have you?" Saina laughed.

"Looks like Lilith is the one that needs saved," Sandra said looking at the cage.

"So you think you are going to free her?"

"Saina, you don't have to be like this, you don't have to get revenge on her for what she did to you," Samantha said.

"Huh? Oh you're talking about the vision of me in the cage and her mistreating me. Yeah, that isn't quite what happened. She did lock me in there but only to teach me a lesson."

"Just let her go," Sandra said.

Saina laughed, "Why would I want to do that?"

"Because we are your sisters and there are two of us," Samantha replied.

Sandra felt bad for Lilith, if everything she had just heard was true then their father had a lot to answer for.

Saina stepped forward and grabbed both of her sisters by the hand. They appeared on a dead planet. Samantha thought it looked a lot like the Underworld except here there were dead trees scattered around.

"Saina, don't do this," Sandra warned.

Saina threw a red ball of fire at them. Both girls ducked and it flew over their heads.

Samantha looked at Sandra and they both nodded. Samantha started pulling lightning bolts down from the sky hitting the ground around Saina. Meanwhile, Sandra threw an ice ball at Saina's feet, freezing her to the ground.

Saina melted the ice and looked at her sisters, "You can't stop me, without killing me and we all know that neither of you can do that."

"That is not true Saina. They could stop you if they wanted," Bee said from behind her.

"Father!" she said as she turned around, "Why are you here?"

"I am here because I do not want to see my daughters destroy each other."

"Liar! You are here to make sure your precious Samantha don't get hurt," Saina said.

Bee shook his head, "No, Saina. I don't want any of you to get hurt. You are all my children."

"Then why didn't you come for me? You had all kinds of people watching out for her, yet you left me with Lilith."

"I could not find you! She found a way to use your powers to hide you. The same way you hid the cave. I did search for you."

"I don't believe you," she said disappearing.

Bee turned to look at Samantha and Sandra.

"We had this. Why did you come here?" Samantha asked him.

"Let's get out of here," Sandra said grabbing her sisters hand and disappearing.

Once they were back at the castle Samantha pulled Wayne aside, "You do not have to stay. I know you are needed on Mondo Del Lupo. I will be fine."

"I will never leave you, you are my girl."

"No matter where we are I will always be your girl, Uncle Wayne. Promise me that you will go live your life with Jade and your pack. You deserve to be happy."

"What will happen to you?" Wayne asked her.

She smiled and hugged him, "I will be fine. Take Gabby, Cassandra and Ben with you, he will be able to help make your village great. I will come as soon as I can."

Wayne could see that she had made up her mind. He also knew that she had to deal with Saina and that there was no way for him to help her.

After Wayne and the others had left Samantha and Sandra started to form a plan to go after Saina. They had to make her understand that they were not her enemies, they were sisters and needed each other.

Zeus and Hercules put their plans in motion. Hades joined Zeus and Hermes to track down and trap the Titans.

"Where are we going to trap them? They have control of the Underworld now," Hermes said.

"Dimension nine," Zeus replied.

Hades' face looked as though Zeus had hit him with a lightning bolt, "Dimension nine? How are we going to keep them there?"

"With this," Zeus said holding up a piece of wood wrapped in cloth so that he wasn't touching it. "This is wood from the trees of Dimension nine, we can turn it into dust and just a small amount will render them powerless."

"What about Coeus and Themis? They won't be with the other Titans," Hades informed them.

"They will have a choice to make. They are either with us or against us."

The three of them went to the Underworld to talk to Themis.

"Will you stand with us or fight us?" Zeus asked.

"I am with you," Themis declared.

Hermes looked confused, "Why? Why would you stand with us?"

"Kronos has handed over everything to a child. He expects us to bow down to her. I refuse to follow her which is why I agreed to stay here."

The four of them went to the New World to recruit Coeus.

"I do not think it's a good idea to go against Kronos," he said. "He is too powerful."

"Not against this," Zeus replied showing him the dust. "This is the dust of a tree from dimension nine."

"That will do. I am with you."

They found Kronos and the other Titans on Mermaid Bay. Kronos had turned the land there into a home for the Titans. Zeus flew over the land and sprinkled enough dust over them to render them each powerless.

"Do not touch them with your bare hand or the dust will block your powers as well," Zeus reminded them all.

They gathered the Titans and took them to Dimension nine, leaving them trapped there.

Zeus knew that Bee would try to find them and so they all went back to Mermaid Bay to wait.

As Zeus had predicted, Bee showed up and the moment Zeus saw him he blew the dust in Bee's face. They placed him alongside the Titans.

Zeus decided that it would be too dangerous to leave the witches free so he captured Kevin and Tony and added them to the population of the ninth dimension.

"All that is left are the three girls," Zeus declared. "The third dimension will soon be ours again."

Samantha and Sandra found Saina in dimension two. She had gone there with hope that no one would bother looking for her. When they found her she was sitting in the middle of an empty field looking at the stars.

She had always known that her father didn't care about her but she had hoped that her sisters would stand with her.

"Why are you here?" Saina asked them.

"You are our sister. We will always come for you," Samantha told her.

"You attacked me."

"You attacked us first!" Sandra said. "What were we to do, stand there and let you kill us?"

"Look, Saina, we are not perfect..." Sandra started.

Saina cut her off with a laugh, "She is," She said pointing at Samantha. "Father even said so himself. Sandra is the good one, Saina is the evil one and Samantha is a mix of both, the perfect balance."

"No matter what he said, I am far from perfect!" Samantha said.

Sandra smiled at Saina, "Sister, will you accept us and be a part of our family?"

Before Saina could answer, Zeus appeared and a dust settled down over the girls. They tried to use their powers to defend themselves but found that their powers were failing them.

Samantha watched as her sisters were grabbed by Hermes, Coeus, Themis and Hercules who took the two and disappeared, leaving Samantha alone with Zeus and Hades.

"Will you surrender to me?" Zeus asked her.

"Why would I surrender to you?"

"I am the king of the Gods. You are nothing but a child." Zeus waved his hand as if he were swatting a fly away, "If I have my way, you would die for going against me."

"If you have your way? Who is stopping you?" Samantha said standing her ground.

"My son swears he can not live without you. So you shall marry him and learn your place or be banished along with the rest."

Samantha closed her eyes and saw Kronos and her sisters running from a creature. The creature had huge crazy looking eyes with two sharp teeth that reached the bottom of it's jaw.

"Let them go!" She screamed as she opened her eyes to look at Zeus.

He smiled, "Marry Hercules and I may allow them to live."

"That creature can not kill them."

"That is where you are wrong. You see, dimension nine is where Kronos put creatures even more vicious than the Forbidden. Creatures that he created too strong to control and that can kill even a Titan."

Samantha couldn't believe that Kronos would create anything that could kill himself. Then again Kronos was running alongside her sisters in her vision.

She couldn't see a way out at the moment. She knew she couldn't give in to his demands but could she allow possibly everyone that she loved to die? She knew that Zeus had her sisters and Kronos but what if he had captured everyone, including Ben and Wayne?

She still didn't have her powers so she could not teleport away from them. She had no choice.

"I...." as she started to speak a strange silence fell over them.

A bright light shone down from the sky, blinding Samantha. She had seen that light before in a cave, just before her father had appeared.

She shut her eyes tightly and waited for the light to fade. Once it started to fade, Samantha saw that she was no longer in the field. She looked around and saw that it was not her father that had saved her but a beautiful woman.

Samantha looked around and realized that she was back in Lilith's cave. The woman leaned against a rock watching her.

"Who are you?" Samantha asked.

The woman had a gentle smile as she said, "My name is Katrina. I am Lilith's oldest friend. I was there in the beginning and I will be there at the end."

"What does that mean?"

"That simply means that I am a higher power than Zeus had thought possible. I knew Lilith when she was the Princess, I watched as she made the deal with your father. I saw her take your sister. I know and see everything. Like the fact that your mother is alive."

Samantha gasped, "No, my mother is dead. She died when I was three."

"No, her body died. Bodies can be remade. She still lives," Katrina told her.

A tear rolled down Samantha's face, "So the waterfall..."

"Is real, yes. However, it is in a place that very few can go."

"How can I save my sisters and friends?" Samantha asked.

"Unfortunately, I can only risk being in dimension nine for a short time. I can take only two. You will have to decide between your sisters, your friends or your father."

"My father is there?" Samantha said in surprise. "How did they capture him?"

"I'm afraid that Zeus figured out a way to get the wood of a thapis tree. The tree has very powerful magic, stripping even the most powerful being of all powers as long as they are exposed to it. That's why you can not use your powers, the dust is from a thapis."

Samantha started to dust herself off and immediately started to feel the effects wearing off.

"Once I get this off me I can help rescue everyone," Samantha said.

"You must stay here. I am afraid of what Zeus might do to you if he finds you again."

"I will not sit here while my family and friends are in danger!" Samantha yelled at her.

Katrina's expression didn't change as her eyes lit up like bright diamonds, "You will do as I say, at least for now." Her eyes changed back to normal.

"What are you?" Samantha asked.

"I will return with your sisters and then we might stand a chance."

After Katrina left Samantha sat down feeling completely helpless for the first time since she found out that she wasn't mortal.

It didn't take very long before Katrina returned with Sandra and Saina. Both of her sisters ran to her.

"I am so sorry," Saina cried.

"Shh, you're fine now. As long as we are together we are stronger than any of them," Samantha told her.

"I don't know if I can, Father said…"

"I don't care what he said about any of us! We will prove him wrong," Sandra said.

"That's right, we will prove them all wrong. We are the most powerful and we will prove it," Samantha said to her sisters. Then turning to Katrina she added, "Now take us to our mother!"

The other two looked at her in confusion.

"As you wish," Katrina said.

Dust from the cave floor started to swirl around them until they could no longer see Katrina. As the dust started to settle Samantha could see the waterfall.

"Mother!" she called out.

"Samantha, our mother is dead," Sandra said.

"It is not that easy to kill me," Athena said from behind them.

They all ran to her and she opened her arms to hug them.

"I am sorry I wasn't able to protect you. I tried but in the end he was right, I belong with him."

"Who?" the three asked together.

"Your father. He deserved his family and I took the three of you and hid you away. Naturally he found us and took the two of you," she said pointing to Saina and Sandra. "Before he could return for Samantha, Kappas showed up and, well, without my powers I was no match for him. Your father returned, but my body was to damaged so he pulled me from it and brought me here. He made me a new body so here I am."

"So you have been trapped here the whole time?" Saina asked.

"No, I can go from here to home. I grow stronger everyday. I'm even getting my powers back."

"Mother, where is Toby? I saw him here before when I visited you," Samantha said.

Athena pointed to the waterfall and Samantha saw Toby walk out through the waterfall the same way her father had done. Instead of walking casually he ran across the water and wrapped his arms around Samantha lifting her off the ground.

"Samantha, I am so sorry that I left you."

"Not like you had a choice," she said smiling at him as he put her back on her feet.

He kept his arm around her as if he would never again let her go.

Athena smiled, "I have been watching you, all of you. I am so happy you are all together finally. And now to see the two of you together, well it's just too much."

They all laughed except Samantha, "How are we going to rescue everyone else?"

The laughter died instantly, "I don't know if we should," Athena said.

"What about father?" Saina asked.

"Of course I want to free your father, but the rest I think we are better off leaving them where they are."

"Tony is there!" Sandra said, not trying to hid her anger.

"Tony? I didn't see him," Samantha said.

"You wouldn't have, you saw who was most important to you." Athena replied.

"If Tony is there then Kevin is probably there. And what about Ben?" Samantha thought that by her showing concern for Ben, Toby would get upset. If he did she couldn't tell.

The three girls held hands, closed their eyes and focused on dimension nine. They started searching for everyone they thought might have been taken there.

Sandra found Tony hiding in a cave alone. Samantha saw Kevin standing on the edge of a cliff. Saina found Bee, he had built a small teepee and was sitting in the middle of it trying his best not to make a sound.

All three opened their eyes at the same moment and at the same time they all started talking.

"Settle down, tell me what each of you saw," Athena directed.

After the girls had told her what and who they had seen, Athena started to pace along the water's edge.

"We can rescue the witches and your father, but the Titans will have to stay trapped until we can figure out how to free them later," Athena said after a few minutes.

"Why can't we just go get a few and go back?" Sandra asked.

"Because the ninth dimension is unforgiving. You have already been exposed to the wood of the thapis tree, the effects will not wear off completely for a long time. It will be risky to make even one trip, let alone multiple trips."

The three girls nodded in understanding.

"Do each of you have your stone?" they nodded once again. "Now go get them and bring them all here, Zeus can not come here. They will all be safe," Athena told them.

Right after the three girls left, Katrina appeared. "Athena, Zeus is destroying any planet that has gone against him. He already destroyed Non Morti and they are heading to Mondo Del Lupo soon."

"I must warn Wayne before it's too late. He may have a way to stop it."

"No one can stop it, I have orders to allow Zeus to do as he pleases with this dimension," Katrina said.

"Orders from who?" Toby asked stepping closer.

"That is not for you to know right now. Ben is with Wayne, he can help them escape. Just warn them so they can save as many people as they can before it is too late!" Katrina said as she disappeared.

Athena looked at Toby, "Reach out to Ben I will try to warn Wayne."

CHAPTER 18

Wayne had been out in the fields working all day with Ben and Hawk. Gabby had been bringing water every few hours for each of them. They had just finished in the last field and were headed back to the village when they saw Gabby walking towards them.

"We are done for the day and heading home," Wayne said wiping his mud covered hand across his forehead, leaving a trail across half his head.

Gabby tried to hold in her laughter as she replied, "I came to tell you that dinner is almost done."

As they reached the top of the last hill they could see the flickering of the torches in the village.

"Ben, you need to get out of there."

Ben stopped as he looked around at the sound of Toby's voice. After he didn't see Toby he figured he had imagined it and started walking again.

"Zeus is coming to destroy this planet. Leave now!" Toby's voice.

Ben grabbed Wayne's arm, "Did you hear that?"

"Depends on what you're talking about."

"Toby, I heard Toby's voice, warning me that Zeus is coming."

Wayne's face turned white, "I heard Athena warning the same thing."

They looked towards the village lightening bolts were slamming into the ground. Wayne and Hawk could hear screams coming from the village, they both ran as fast as they could, trying to reach the people trapped inside.

Gabby followed Ben as he hurried to reach Wayne and Hawk. She watched as the flames grew, overwhelming the entire village.

A bright light came down from the sky and engulfed Wayne, Hawk and Ben.

"Ben!" Gabby yelled as the light came towards her. She turned and started to run but the brightness surrounded her.

Wayne saw the light and was pulled backwards and then up into the sky. He saw his entire village burning and then with a bang the planet exploded.

The four of them had been passed out when Katrina laid them down beside the waterfall. Athena and Toby ran to the water's edge and splashed water on each of them to wake them up.

"Ben! Wake up." Toby was saying as Ben opened his eyes.

"Toby? What happened?"

"I tried to warn you," Toby said with a smile. He stood up and extended his hand down to Ben.

Ben grabbed his friends hand and got to his feet. He looked around, "Where are we?"

Gabby screamed, Ben and Toby looked over to see what was wrong.

"Gabby, calm down," Athena was saying.

"I can't believe I'm dead. I wasn't supposed to die this young. What did I do to deserve this?" Gabby ranted.

Athena couldn't help but laugh a little before saying, "Gabby, you are not dead!"

Gabby fell silent and then hugged Athena, "I'm really not dead?"

"You are really not dead," Athena assured her.

"What happened?"

"Zeus destroyed Mondo Del Lupo," Katrina answered.

"Who the hell are you?" Ben said walking towards her.

Toby grabbed Ben's arm, "Calm down, she is a friend."

"I disobeyed saving you and you question me? You should bow at my feet, boy!" Katrina said.

"Bow...."

"Ben, that's enough. You need to settle yourself before you regret it," Athena scolded.

Ben looked at her, trying to remember where he had seen her before.

It didn't take long before he remembered being on Mount Olympus. "Athena? How are you here?"

"That does not matter right now," Athena said looking towards Wayne and Hawk. "Why haven't they woke yet?"

"They will wake up when the transformation is complete," Katrina answered.

"What transformation?" Athena asked.

"Zeus has cursed all wolves who survived the destruction of their planet. Not all the wolves had made it back and of course they escaped," she said pointing to the two men still lying beside the water.

Sandra appeared just outside the cave where she had seen Tony hiding. She slowly started walking into the darkness. Her foot slipped and she slid down the rocky slide and landed hard on her left foot.

Sandra pulled the blue and green stone from her pocket, the stone gave off just enough light for her to see around her.

She could hear muffled cries that echoed off the cave walls. She quickly followed the tunnel until it opened into a small cavern.

The light from her stone reached across the space lighting up a vine that was slowly tightening around Tony's body. Sandra couldn't see his face but knew by the clothes that it was him.

She sat the stone down and hurried over to free Tony but the vines were too thick and strong for her to break with her hands.

She started to panic as the vine started to pull Tony down into the ground. Sandra punched the ground in frustration and the dirt loosened around her hand.

She smiled to herself and punched the ground harder, breaking through the top and reaching down to the roots of the vine.

She tightened her grip and watched as the plant started to freeze, the green color faded as the ice formed over the surface. Once the vine was solid, she started to break it into pieces.

After a few minutes Tony was free. Sandra picked up her stone and then reached out her hand. Tony grabbed her hand and they disappeared.

Samantha looked around and saw Kevin still standing at the edge of the cliff but now he was screaming something that Samantha couldn't understand.

"Kevin!"

He continued yelling at nothing at all.

Samantha walked up behind him and gently touched his shoulder, "Kevin?"

He stopped screaming and slowly looked at her with a blank expression. Then without warning he started hitting Samantha, "You are not real! Leave me alone!"

Samantha tried to back up away from him but he stayed right with her. She glanced over his shoulder and saw that there was what looked like a grey woman floating in mid air. Her mouth wide open but no sound came out.

"Aberous!" Samantha said out loud.

The floating woman shut her mouth and Kevin fell to the ground. She floated over to Samantha and without moving her mouth asked, "how do you know my name?"

"I don't know but you are Aberous, aren't you?" Samantha replied.

"Yes." Then she opened her mouth again.

Samantha still could hear nothing but she knew that Kevin could. He screamed again but this time Samantha could tell that whatever the silent scream was doing caused Kevin a lot of pain.

Kevin stood up and jumped off the cliff. Samantha screamed his name and ran to the edge. She looked down and saw that he had landed in a pool of water at the bottom. He started to slowly swim towards the edge.

Samantha looked back and saw that Aberous was smiling.

Raising her hand, Samantha shot a blast of lightning, hitting Aberous in the chest. Samantha watched as the creature fell to the ground in pain.

Looking over the edge of the cliff again, Samantha saw that Kevin had managed to pull himself out of the water but was now lying in the dirt, not moving. She appeared beside him she knew he needed help. Samantha bent down and picked him up, then disappeared.

"Saina?" Bee said as his daughter appeared beside him in his pathetic little teepee. "How did you get back here? Did Zeus…"

"No, I came back for you," she said with a shrug.

Bee was touched that she came back for him but at the same time he knew that she should have stayed away. "We need to get out of here!"

Saina jumped as something very big slammed into the teepee knocking it over. They were surrounded by trees.

She looked around to see what had hit into them when something huge swooped down and knocked her to the ground. It was gone before she could get a look at it.

"Saina!" Bee yelled.

Saina stood up and realized that the creature had knocked her more than ten feet backwards. She started walking back towards her father.

"What was that?" she asked when she was close enough for him to hear her.

"Bragle. One of the most vicious creatures I ever created," he replied.

There was a loud hiss behind her, she turned and saw a giant snakehead flying towards her, brown wings spread over forty feet wide.

"Run!" Bee yelled.

But it was too late, the creature picked Saina up in massive claws and Bee watched as the monster carried his daughter away.

When Sandra appeared with Tony, Athena ran to her and hugged her tightly.

"Are you alright?"

"Yes mother, we are both fine. It's a good thing I went when I did though," Sandra said with a smile.

"She got there just in time to save me," Tony added.

"What happened?"

Sandra told her mother about the vines and how she had punched a hole in the ground to get to its roots.

"I never saw anything like it before," Sandra finished.

"That was Ilkous, a living vine that feeds on mortals," Katrina explained.

Athena looked at her, "How do you know what it is?"

"The reason dimension nine exists is for creatures like that. They are the worse of the worse. Created out of hate and fear by the superior beings."

"Help!" Samantha said as she appeared just behind Athena.

Katrina and Athena helped lay Kevin down on the ground. After a few moments Katrina shook her head.

"You mean, there's no hope. Can't we help him?" Samantha fought to hold her tears in.

"You must be able to help?" Athena pleaded with Katrina.

Katina knelt down beside Kevin, she reached down to touch his forehead.

"Katrina stop!"

A man appeared behind Katrina. Long brown locks laid neatly down his back. He was dressed in a long flowing robe that brushed the ground.

"Gabriel?" Katrina gasped as she quickly stood up to face him.

"You must stop overstepping. This is not for you to decide," he told her in a gentle voice.

"You know who he is?" she asked.

"I do. It changes nothing. You must not continue on this path. The consequences are too great."

"But Lilith…"

The two of them disappeared before she had finished speaking.

Samantha knelt down beside Kevin, putting her hand on his chest she felt him take his last breath. Tears rolled down her face but she wiped them away.

She stood up with determination and looked at Sandra.

"No," Sandra simply stated. "We are not strong enough yet."

Samantha shook her head, "Zeus has to pay for this!"

"I know and he will. I promise you he will."

Meanwhile, Wayne had been reliving the nightmare of watching his home planet exploding. He knew Jade was at home helping Cassandra finish dinner for the rest of them. There was no way she could have survived, yet he held hope that she had.

He opened his eyes and saw Athena. He thought to himself, 'perhaps Jade survived and I died.'

Athena turned around and saw Wayne looking at her. She smiled as she walked over to crouch beside him. "How are you feeling?"

"As well as I can for a dead man," he said with a small grin.

"Dead man? Wayne you aren't dead."

A confused look crossed his face, "If I am not dead how am I here with you?"

"Dead?" Hawk mumbled.

Athena looked over and for the first time she recognized him. "How are you with Hawk?" She asked.

"My brother had been helping me restore my village."

"Your brother!" Athena was staring at Hawk. He was wet with sweat and his face was pale.

Hawk opened his eyes and looked up Athena, "I knew you would return to me someday."

He reached out to touch her face, Athena did not stop him. She felt his cold hand touch her cheek.

Wayne got to his feet and saw Samantha standing with Sandra, tears fell down her face and he felt the familiar stab of pain he always felt when she was hurting.

Samantha had not noticed that Wayne was awake until he pushed passed Sandra and wrapped his arms around her. She put her head to his chest and cried.

Toby and Ben stood off to the side talking.

"Saina should have returned by now," Toby told Ben.

"How long has she been gone?"

"Since before you all got here. They all left at the same time."

"Where did they go?"

"To dimension nine to rescue Tony, Kevin and Bee."

Ben's face fell in shock, "How did they end up there?"

"How do you think they got there?" Toby asked.

"Zeus!" Ben answered.

"With the help of two Titans, another God and your father."

"Hades helped him do this?"

Once Samantha had calmed down Wayne said, "I want to go back to Bella Isola."

"There is no one there. Everyone left."

"There is something I need to get. Please take me?" he begged.

"If you are leaving, I am going with you," Hawk said walking towards his brother.

"Samantha and I will take you," Ben told Wayne.

Samantha nodded in agreement. She knew that sooner or later she would have to face Toby and Ben together but she wasn't ready for that yet.

The castle had been all but destroyed. The barrier was down so they were able to appear inside the castle foyer. The walls around them were cracked and parts had crashed to the floor.

Samantha started grabbing torches off the walls and lighting them. They could see outside through a hole in the wall that had fallen or knocked down. The sky was cloudy and it was raining. Samantha had never seen rain on the island before.

"What happened here?" Ben asked looking around.

"Looks like our home wasn't the only one that Zeus decided to destroy," Hawk said.

"Samantha, did you take my journals with you when you left here before?" Ben asked her.

"No, I figured I would be back for them. I left them in my room."

"You two go ahead up. Hawk can help me down here," Wayne told them.

Samantha was saddened to see that the once beautiful room was now destroyed. Most of the ceiling had fallen down crushing two of the posts on the bed. The once spectacular fireplace was now a pile of rocks and debris.

"Where did you put them?" Ben asked her.

"Under the mattress."

Ben stepped over the fallen ceiling and crouched down. He reached under the mattress and pulled out the journals.

Samantha looked out of the broken window and saw that the sky had cleared and the full moon was shining bright.

"Did you hear that?" Samantha asked looking back towards the door.

"No..." Ben started to say but then he heard the growling coming from the hallway.

Samantha moved closer to Ben and saw two massive wolves appear in the doorway.

"Wayne?" Samantha whispered as the wolf on the right lunged for her.

The wolf bit down into flesh as Samantha screamed. Ben pulled Samantha back as the second wolf lunged. Both wolves now had their teeth deep in Poseidon's skin.

The second wolf let go, Poseidon looked at Ben, "Get her out of here!"

Ben grabbed Samantha and disappeared just as the wolf's mouth closed over Poseidon's throat.

Ben took her to the first place that came to mind, the lake by the farm.

"We have to go back! We have to help him!" Samantha screamed.

Ben held on to her as tight as he could, hoping that he could stop her from teleporting back to the castle.

"Samantha, Ben," Hermes said appearing with Hades beside him.

Samantha looked at Hades and all the pain she felt came pouring out. Samantha threw purple balls of electric balls at Hades. He dodged every one of them.

He knew that she would blame him for everything that had happened and she was partially right. He had taken Zeus' side once again when he should have been against his brother. Now his favorite brother above all was dead and there was nothing he could do to help Poseidon or Samantha.

Ben stepped in front of Samantha, "Stop! This is not their doing."

Samantha dropped to the ground.

"Unfortunately that is not entirely true," Hermes said.

Ben looked at him, then to his father, "What did you do?"

"I did nothing," Hades replied.

Ben took a step towards his father and pulled his hand back, a black spear appeared in his grip. "Tell me what you did!"

"I did nothing to stop him. He cursed them. I did not know the extent of what the curse was and so I did nothing. Had I known that the wolves would be able to kill us I wouldn't..."

"Zeus did this!" Samantha said. She stood up, wiped her face and brushed the dirt off her knees. "We need to go back. I have to see for myself."

Ben nodded, then to his father he said, "You will come with us!"

"Of course."

The four of them went back to the castle. When they got to the doorway of Samantha's room they could see the blood splattered everywhere.

Samantha covered her mouth in shock. Ben put his arm around her. Hermes and Hades walked into the room and knelt down beside Poseidon's body.

He had deep gashes all over his arms. His throat was ripped open and half of his face had been torn away.

"How is this possible? They are only wolves. You don't think that Zeus meant to give them this much power, do you?" Hermes quietly asked Hades.

"This would not be the first time. Question is why would he do this."

Samantha walked into the room, "Help me, we have to take him to my mother."

They started to pick Poseidon's body up but stopped when they heard a scream. They laid him back down and realized that they were back at the waterfall.

Athena ran to her father's side and looked at Hades, "What happened?"

"Zeus turned the wolves into powerful creatures. They attacked him," Hades replied.

"Are you trying to tell me that Wayne did this?" she asked.

"Mother, it's true. Grandfather appeared in front of me just before Wayne attacked me," Samantha told her.

Athena was quiet for a long moment and then she turned on Hades once more, "You knew he was cursing them and did nothing to stop it? What kind of a God are you to stand idly by and watch one brother murder another?"

Samantha and Sandra wrapped their arms around their mother. Athena hugged them and they cried together.

Hermes saw Toby sitting beside Gabby and wanted so badly to reach out to his son. He had longed for the day when they would be reunited.

Gabby saw Hermes looking at them and she nudged Toby's arm, "Go talk to him."

"Why would I want to talk to him? He helped Zeus," Toby replied.

"He is your father, Toby," she told him.

Toby stood up slowly and stared at Hermes.

He saw his son looking at him and decided he had better say something to him. He slowly approached Toby.

"Are you really my father?" Toby asked.

Hermes smiled, "Yes, I am."

"Where have you been? All these years, I was raised thinking that Kim was my mother. Which I now know is bullshit!"

"I know I have a lot to answer for and not just to you. I am sorry that I gave you up," Hermes said.

Hades had watched Hermes walk over to Toby and he felt the guilt wash over him. He had abandoned his son, only in a different way. Hermes had thought what he was doing was for the greater good. Hades had only used his son to accomplish his own goals.

"Ben," Hades called out to his son.

Ben looked at him, nodded his head and then looked away.

Hades walked over to Athena and the two girls, "Athena, we need to give him a send off."

Without looking at him she said, "Did you really not know what Zeus was doing when he cursed the wolves?"

"I really did not, I swear."

"Then I think it best if you do it," she told him.

He nodded once and then stood beside Poseidon's body.

Everyone gathered around as Hades started to speak, "I send you off into the unknown, not as a God but as my brother. You stood by us all, fought for us and gave your life for us. For that, you died a hero. You shall never be replaced by another. For today, all the oceans cry out in heartache."

Hades placed his hand over Poseidon and slowly moved from head to foot. Poseidon's body turned to ash as Hades' hand moved over his body. Once his body was replaced with ashes, Athena scooped some of the ash in to her hand and walked to the water's edge. The others followed her lead.

As they stood there looking out at the waterfall Athena said, "We will find Saina and Bee then Zeus will pay for killing you, father. I swear this to you." She blew the ashes into the air.

Samantha and Sandra blew the ashes they held into the air and together added, "And we swear."

... to be continued...

About the Author

Laura Lynn has always been fascinated by the Gods and mythical beings. Her writing is inspired by her father who always encouraged her creativity. She currently resides in Boswell, Pennsylvania. The Mystical Ones: Rise to Power is her debut novel.